Scuttle Watch

The Crosbys

SCUTTLE

WATCH

By

MARION CROWELL RYDER

Illustrated by

ALEX RAYMOND

The reprinting of this book
is sponsored by the
DENNIS HISTORICAL SOCIETY
Dennis, Massachusetts

TO

My Father

WHOSE REMINISCENCES AND
BOYHOOD DIARIES
HAVE MADE THIS BOOK POSSIBLE

FOREWORD

A number of years having passed since the first edition of "Scuttle Watch" was sold out and a whole generation having grown up without any knowledge of what Cape Cod used to be like, I believe this is the time to have the story reprinted. Interest in the Pilgrim 350th Celebration and the increasing popularity of the Cape as a permanent home as well as a vacation land, seem to make this the appropriate moment for the reappearance of the book. I welcome the paper back edition with its opportunity to make the book available to more people who love the Cape.

October 30, 1970

CONTENTS

I ·	*John Sets Sail*	3
II ·	*An Unexpected Port*	29
III ·	*Off to the Grand Banks*	50
IV ·	*The Chesapeake Present*	69
V ·	*A Narrow Escape*	91
VI ·	*By Lantern Light*	115
VII ·	*The Wash-Out Dinner*	142
VIII ·	*The Fight in the Snow*	165
IX ·	*Christmas*	182
X ·	*The Rescue*	200
XI ·	*Mittens*	213
XII ·	*The Secret of the Old House*	233
XIII ·	*Sailors All*	265

Scuttle Watch

John Sets Sail

"LAST ONE UP to the green fence is a horseshoe crab!" shouted a small boy as he dashed around the corner by the white church and darted up the sandy lane. With a twinkle in his eyes he looked over his shoulder and grinned at the boy who was some distance behind him.

"Aw, that's no fair, John!" gasped the laggard. "You know your legs are longer'n mine; and besides, you had a head start from the store."

Reaching his goal John leaned on the fence and called, "Hurry up, Joe! Crabs can go a heap faster'n that."

"I don't care," panted Joe, as he threw himself on the ground to rest. " 'Twan't a fair race! And anyhow I'd ruther be a crab than a slippery ol' eel."

Both boys fell silent, chewing thoughtfully on pieces of grass until a sudden sound of whistling, coming from the near-by house, attracted their attention. Looking up quickly, they watched the head and shoulders of a boy a year or so older than John, appear in the small doorway that was set in the roof near the ridgepole. Reaching out, the boy grasped the door and retreating from sight, closed it down with a bang.

"Aw, gee!" exclaimed John. "Eben's closing the scuttle. Do you s'pose that means it's goin' to rain tomorrow?"

John looked so anxious that Joe hastened to reassure him. "Naw, those clouds don't mean rain. Most likely Eben was closin' it so's to have it off his mind, bein' as there won't be any vessel they'll need to be watchin' for, for a spell."

"Maybe so," assented John doubtfully and then both boys were silent again, each intent on his own thoughts.

The house, in front of which the boys were standing, topped a gradual rise from the main road so that the scuttle in the roof, which Eben had just closed, afforded a wide view of the countryside and of Vineyard Sound. It was there that watch was kept whenever Captain Benjamin Crosby, John and Eben's father, was expected home from a voyage in his three-masted schooner, the *Good Fortune*. The vessel could be recognized by her owner's flag as she sailed down the Sound or came to anchor inside the breakwater, a mile off shore.

With a sigh Joe said enviously, "You're awful lucky,

John, to be goin' on a voyage on your father's vessel. You'll get out of goin' to school and have a heap of fun besides. I wish my father was a sea captain. It must be awful excitin'."

"It is!" said John proudly, thinking of Father's voyages to far places. Then he added, half-hesitantly, "But sometimes I almost wish he was in the grain business or something, like your father, 'cause then he'd be home all the time. Seems like Father's always away!"

"Say, it does mean that you and Eben and Peter have to do the heft of the work around home, sure enough," sympathized Joe.

"Oh, we can manage the *work* right enough," retorted John staunchly, "but it's lonesomelike without Father."

"Just the same," said Joe, unimpressed, "I wish I was a-goin' to sea like you be! How long do you s'pose you'll be gone?"

" 'Bout a week I guess," answered John, his eyes kindling as he thought of the adventure that would begin for him the next day.

Then as the church clock struck five John said reluctantly, "Well, I gotta get my chores done 'fore dark. I'll tell you all about the voyage when I get back and maybe some day we'll go on one together."

"Gee! That'ud be dandy!" exclaimed Joe, his freckled face one broad grin. Then, as he started across the fields to his own home and chores, he called back, "Good-bye, ol' eel. Don't go and fall overboard."

"Don't study too hard in school, ol' horseshoe crab,"

replied John, running along the lane and around the house to the woodshed.

The house had been set by compass to face directly south and so its west side, instead of its front, was toward the lane. In one ell John's grandfather, Captain David Crosby, a retired sea captain, kept his ship chandler store where he sold supplies and gear to the local fishermen, and also outfitted the fishing fleet that he, himself, sent to the Grand Banks each year.

John set about piling wood, whistling lustily all the while. Grandfather, on his way home from the store, heard John at work and called out to him, "Ahoy, young sailorman! Going to set sail on your first voyage tomorrow?"

"Yes, sir," replied John respectfully, trying hard to appear casual as he dropped an arm-load of pine sticks and came to stand by Grandfather in the path.

"Well, it's in your blood to love the sea, John," continued Grandfather, "and I'm hoping it'll give you a civil welcome. I mind how it treated me when I first signed on as cabin-boy—one storm after another till I came to think it hadn't any other way of acting. I was plumb surprised at the first spell of fair weather we had." Grandfather chuckled at the recollection but added hastily, when he saw the soberness of John's expression, "But that was the November-gale season when I shipped aboard the *Eliza M*, while you've got the pick of the spring weather ahead of you." Satisfied with John's look of relief Grandfather went on his way, turning after a few steps to call back, "Mind you learn to box the compass for me, real smart, by the time you get back."

John finished up his chores with a rush and hurried into the lamplit kitchen. Father, tanned and hearty-looking, was reading the newspaper, while Mother stepped briskly about the kitchen getting supper. She looked very trim in her starched print dress, her dark hair drawn smoothly down on either side of her face. Peter, thirteen years old, was filling the wood-box back of the stove and Eben, aged eleven, was just setting a full water pail on the shelf by the sink.

John's first remark made them all look at him and smile. "Say, Eb," he blurted out. "did you close the scuttle 'cause you think it's goin' to rain?"

Father answered for Eben, "No, son, I think we're fixing to have fair weather tomorrow. I just sent Eben aloft to make everything snug and shipshape against our going off in the morning."

Captain Crosby had taken each of the older boys on a voyage the year before, and now at last, after ages of impatient waiting, it was John's turn to go. Since he was only eight, Father thought that a short trip would be best for him. The *Good Fortune* was to sail from Boston to Maine for a cargo, so it had been decided that John would go to Boston with Father and sail aboard the vessel to Maine. Then on her passage south around the Cape he would be landed at the mouth of the river. In that way he would have his longed-for taste of the sea without being too long away from home and school.

When John opened his eyes next morning, he was out of bed in a flash and at the small window that looked across the Cove toward the east. When he saw the clear sky he heaved a great sigh of relief, exclaiming, "Father was right—it's going to be a fine day." Since it was much too early to get up, he snuggled under the patchwork quilt again, trying to realize that *the* day had come at last!

Finally, unable to lie quiet a moment longer, he slipped out of bed and dressed quickly in the clothes that had been carefully laid out. As he inspected with satisfaction the little satchel all packed for the voyage he heard Mother's voice calling to waken him. She smiled when, a moment later, he came clattering down the steep back stairs.

"Well, you're up with the sun and no mistake," she said as she moved around the homey kitchen.

As John watched her he suddenly realized that tomorrow morning, for the first time in his life, he would not be in that familiar room. That would seem *queer*!

"You might fetch the bell from the lamp shelf, John, and wake the boys," suggested Mother, stirring the porridge on the stove.

John, itching to get things started, grabbed the brass bell and gave it a lusty ring at the foot of the back stairs. When its clamor died away and he heard grumbling sounds from above, he shouted, "Avast there, my hearties, tumble up!"

Presently Peter and Eben came slumping down the stairs, cross and sleepy. "I'd like to tumble *you* good and hearty," growled Eben, rubbing his eyes.

"Oh, he just thinks he's smart 'cause he's going away today, but 'bout this time *tomorrow* morning he won't be feeling so spry—he'll be awful sick!" offered Peter in a lofty tone.

"I will NOT!" protested John hotly. "I'm just as good a sailor as you are and you *know* it, Peter Crosby!"

Father's entrance at this point silenced the boys. With a twinkle in his eyes he said, "I guess likely school and chores don't look so interesting this morning. Like enough I'd better hire 'Lonzo Small to see to things around here while I'm gone, Mother."

Peter and Eben, ashamed of their crossness, grinned at Mother. She knew she wouldn't need any outside help.

"Well, son," said Father, looking at John, "we're going to have a prime day to start off. Now eat a good breakfast for it's a long journey to Boston and we'll not get dinner till we're aboard the vessel."

Excitement made it almost impossible for John to swallow the good breakfast that Father advised and finally he pushed back his plate with the excuse that he must run over and say good-bye to Grandmother and Grandfather. He found that Grandmother had a little paper sack of striped peppermints for him to take in his pocket, "to eat on the cars." Clutching his present John dashed home again.

Back at home John found himself the center of the pleasant bustle of departure. Eben had been sent out to the fence to watch for the stagecoach, and in a moment they heard his shout of "Here she comes!"

The driver swung the coach around and drawing up to the gate, hailed Father. "Morning, Captain Crosby, so the youngest sailor's goin' to sea, is he? You've pretty nigh got a hull crew of your own."

Father and John climbed to their places on the carpet-covered seats. Father's valise was hoisted to the baggage rack on top of the coach, but John kept tight hold of his little satchel and sat with it on his knees. In a chorus of good-byes the stagecoach started and John, poking his head and one arm out of the window in the coach door, waved wildly back at Mother and the boys until the coach swung around the corner into the main road.

Though the scenery for the first part of the journey was familiar to John he found that, seen from the seat of the stagecoach, it looked more interesting than usual. He enjoyed the way they rumbled heavily across the wooden drawbridge and was sorry when the noise ceased as they turned into the sandy road that led across the Cape to Yarmouth where they would take the train. Jogging through the woods was so tedious that John fidgeted about on the seat, sighed heavily, and kept peering ahead over the bobbing ears of the horses for a glimpse of the village in the distance. Just as the ride was beginning to seem endless they rounded a bend and were on the main street of Yarmouth.

As they neared the railroad station John bounced up and down on the seat, craning his neck for the first sight of a locomotive. With mouth and eyes wide open he climbed out of the coach and stared about him at the stir and confusion of the platform. He had never seen so many stagecoaches or heaps of luggage or hurrying people and they almost distracted his attention from the snorting engine and its string of smoke-blackened cars.

Threading their way through the crowd Father and John climbed aboard the train, found a seat and settled their baggage. They had not long to wait before the train started with a din of bell-ringing and shouting, and a great puffing of steam. At first John tried to see everything that they were passing although they were going at what seemed a terrific rate of speed. But, before long, he grew tired and his eyes drooped heavily. He fought against his drowsiness, hating to miss any part of the journey, but at last he gave in and dropped off to sleep.

The next thing he knew he was awakened by a series of jolts, a roaring of steam, and Father's voice saying, "Come on, boy, wake up! This is Boston."

Bewildered by the confusion of the big station John stumbled along in a daze as Father led him out to a waiting hack. But as they jounced over the cobblestone streets he was soon wide awake and pressed close to the tiny window of the cab to get the first glimpse of the ships that thronged the water-front, their masts and rigging making a maze of lines against the blue sky. He had not thought there were so many ships in the whole world!

As they drove down to one of the docks John quickly

singled out the *Good Fortune* and shouted excitedly, "There she is, Father! I see her!"

Almost before the hack had stopped he was out the door and dashing along the dock until he stood opposite the vessel and could feast his eyes on her trim lines and spotless paint. With rapidly beating heart and shining eyes, he was soon following his father up the gangplank.

The mate and crew were on board and greeted Captain Crosby and his small son with respectful salutes and broad grins. Going below, John was shown his bunk in a little stateroom, opening from the after cabin where Father kept his books and charts, and where he and the mate ate their meals. Scarcely had John stowed his satchel in his bunk and hung jacket and cap on a peg, when the cook came into the cabin to lay the table and say, "Dinner's ready, sir." Those were welcome words to John!

During the meal Father discussed the final details of the voyage with Mr. Gibson, the mate. They were to sail at flood tide that night, in ballast, for Gardiner, Maine, where they would take on a cargo of ice for Savannah. Father explained his plan to put into the river and land John on their way south around the Cape and through Vineyard Sound. The *Good Fortune* would then continue on her way to be absent weeks or even months, for it would depend on what cargo Father found waiting for him in Savannah as to whether he would make the return voyage directly to Boston or to some other port on the coast.

John spent the afternoon exploring the vessel from stem to stern and getting acquainted with the sailors. Father had gone ashore to get the ship's clearance papers from the Custom House and came aboard again toward sunset. At once he called the mate and gave the order to warp the *Good Fortune* away from the dock and make ready to hoist sail so as to be away on the evening tide. John found a corner of the quarter deck where he could watch the orderly preparations and yet be out of the way of the hurrying seamen.

As soon as the vessel was clear of the dock and drifting out into open water, the sailors hoisted the great sails, heaving on the halyards together as they sang:

> *Lather and shave,*
> *Lather and shave,*
> *And frizzle come bum.*

As the light westerly breeze filled the sails the vessel heeled gently and began moving swiftly through the crowded waters of the harbor. Watching the sails catch the sunset glow, and the white water foam away behind the *Good Fortune,* John thought there could never be anything more beautiful than the departure of a vessel bound to sea.

When they were out past the harbor light, the cook came on deck, ringing the supper bell. Sitting in the warm, lamplit cabin, eating and listening to the quiet talk of Father and the mate, John grew sleepier and sleepier until finally Father noticed his drooping head. "Bed's the place for you, son," he laughed. "Time enough tomorrow to learn to work ship."

Half awake, John managed to get undressed and snuggle into his little bunk. The gentle swaying of the vessel and the gurgle of water against the planks beside his head lulled him to sleep, and he was soon dreaming of his little attic room at the Cape.

The next morning he was awake early and lost no time in getting on deck. It was a sunny morning with a fresh breeze blowing. The *Good Fortune* was flying along before it with all sails set. He strolled along the deck and paused to peer into the galley where Alec, the cook, was rattling stove lids and singing in a booming voice as he got the breakfast. John hesitated at the door for he knew that it was bad business to bother the cook. But Alec was good-natured so, when he saw the figure in the doorway, he grinned broadly and said, "Ahoy there, my lad. How'd a sinker suit you to start the day proper?"

For a moment John looked puzzled, but when the cook held out to him a fat, brown doughnut he seized it with delight, mumbling, "Aw, gee, thanks," as he bit into it hungrily. Then, made bold by Alec's friendliness, he stepped over the high sill into the galley and chatted sociably while he munched his sinker. Alec clattered and banged around the snug little galley but he worked quickly and tidily for all the commotion. John thought of Mother moving around the big kitchen at home, and then he chuckled to himself as he remembered Peter's dire prophecy as to the way he would be feeling. He wondered if they would be eating breakfast yet and if they were thinking and talking about Father and himself at the same time that he was thinking about them.

Alec's voice broke upon his thoughts. "Want to give your sea-legs a trial and see what a stiddy hand you're gonna have for luggin' vittles along a crazy deck?" he asked as he fixed a tray of breakfast for the captain's cabin.

Glad of something to do John grabbed the tray eagerly and started confidently along the deck with it. The vessel heeled slightly and he staggered in his gait. To his dismay, the loaded tray gave a lurch. He tried with all his strength to steady it but, in spite of his efforts, a pile of sliced bread and a platter of fried ham slid off the tray, crashed to the deck, and slithered away into the scuppers.

Crestfallen, John stood still, eying the wreckage. He was undecided whether to set the tray down and gather up the scraps or leave them and go on. He felt that he had better get the remaining contents of the tray to the cabin in safety—IF he could. He heard Alec shouting with laughter behind him. Setting his mouth in a determined line he started on, plodding slowly and cautiously and stopping often to make sure of his balance. It was a nerve-racking trip but he reached the cabin without further mishap and set the tray down on the table with a whistle of relief. Resolutely he started back to pick up the remains and face Alec's laughter but he found that the cook had good-naturedly cleaned up the deck and prepared another lot of bread and ham.

On the second trip to the cabin Alec went ahead with the steaming coffee pot. John was tempted to laugh at his wide, high-stepping gait as seen from behind, but now he realized that it was the only way to walk on shipboard.

Later in the morning Father called to John, "Want to take your trick at the wheel, son?"

"Yes, sir!" John answered, his heart racing at the thought.

"Aye, aye, sir, you mean," corrected Father. "Now stand here. Take a firm grip on the wheel and hold her steady."

John braced his feet far apart and gripped the hand-spokes of the big wheel with all his strength. How the vessel pulled and tried to jerk the wheel out of his hands! Now and then she would give a tug and swing off her course in spite of all his efforts.

"Steady there," cautioned Father and then he laughed as he glanced over his shoulder at the wake foaming away behind them, "Looks like there's an eel following us."

John didn't have any time to look around! And besides, he knew well enough how the wake must look and he wanted to wait until he could point with pride to a straight, clean course. Gradually he began to discover a knack to steering and found that he could meet the vessel's surges with more skill and use less strength. When Father, watching him closely, noticed this he decided it was time for the next step in the instructions.

"Now that you begin to get the hang of it, John, try

keeping her up by compass."

John glanced up uncertainly, hating to admit that he did not know exactly what that meant. But Father, seeming not to notice his hesitation, went on. "You see that heavy black line on the swinging compass card? Well, that's called the lubber line. You want to keep that opposite the point of the compass toward which you are steering. The course she's on now is East-No'th-East."

With his eyes glued on the teetering compass card John wished fervently that it would stay still for just a *minute!*

"Hold on!" cautioned Father. "Give her two spokes. See, the spanker was beginning to shake close to the mast. Keep her full. There! Keep her steady—steady as she goes."

John thought there were an awful lot of things to attend to all at the same time, but he worked until his face grew red and his tongue stuck out between gripping teeth. Finally Father took the wheel from him saying, "That's well done for the first try, son. We'll make an able seaman out of you and no mistake."

John could not repress a little strut as he sauntered away feeling so pleased with himself he quite forgot how his arms were aching. He climbed on top of the cabin and lay down, beside the skylight, picturing himself, one of the youngest captains afloat, proudly treading the deck of his own three-master.

In the afternoon the wind freshened and the *Good Fortune* raced along, dipping and rising over the white-crested waves. One of the sailors noticed John studying the sky, which was flecked and streaked with small, white clouds, and said, "Mackerel backs and mares' tails make tall ships take in their sails."

Just as John was wondering about the truth of the saying he heard Father order, "Take in the topsails!" The seamen sprang to their work and John held his breath as he watched them swarm aloft and move about quickly and easily where there seemed to be no safe footing at all.

A few moments later Father called to the mate, "Go aloft, Mr. Gibson, and keep a sharp lookout. We ought to be off the Kennebec in half an hour."

With a brisk "Aye, aye, sir," the mate sprang nimbly up the shrouds to the crow's-nest.

Full of admiration for such agility John hurried aft to Father and asked when he could learn to climb aloft.

"You'd best try it first some day when we're anchored in the river," answered Father. "Then, when you get used to feeling the shrouds sway with your weight, you can try it some moderate day at sea." With that, John had to be content.

In a few moments they had proof that the *Good Fortune's* course had been accurately laid, for, just as Father began to look expectantly up to the crow's-nest, the mate sang out, "Lighthouse, two points off the weather bow, sir."

They entered the river at sunset, lowered sails, and dropped anchor opposite the town of Bath. After supper Father went ashore to arrange for a towboat to take them up the river the first thing in the morning. John wanted to go with him but the long day in the wind and sunshine had made him so sleepy that he was easily persuaded to stay aboard and listen to one of Job Handy's sea yarns before he turned in.

The towboat came alongside before John was awake the next morning so, when he went on deck, he found the vessel slipping along steadily between rocky, wooded shores and past occasional villages. By three o'clock they reached Gardiner and were tied up at the dock, and this time Father took John ashore with him when he went to make arrangements for taking on his cargo of ice.

At the ice company's office they learned that the loading would not begin until the next day so Father and John turned from the dock and went on up into the town, to the elm-shaded white house that belonged to a sea captain whom Father knew. They found that Captain Stevens was away at sea, on a voyage around the Horn to San Francisco, but Mrs. Stevens welcomed them cordially and insisted that they stay to supper. She led John out to the back porch and called to a girl and a boy about his age, who were working near the wood-pile, the boy splitting kindlings and the girl collecting them in a basket. "Come, Jane and Obed," called their mother, "you can leave the kindlings. I want you to show John Crosby around the farm and make him welcome."

The two children were very friendly, and in a few minutes John was running off with them to see the

horses, cows and pigs. After he had made the acquaint-
ance of all the farm animals John said, "Gee, it must
be dandy fun living on a real sure enough farm like this
all the time. Do you ever *ride* on the horses?"

Obed laughed at the awe in John's tone as he answered, " 'Course we do, but they're so fat and slow
you can't make 'em go faster'n a plowing pace. Seems
like it would be a whole lot more exciting to go to sea,
like you're doing."

"Father always leaves his vessel in Boston when he
comes home so we haven't ever even *seen* her or been
aboard," said Jane wistfully.

"Say, how'd you like to come aboard the *Good Fortune* tomorrow?" suggested John eagerly. "I'll ask
Father straight off if it'ud be all right, and I'll show you
all around and then we could play going to sea."

When Father had been consulted and had given his
consent all three children were jubilant; John, at the
prospect of showing off his knowledge of nautical affairs, and Obed and Jane, at the chance to satisfy their
long-felt curiosity about ships.

Much to Father's annoyance the loading did not start
the next morning and there was no sign of activity
around the big ice house on the dock. Aboard the vessel
the hatch-covers were off so that the holds might be
well aired, and everything was in readiness for the
cargo.

Obed and Jane arrived promptly after breakfast and
were eager to begin exploring the vessel. As they went
about on their tour of inspection the shadowy depths

below decks fascinated the children. They peered down
through the open hatch-ways and speculated on what
the darkness hid until they could resist their curiosity
no longer. John found Father in the cabin and asked if
they might go below and explore. Father hesitated a
moment and then said, "There's nothing to see in an
empty hold, but I guess you can go if you've a mind to.
There's no chance of their commencing to load this
forenoon as I can see! Take care you don't get a tumble
on the ladders."

Waiting for no more warnings John dashed off to
join Obed and Jane. They made for the main hatch and
down they went with more haste than care. At the foot
of the ladder they paused and drew together. The patch
of light from the open hatch-way did not seem to pene-
trate beyond the little space at the bottom of the ladder,
and to their eyes, accustomed to the sunlit deck, the
darkness looked solid and inky black. Gradually they
grew used to it and the heavy beams and oaken ribs of
the ship began to be dimly visible in the gloom. The
children moved cautiously away from their lighted spot.
Every step or scraping sound they made echoed with
a hollow, ghostly noise. Jane giggled nervously and
then caught her breath as a weird cackle seemed to
mock her from the dim corners. That instantly suggested a new idea to the boys and they tried out the
echoes with every sort of sound they could think of.
Then they started on their way again, tiptoeing ahead
until they reached the forward bulkhead. Working
along the side they poked into the dark recesses be-

tween the jutting ribs and braces of the hull till they came to the corner near the after bulkhead.

The children were about to move on when Jane whispered, "Hush! Did you hear a little, funny noise?"

"How could we hear any *little* noise when every sound we make booms 'round this place somethin' terrible?" retorted Obed.

"Well, hush up and see'f we can't," urged Jane anxiously.

All three stood silent, listening intently, and, sure enough, there was a scratching sound coming from behind some casks in the corner. John began to recall all the stories he had heard about rats aboard ship and hoped they weren't trying to get out and leave the vessel, for that would mean bad luck.

"Come on, John, let's shove away those casks and see what it is," suggested Obed.

Jane hung back fearfully as the two boys went vigorously to work. They rolled the small casks out of the way easily but a big hogshead was a harder job. They shoved and tugged at it but it would not budge. When they stopped to rest a moment they heard the scratching more plainly, accompanied by a faint squeaking sound.

"It must be rats and they *bite*," offered Jane. "Let's not look any more. Maybe it's time we went home." As she was speaking she edged toward the ladder and its reassuring patch of light. But the boys were intent upon their search and paid no attention to her.

Finally the big barrel moved a little, and by twisting

it around the boys got it away from the wall. They knelt down and peered into the space behind it.

"Say, look'ut, Obed, there're two shiny green eyes!" breathed John.

"Sure, I see 'em. And lissen!" whispered Obed.

The scratching had become more of a scrabbling noise and the squeak sounded like a feeble "mew."

"I believe it's a *CAT!*" exclaimed John, "and I'm gonna get it out."

"Look out—it'll scratch you!" warned Obed. "I'll shove this hogshead 'round further so's you can get in behind it."

At the word "cat" Jane had paused in her retreat and turned back toward the corner. Now she crept up beside Obed as John squirmed his way behind the barrel. They held their breath when they heard John saying coaxingly, "Nice pussy—we won't hurt you."

In a moment he said in a muffled voice, "I've got it!"

Obed and Jane moved back a few steps to give John room to back out and straighten up. Then they all hurried over to the ladder to see what they had found. There in John's arms lay a small, grey cat, hardly more than a kitten. It was pitifully thin and so weak it could barely move or cry. Jane was all sympathy at once, talking to it soothingly and smoothing its matted fur.

"It must have gotten aboard at the dock in Boston," said John, "and been caught in that corner when the hands shoved those casks around. It couldn't get out and it's been starving to death. Poor little thing!"

"Let's take it up to the cook and get it something to eat," suggested Obed.

But how could they climb the wobbly ladder and carry the cat at the same time! Suddenly Jane said, "Here, put it in my skirt. I can hold it up, like this, with one hand, and then you can boost me up the ladder."

Jane hung on with her one free hand. The boys pushed and bundled her from rung to rung. The ladder wobbled. Jane screamed as she felt herself swaying dizzily. The boys laughed until they were almost helpless, but somehow they all managed to gain the deck in safety. They hurried to the galley, exhibited the forlorn little cat, and all three talking at once told Alec the story of the rescue.

Luckily Alec was very fond of cats! Without a moment's delay he fixed a dish of warm milk and they all watched anxiously while the kitten feebly lapped up a little of it. Then Alec hunted about and found an old wooden peck measure which he lined with pieces of frayed canvas. When the cat had lapped a little more milk and the children had put it gently in its bed, close to the galley stove, they were convinced that they could hear a faint murmur of purring.

"I guess it'll be all right for us to take it home with us. Mother never minds an extra cat," said Obed as they stood about, still talking of the rescue.

John, dismayed at Obed's suggestion, glanced swiftly at Alec. To his joy Alec said quickly, "You talkin' about takin' our cat home with you? Well, I guess not! She shipped aboard this vessel and aboard this vessel she's goin' to stay. Why, she's our own pertic'ler stowaway."

"You've given me an idea for a name for her!" exclaimed John. "Lets call her Stowie."

"That's capital! Capital!" roared Alec, slapping his knee in delight.

So the fate of Stowie was settled and John was jubilant.

"I'm real glad you can keep her," Jane said generously, "'cause we've got *lots* of pets on the farm and you haven't anything alive here on the boat."

"Say, why don't you ask your father if you can come up to the farm tomorrow?" suggested Obed. "Maybe the hired man'll let you ride one of the horses out to the field."

Once more John burst in upon Father, who was working at the chart table in the cabin, and asked excitedly, "Please, c'n I go to Obed's farm tomorrow and ride on the horses?"

"I'm willing that you should go to the farm, if it's no trouble to Mrs. Stevens, but I reckon the horse-riding part will likely be the hired man's say-so," answered Father, smiling.

"I c'n come, Obed," shouted John as he ran up on deck again, slamming the cabin door behind him with a resounding clap.

The following days were vexing ones for Father because, even after the loading of the ice finally started, it went forward slowly and there were delays of every sort. With such a perishable cargo speed was important and already the loading had taken four days longer than Father had expected. He was troubled and impatient.

But the days passed happily for John. Once the loading commenced it was not safe for the children to play aboard the vessel, so, each morning, John ran up to the white house and spent the day sharing lessons, chores and playtime with Jane and Obed.

At last the day came when the final block of ice was below deck. Good-byes were said and soon the towboat was taking them down the river again to Bath, where they anchored for the night. Early in the morning John was on deck, impatient for the *Good Fortune* to be under sail again. This time he felt like an old hand at the game, and when the longed-for orders came, he darted around, coiling a rope here and running an errand there, as busy as any of the crew. He capered around the deck in delight at the feel of the wind and the lift of the open sea and ended by giggling at himself when he discovered that he had to find his "sea legs" all over again.

As twilight came on, John took his place by the rail and stated that he was not going to budge from the deck until he had caught the first glimpse of Highland Light on the Cape. He peered hopefully through the gathering dusk, as the *Good Fortune* dipped and swung on her way. After an hour of fruitless watching John grew restless and, seeing the mate coming toward him along the deck, questioned him anxiously. When Mr. Gibson told him that they would not be off Highland Light until midnight or even later, John exclaimed in disappointment, and reluctantly giving up his watch, went below.

When he climbed into his bunk sometime later he was glad to hear again the soft chuckle of the water along the side of the vessel and fell asleep, quickly, to its pleasant song.

☀ 2 ☀

An Unexpected Port

"I SEE IT! I see the Cape!" yelled John dashing up on deck the next morning and darting to the starboard rail. Gazing at the green-topped dunes rising out of the sea John stood, elbows on rail, planning all the things he had to tell Mother and the boys when he reached home that afternoon. He was thinking that Peter and Eben had probably been on watch from the scuttle for several afternoons, puzzling over what could have delayed the *Good Fortune*. John felt as if he had been away a long time and he wondered if there would be many changes around home. He was eager to get back to school again and be with Joe and the other boys. They would envy his having been on a real voyage. His heart was light as he turned to pace the deck. He whistled, hands in pockets, and watched until the *Good Fortune* made the Cross Rip Lightship and changed her course to head down Vineyard Sound. Feeling that he had seen her started on the homeward reach he went below, content.

At breakfast Father was unusually quiet, but John was absorbed in his own thoughts and did not notice it. When he had finished eating he repacked his satchel and then went on deck again to watch for familiar landmarks as they approached the mouth of the river.

Job Handy, passing along the deck, stopped to ask him if he was sure he could tie a bowline knot for the boys at home. John grabbed up an end of rope and was demonstrating his skill when Father called him. Dropping the rope John ran to where he stood on the after deck near the wheel and, glancing up expectantly, found Father looking down at him seriously. After a moment's hesitation Father said, "Son, I'm afraid you won't see your mother tonight. I must make the most of this fair wind. If I stop now to beat in to the river and land you, I'll lose another day. I don't see my way clear to do that after the delay we've had. I'm sorry, John, but I guess likely you'll have to turn able seaman and make the whole voyage with us."

John's heart stood still in amazement at Father's words. He could not believe his ears! As he looked at the white tower of the distant lighthouse near the mouth of the river, he felt a huge lump rise in his throat. He swallowed hard, determined not to show his feelings before Father and the men. Thrusting his fists deeper in his pockets he walked away along the deck, with chin up and teeth set hard.

Just as he was passing the galley door Stowie, now fat and fluffy, ventured out over the high sill. The sight of her comforted John at once. Stooping to pick her up he said, "It looks like I'm kind of a stowaway too! It's a pretty sudden trip for both of us, Stowie. I wonder if I'll get as fat as you have in a few days." Grinning as he pictured himself round and chubby John cuddled Stowie up under his chin and found her loud purring very cheering.

Carrying the kitten, he went down to the cabin where he could think over the abrupt change in his plans and get used to the idea. He was troubled most of all about Mother, waiting and watching for him to come home. What *would* she think! If only she could know that everything was all right he knew he would enjoy the extra voyage. What a lot he would learn about handling a vessel! He could almost catch up to Eben and Peter whose greater knowledge and experience had always made them the unquestioned leaders in everything the boys did.

Presently the sound of shouting and thudding footsteps on deck brought John to his feet. Picking up Stowie, he ran up the companionway and saw that a schooner was approaching on the starboard quarter, heading in to the river. Father, recognizing her as the *Oriole*, bound into the river from Philadelphia, was altering his course so as to come up and speak her. In a flash John realized what this lucky meeting meant and ran to Father's side to wave his arms and have his share in the exchange of messages. Through his speaking trumpet Father hailed her master, Captain Baxter, and asked him to report to Mrs. Crosby that he had spoken the *Good Fortune* and learned that John was well and was going to make the voyage to Savannah.

Father was pleased that he had found means to relieve the increasing anxiety that Mother would have felt as the empty days dragged by, and the meeting with the *Oriole* took a huge load off John's mind, too. Now he could think of home without a feeling of distress and he began to picture the surprise of Mother and the boys when they received the message from Captain Baxter.

During the afternoon watch the mate brought out some pieces of wood and said to John, "How'd you like to make a board to play dallies on? You know how to play, don't you?"

"Oh, yes, Mr. Gibson, we play a lot," answered John. "We shake our dice in a gourd that we grew in our own garden and we move the pegs along from the side rows into the center row of holes. I do have the dreadfulest luck havin' the other player land in the same hole I'm in and then I have to go clear back to the start of my own row again! I'd like it fine to make a real good board 'cause the one at home is kinda old. I could take it back as a present for Peter and Eben, couldn't I?"

"I guess likely they'd set great store by something you made aboard the vessel," commented Mr. Gibson.

Together they looked over the wood, deciding on the

best piece to use for the board and setting aside some scraps to cut up for pegs. John admired the wood, smoothing it with his hands as he said, "Gee, Mr. Gibson, this wood's got a dandy grain. It'll make a real handsome board."

"It will so," agreed the mate. "Now here's a piece of shark skin you can use for sandpaper, to rub down the pegs when you get them whittled out. I'll trim off the board so's you can work on that next."

The afternoon passed quickly while John was busy whittling and polishing the pegs and he was really surprised when Alec came out on deck to ring the supper bell. His broad grin was explained when he proudly served up hot soda biscuits and beach plum jam in honor of John's signing on for the whole voyage.

When John went on deck again he found that they were sailing out past Block Island into the open Atlantic. The increased heave of the vessel made him stagger across the deck until he grabbed the shrouds and clung to them as he gazed in wonder at the waves mounting all about them. He was excited by the new rush and surge of the *Good Fortune. This* was really being at sea!

Suddenly he was startled by a hail from the port watch—"Thar she blows!" It simply could not be true! But he raced for the port rail and there, sure enough, were three whales, close to the surface and spouting like geysers! One great black fellow swam along within thirty feet of the vessel and John, gazing wide-eyed, had a rare chance to see its huge bulk. He hung over the rail watching until the gathering dusk hid the whales from sight.

The wind held most of the night but lightened toward morning so that Father was on deck early, ordering on more sail, and John awoke to hear the men singing:

> *The shark he rose up with his seven rows of teeth,*
> *You eat the pork, boys, and I'll eat the beef!*
> *Wednesday morning, cold frosty morning,*
> *Wind is fair, boys, ship she will go.*

Sitting atop the cabin, a little later, John polished dally pegs and watched Father issue crisp orders to the crew. John thought it was a splendid thing to be in command of a vessel. His hands fell idle while he pictured himself striding about, roaring orders and seeing men jump to obey them.

Suddenly there was a cry from the lookout. He had sighted a school of porpoises rolling and plunging toward them. John scrambled down from the cabin, scattering his work in all directions, and raced forward. At the lookout's hail the mate had darted below and grabbed up a small harpoon. Reaching the deck again in two bounds he ran out along the bowsprit and stood, one hand grasping the stay and the other balancing the harpoon while he scanned the water intently. Suddenly Mr. Gibson flung the harpoon. John let out a whoop when he saw that the mate had struck a porpoise, and he held his breath as the line was drawn in. It actually looked as though they were going to land

one on the very first try! But just as it was almost to the surface of the water, the porpoise thrashed himself clear of the barb and dove out of sight.

On the second trial Mr. Gibson made another strike but the porpoise made such a violent lunge and swam away so fast that the line caught and snapped in two. In his excitement John was hanging far out over the bow rail when Job Handy seized him firmly by the seat of his pants and jerked him back to the deck again, saying sternly, "Like enough you need to go to school for a considerable spell yet, but we don't aim to have you joinin' no porpoise institootion!" John grinned but edged up to the rail again as soon as Job's back was turned.

Father handed out a new harpoon and the mate watched his chance. Balancing on the swaying bowsprit he made a third, mighty cast and a porpoise was securely caught. Slowly and cautiously the line was drawn in and the creature was landed on the deck amid the cheers of the crew and John's lusty yells.

In the afternoon the wind was so light and the ship so steady that Father let Job Handy give John his first lesson in climbing aloft while at sea. He had tried it once when they were anchored in the Kennebec and found it not quite so hard as he had expected. However, the spaces between the shrouds were wide and it took plenty of stretching and clinging and scrambling to go up even a few steps. The vessel was swaying and dipping. The deck below looked so tiny in the great circle of blue sea! John thought if he did slip he could *never* manage to land on that small, moving area of planking. He hung on for dear life, looking all around the horizon and since he could not see the coast line he thought he could truthfully tell Peter and Eben that he had been out of sight of land.

After a supper of fried porpoise liver, which tasted good as a change from the salt beef and pork that made up their usual fare at sea, John cleared the cabin table and carried the dishes, without mishap, back to the galley. It was part of his daily chores to help the cook, for he and Alec were great friends and John liked having something to do. With everyone else busy around him time would have hung heavy on his hands. One job in particular was a never-failing source of delight to John—to lift up a small scuttle in the cabin floor and store away the butter and fruit on top of the cargo of ice.

The sun set in a dull, murky sky and a chill in the air made the lamplit cabin seem cosy and pleasant. John was afraid the fine weather was spoiling but when a flaming sky greeted him next morning, he cheerfully laid his plans for a busy day as able seaman. Job, however, shook his head dubiously as he looked at the color in the east. "See that, boy," he said soberly. "Red sky at night, sailors delight; red sky at morning, sailors take warning."

John scoffed at his gloom but, as the day advanced and the sky grew grey and lowering, and the wind came in sudden gusts, his face began to reflect the soberness all around him. He gave up all thought of going aloft and set himself to rigging a fishing pole.

By afternoon there was a feeling of anxiety in the air. Father's face was grave and John heard him say to the mate, "We ought to make Hatteras just night and I don't like the look of that sky. Set all hands to shorten sail and take a single reef."

The vessel rolled and jerked in the choppy sea. The wind was squally and baffling. John was too uneasy to settle to any of his usual tasks. He wandered aimlessly about the deck. The men were busy battening down the hatches and making all tight against the coming storm and for the first time since the voyage began, they were impatient and spoke gruffly when John got in their way or asked anxious questions. He began thinking how warm and cheerful it would be in the kitchen at home on such a chilly, grey afternoon. The fire would be crackling in the stove and very likely Mother would let the boys pop corn. With these thoughts, homesickness, for the first time, closed down upon a lonely, forlorn small boy.

The galley seemed the nearest approach to the home kitchen, so John sought its comfort; but even Alec was too busy to notice him today. He was hastily cooking up a batch of doughnuts to go with a constant supply of hot coffee for the men who would soon be battling the storm on the cold, wet decks.

After looking longingly inside, John sat down in the galley doorway, on the high, brass-bound sill. He sat disconsolately, elbows on knees and chin in his hands, gazing out rather fearfully at the grey sea. A sudden exclamation from the cook made him turn quickly to find Alec looking at him with a mixture of laughter and dismay.

"Avast there! Belay, my lad!" Alec shouted. "Up with you! Didn't you see I'd been scouring my bright work and had the sill covered with lye?"

At his words John leaped to his feet and clapped his hands to the seat of his trousers. His heart sank when he felt two dampish, sticky spots where he had been sitting. At sight of his plight Alec doubled over in help-

less laughter and then, sobered by the look of distress on John's face, he said kindly, "Come here, boy, and let's see what the damage is. Maybe we won't need to lay up in drydock after all."

John entered the galley and stood craning his neck so as to see as much as possible of his back while Alec examined the rear of the trousers. Alas for John's hopes of escaping unharmed from the lye—at the touch of warm water the cloth of the trousers fell away in shreds, leaving two ragged holes!

"It looks like your craft needs a new suit of sails, sonny," was Alec's decision.

"But I haven't any others with me!" protested John desperately.

Father was too busy handling the *Good Fortune* in the increasing gale to be consulted in this emergency so John, at Alec's suggestion, took off his trousers and huddled close to the galley stove while Alec fetched some scraps of sail cloth from a locker in the fo'c'sle and sewed two white patches on the seat of the trousers. When he had finished Alec gazed at his handiwork with great pride but John eyed the patches with a sinking heart. "Have I got to wear 'em like THAT?" he cried.

"Sure, my lad, you're a lightship now and those are your day marks," replied Alec with a chuckle as he hustled back to his interrupted cooking.

John donned the trousers without further protest but he secretly determined to spend the rest of the voyage *sitting down*!

As he stepped outside the galley door the wind caught him in a wild buffet. He made a dash for the rail and clung to it. When he had gotten his breath he worked his way aft, hand over hand, toward where Father stood beside the man at the wheel. He looked anxious as John was swept along the deck in a rush, the moment he loosed his hold of the rail. Father grabbed him and leaning down, shouted in his ear, "Go below, son! The deck's no safe place for you in this sea!"

John clung to Father's arm an instant to ask if the *Good Fortune* was going to be all right. "Certain sure, she is!" Father replied heartily. "This is only about half of what Hatteras can do in the way of a gale."

Reassured, John waited for a moment's lull in the wind and darted to the cabin companionway. He passed one of the sailors rigging lines for the men to grasp as they made their way along the slanting deck, awash with big seas. He glanced up at John and catching sight of the patched trousers, hailed him as "White-eyes." John ducked below without any reply realizing what life would be like for him when the storm cleared and he had to be on deck among the sailors.

Supper that night was a strange meal with wooden racks fastened to the table to keep the plates from sliding off onto the floor when the vessel rolled and plunged. John amused himself by making a game of eating; timing his mouthfuls to the moment when the contents of his plate and cup surged toward him, and giving himself a black mark every time anything spilled over.

Father and the mate, throwing off their streaming

oilskins as they clumped down the companionway, came, one at a time, to snatch a bite to eat before making for the deck again. They were too sober and preoccupied to invite John's questions though he was bursting with things he wanted to ask. Ordinarily it was Father's habit to sit sidewise at the end of the cabin table so that he could look up through the open companionway and keep an eye on the man at the wheel. Tonight Father did not even take time to sit down at the table. He ate while he studied the chart, spread out on its wide shelf. His face was intent and he stood with legs braced far apart, seeming to feel and judge the strain of the plunging, groaning ship. Watching him, John felt for the first time a chilling doubt about the complete enjoyment of being in command. What if you gave the wrong order and something awful happened! Father was making up his mind right now what to tell the crew to do to bring them all safely through the storm. He had to be awfully sure he was right. Sensing Father's responsibility, John suddenly realized that it was really a *solemn* thing to be captain.

However, so great was his trust in Father and the *Good Fortune* that he did not have any trouble getting to sleep once he was snug in his rocking bunk.

During the night he was awakened by a swashing of water close at hand. With sudden fear gripping his heart he looked over the edge of his bunk. The floor was covered with water! What had happened? Were they sinking?

In the dim light from the cabin lamp he saw his

satchel floating in the water. As the vessel rolled the water rushed from his stateroom, carrying the bobbing satchel through the door into the cabin. With pounding heart and racing thoughts John watched for the next roll of the ship to bring the water back toward him. Fearfully he measured it with his eye. No, it wasn't getting any deeper. They couldn't be sinking very fast.

He heard the satchel bumping against the cabin table and wondered if the surging water would bring it back where he could reach it. On the next heavy roll the satchel came dashing through the doorway again. John grabbed it and clutched it to him as he lay, rigid and frightened, straining his ears to catch some hint of what was happening. There were no sounds he could hear above the howl of the wind and the creaking and groaning of the laboring vessel.

After an age of suspense he heard the opening of the door at the top of the cabin companionway and Father's voice exclaiming at the sight of the water on the floor, "Well, I snum! Some lubber must have left the slide pushed back a mite and we've shipped a sea clear down here."

Overwhelmed with relief at the hearty, usual sound of Father's voice John swallowed hard and then was able to command an ordinary tone as he called out, "Father, is the storm getting worse?"

Father strode into John's room and told him that they had rounded Hatteras and would soon be in quieter water. He explained that he had left Mr. Gibson on duty and had come below to rest a little and have a cup of hot coffee. John took the opportunity, while they waited for Alec to bring aft the coffee and sinkers, to tell Father about his mishap that afternoon. Father laughed heartily at the story but comforted John with the assurance that they would soon be in port where they could buy some new clothes.

By the time John went on deck next morning the sky was blue, the sun warm and bright, and a brisk wind was speeding the *Good Fortune* on her way. Save for the tumbled, foam-streaked waves there was no sign of last night's storm. John leaned on the rail, enjoying the warmth and idly watching two schooners and a steamer passing them, headed north. He turned at the sound of a suppressed snicker and saw Job standing behind him. With a solemn face Job raised his hand in salute, saying, "Ahoy there, White-eyes."

John, suddenly remembering his awful trousers, flushed to the roots of his hair. Shutting his mouth in a tight line he sat down hastily on a handy coil of rope and frowned deeply as he racked his brains for some way out of his plight.

In a flash an idea came to him and he set about carrying it out without a moment's delay. He sat down and scrubbed around on every rail and hatch-cover that might possibly be grimy. If only he could blacken the canvas patches they would look more like the rest of his dark trousers and he could no longer deserve the hateful name of "White-eyes." For once John was sorry that the vessel was kept in such spick and span condition for it was hard to get dirty enough. He worked

diligently all morning while the sailors, repairing a spar
that had snapped during the gale, were too busy to
notice what he was doing. Finally he screwed himself
and his trousers around so that he could inspect his
work. He was quite satisfied with the result. Now he
could walk the deck boldly once more without fear of
teasing.

In the afternoon the mate told him that they were
in the Gulf Stream which explained the sudden warmth
and softness of the air. To his delight John soon saw
flying fish rising from the water as they were chased
by dolphins.

That night they had a head wind and beat back and
forth, making very little progress. But in the morning
the wind shifted and blew stronger so that they slipped
steadily along all day and by nightfall were nearing the
Savannah river where they took the pilot aboard and
made into the river mouth.

It was slow work drifting with the tide up the river
but it gave John plenty of time to see everything along
the banks. He climbed on top of the cabin from which
vantage point he could watch both sides of the river
at once. It did not seem quite possible that he was actually seeing rice and cotton fields. He decided, without hesitation, that seeing geography was preferable
to reading it.

At dusk they reached Savannah and were eventually
tied up at the ice wharf. After the exciting business of
docking was over John found that he was tired yet it

was strangely hard to get to sleep on such a silent and motionless vessel.

Father woke John early in the morning so that he could go ashore with him and see the market.

John stood amazed in front of piles of fruits and vegetables he had never seen before, and was equally surprised to find all the familiar kinds ripe and ready to eat. Gardens on the Cape were only just being *planted*! And how he wished for Peter and Eben when he came to the stalls where new kinds of fish lay glistening in their rainbow colors!

When Father began his marketing, he bought so generously of fresh fruit and vegetables—even strawberries, peaches and plums!—that several little, grinning negro boys were soon loaded with bundles to be carried down to the *Good Fortune*. After starting them on their way to the dock he and John went on up into the town, to a big store where John was fitted out with a linen suit and a straw hat. Looking at his reflection in the store mirror he could not suppress a glow of pride and he actually felt kindly toward his dejected "whiteeyes" trousers for their share in his unexpected elegance. He decided then and there to continue to wear them aboard ship so that his new suit would still be good when he reached home and would show off at its best.

The idle days in port dragged for John and he grew constantly more restless and impatient to be headed home. His thoughts surged back toward the Cape until he felt that he was ready to burst with all the things he had to tell Mother and the boys.

The unloading of the ice went forward swiftly and when Father learned at the agent's office that a return cargo of lumber for Boston had been assigned to the *Good Fortune* his relief almost matched John's high spirits at the news.

Just before leaving Savannah Father took John up-town again. He had two silver dollars in his pocket to spend for presents for Mother, and Peter and Eben. John was bewildered by the array of fascinating things in the stores. He finally chose two bamboo fishing poles with lines and trimmed hooks for the boys and for Mother, a bamboo workbasket lined with gleaming red satin.

On their way back to the vessel Father had one more treat in store for John, his first taste of ice cream! After the first eager attack on the heaped-up saucer John took tiny spoonfuls, partly to prolong the rapture, and partly because he had discovered that large mouthfuls made his teeth ache. John suddenly dug in his pocket and brought out the small bits of change left from his purchases but, seeing how few they were, his face fell.

Father, who had been watching him with curiosity, asked, "What's on your mind, son?"

"I thought maybe I c'ud take a treat of ice cream back to Alec, kinda celebrating 'cause we're going home, but I guess it costs more'n that," answered John, holding out his money.

"I don't know but 'twould," agreed Father, "but it's

a first-rate notion, so, like enough, I could help out a mite. What flavors do you reckon he'd relish?"

After some thought John decided on lemon and strawberry. When it was packed for them in a little paper box, Father and John gathered up their bundles and hurried down to the dock to deliver the ice cream before it melted. Alec smacked his lips over the treat with satisfactory enthusiasm and then suggested that Stowie have a taste, too. She lapped up the melted liquid readily enough but she sent Alec and John into fits of laughter over the way she sneezed and shook her whiskers when she attempted the cold, solid part. "I bet it makes her teeth ache, too!" commented John.

While he was showing the rest of his purchases to the cook John heard running steps and shouted orders on deck.

"Golly, I bet we're casting off!" he exclaimed, grabbing up his things in a rush. Darting aft and clattering down the companionway he dumped the presents, helter-skelter, in his bunk and ran back on deck, to lend a hand in getting the vessel under way—homeward bound.

Off to
the Grand Banks

THE HOMEWARD VOYAGE was a pleasant one. Wind
and weather favored the *Good Fortune* save for one
spell of fog when she hove to for two days, rocking
gently in the midst of the muffling whiteness, with her
sails slatting idly. The rest of the time she drove along
steadily with "a bone in her teeth" as John learned was
the seaman's way of describing the curling, white bow
wave under her forefoot. He enjoyed the voyage thoroughly. He took his trick at the wheel every day;
learned to tie all the sailor knots and to splice rope; and
practiced climbing in the lower shrouds until the crew
called him "the ship's monkey." He finally learned to
box the compass, studying the card each day and reciting the points to Father at supper each night.

The morning they entered Vineyard Sound John was too excited to eat breakfast or do anything but watch for familiar landmarks. Father had not said what his plans were and John wondered whether they would anchor off the river and go ashore, or go straight on to Boston and then down to the Cape by train. It didn't seem as though he *could* go right past the mouth of the river *again*!

Father must have read his anxious thoughts for he joined John on the quarter deck where he stood eagerly scanning the low, wooded line of the Cape, and said, "Well, son, I guess likely we can anchor long enough to set you ashore this time. We've made a good passage and with this wind it won't delay us more than a couple of hours."

"Oh, Father," exclaimed John, his eyes shining, "then I'll be home tonight! Do you s'pose Peter and Eben are watching for us?"

"I shouldn't wonder a mite, not a mite," replied Father, smiling, and he promptly ordered the owner's flag run up to the masthead so that the boys on watch in the scuttle, with the spy-glass, could identify the vessel when she came in sight.

At the first glimpse of the lighthouse on the beach John plunged down the cabin companionway to his stateroom, to snatch up his satchel and precious bundle of presents. Returning to the deck he made the rounds of the crew, to say good-bye, and stopped in the galley for a last chat and a last sinker with Alec.

"We're goin' to miss you, boy, Stowie and I are! I'm

real spoiled, havin' a handy helper and cabin-boy. I am so!" said Alec sorrowfully.

John grinned, picked up Stowie for a last hug, and then ran out on deck again. Father was waiting by the after rail to say, "I can't take time to go ashore with you, John, but tell Mother I'll come down on the train before Sunday and aim to have a week at home."

John was disappointed for a moment to find that they could not go home together, but Father continued, "Two of the sailors will row you ashore and land you at the town wharf yonder. Walk up the lane to Ezra Hallett's house and ask him to drive you over home. By this time of afternoon 'tisn't likely he'll be too busy to hitch up and take you straight off. Here's twenty-five cents to give him for making the trip."

They had reached the sheltered water inside the breakwater and Father gave the order to lower sails and drop anchor. In a moment the *Good Fortune* swung to her cable and the mate gave the signal to lower away the ship's boat over the stern. John climbed nimbly down the swaying ladder and when he was seated in the boat, his satchel and bundle were lowered to him.

As the little boat moved away from the vessel's side John looked up and waved to Father and Mr. Gibson, smiling down at him from the deck, and then fixed his eyes on the wharf inside the wooden jetty. Impatiently he watched the distance between him and the shore lessen slowly. At last they reached the wharf and the sailors steadied the boat while John landed his luggage and scrambled ashore. He waved to them as they shoved off and then, with the money clutched in his hand, he grabbed up his things and marched with an air of great importance, up the lane.

Ezra Hallett, working out by the barn, went at once to hitch up the horse and carry out Captain Crosby's orders. Riding along beside Ezra on the high wagon seat John surveyed the country. He noted each familiar landmark with pleasure. When they crossed the bridge and were driving along the main road, John was fairly bursting with excitement. It seemed good to be going home! At last they were approaching the corner of the lane: they were turning the corner: they were in sight of the house!

He leaned forward eagerly—yes, there were Peter and Eben, waving and shouting! Mother had followed the boys out to the gate and, at sight of her, John leaped down from the wagon and flung himself into her arms. As Ezra turned the wagon and drove away, the Crosbys moved toward the house, all talking at once.

Once inside the house John was so anxious to present his gifts that he fumbled awkwardly with the string, dropped the bundle on the floor and ended by dumping the whole thing in Mother's lap. She undid the bulky parcel and distributed the presents while John looked on expectantly. As the final wrappings were removed the expressions of delight made John's heart swell with satisfaction. Though they were eager to hear about his voyage, they could not help interrupting him every few minutes.

"Were you seasick?" was Peter's first question.

"No, I wasn't—not a *mite*! not that first morning you *said* I'd be, or in the storm off Hatteras, or *any* time," answered John vehemently and continued, with the words fairly tumbling over each other, "and I saw whales and we caught a porpoise and I had *ice cream*!"

"It's plain to see you've been eating something that's hearty and filling, besides ice cream," said Mother, "for you're looking real stout and, I declare, you've grown an inch."

"What was it like in Savannah?" asked Eben and in the same breath Peter said, "Did Father buy you those clothes down south? Do they wear suits like *that*— kinda light and thin?"

John could not forbear strutting a little as he answered, "Oh, it's awful hot down there and all the men-folks dress like this."

"We'll lay that suit right away," said Mother practically, "and keep it nice for Sunday School and Church, come real warm weather."

While Mother was making the final preparations for supper John ran over to see Grandfather and Grandmother. And on the way home again stopped in the woodshed and chicken house to help the boys do the chores. Why! It was actually *fun*, he was so glad to be home!

They sat down to a supper of chicken stew and raisin cake and John thought that nothing in his whole life had ever tasted so good! While they ate they listened to more of John's experiences and told him what had happened at home during his absence. After describing the strange new sights in Savannah John said slowly, "I was just thinkin'—each of us boys has been away on a voyage with Father. It's *your* turn, Mother."

The other two boys seized upon the idea with enthusiasm. "That's so," said Peter earnestly, "you haven't been to sea with Father since I can remember."

"You ought to go, Mother," urged Eben. "Father'd like it fine and I guess maybe you'd kinda relish seein' some new places."

Mother smiled at their serious expressions but shook her head firmly as she said, " 'Twould be real nice to go, sure enough, but while I have you three boys to do for and to keep me company 'tisn't likely I'll take to gallivanting for a spell yet."

She sounded very positive but, nevertheless, the boys could not give up the idea. They talked it over when they went up to bed that night and agreed that they would work and plan so that Mother could be persuaded to take her turn.

The next morning John went back to school. He felt proud and important when all the older boys and girls, and even the teacher, Mr. Parker, welcomed him back and asked about his voyage. At recess time an eager group crowded around him to hear about the whales and porpoises and strange southern fish.

When they were dismissed for the afternoon John suggested to Joe that they go down to the fish wharf and watch the men at work refitting Grandfather's fishing fleet. Already, John was feeling a little homesick for the *Good Fortune* and he thought that even a fishing vessel would be a welcome sight. The fleet was made up of five small, two-masted schooners with bluff bows and hulls wide and bulging so that there would be plenty of space for storing fish below decks. John thought proudly and longingly of the *Good Fortune's* clean lines and towering masts. However, the fishing boats had the satisfying *smell* of deep-sea vessels. All the fishermen knew about John's unexpected voyage and teased him good-naturedly. The afternoon passed quickly as the boys helped the men with paint and tar pot.

On their way home as the boys neared a tiny, white cottage, neat and trim in its bright little flower garden, John said, "I wonder if Aunt Betsy Ann knows I'm home yet? Seems like she must have a right smart store of cookies saved up for me by this time—unless you got a double share all the time I was gone."

" 'Course I did," grinned Joe. "Hadn't you noticed I wasn't *quite* so thin and poor as when you set sail?"

"Huh!" snorted John. "You can't make me believe Aunt Betsy Ann's forgot me all this time."

As if in answer to his speculation Aunt Betsy Ann Eldridge, a brisk little old lady with white hair and bright brown eyes, stepped out of her back entry door calling, "Yoo—hoo," and beckoned to the boys.

Grinning at each other John and Joe obeyed her summons on the run and Aunt Betsy Ann exclaimed, "Land sakes, 'tis you, John Crosby, sure's I live! Thinks I, it looks like him right enough! When did you get home?"

John answered her question and was going on eagerly

to tell her something about his voyage when he realized, in surprise and disappointment, that she wasn't listening to him at all. Ordinarily she would have heard him out with ready chuckles and quick sympathy, but now she looked away from them and seemed so troubled and flustered that John let his recital trail off into silence. For several minutes he and Joe fidgeted around and then started to edge away. Aunt Betsy Ann hesitated and then burst out with, "I was just a-wondering if you boys would know of anyone who'd likely want to buy my Plymouth Rock hen. She's a real good layer, my Mehitable is, and it does seem kinda foolish for me to keep her, all alone like I be. I can't nowise use the eggs fast enough. I thought maybe you'd come across someone as was hankerin' for a good hen."

The boys looked at each other uncertainly and then Joe said slowly, "My father was sayin' the other day as how Captain Chase, down at the point, was lookin' to get hold of some good layers. I c'ud ask him if he'd like to buy your Plymouth Rock."

"Now that'ud be real nice of you, Joe, and I'd be much obliged," said Aunt Betsy Ann, turning abruptly to go back into the house.

As the boys walked along in silence John said, "It seems kinda funny she wants to sell her hen so suddenlike. I thought she set such store by it, always talking about how many eggs she gets and all."

"She must be worked up about somethin' 'cause she clean forgot to give us cookies or *anythin'*, like she usually does," commented Joe ruefully, and then he added, brightening, "say, I'm gonna ask my father if I c'n buy her hen for myself. I'll put her in the Poultry Show over to Barnstable Fair, come September."

"Gee, that'ud be dandy!" exclaimed John. "Maybe you'll get a prize if she's as good as Aunt Betsy Ann makes out."

At that glowing prospect Joe hurried away across the fields to his house while John, seeing Peter and Eben out by the chopping block, joined them to do the evening chores.

Later, as the boys were going in the back door, they saw a horse and buggy stopping at the side gate. Peering through the window of the kitchen they saw the dignified figure of Squire Nickerson climb out of the buggy. What could Squire Nickerson want at this time of the day? Smoothing down her dress, Mother hurried to the door to greet him and usher him into the sitting room. The boys, waiting in the kitchen, wondered what they could be talking about in such low, serious tones. They felt vaguely anxious and uneasy.

They were relieved when, in a few minutes, Squire Nickerson took his leave and Mother came back into the kitchen and told them that Squire Nickerson had driven over, thinking to find Captain Crosby at home. He had wanted to consult him about the affairs of Aunt Betsy Ann Eldridge.

At the mention of her name John looked up quickly and Eben too, seemed about to say something but changed his mind. They were all anxious to find out what was happening to Aunt Betsy Ann, for the cheery little old lady was one of their closest friends and neighbors and a great favorite with them all. Her husband, Captain Elnathan Eldridge, had been one of Father's friends. Father had often told them of the older boy whom he had always looked up to, and with what envy he had watched him go off to sea years before Father was ready to follow him. In later years, as fellow captains, they had thoroughly enjoyed their brief meetings at home. Captain Eldridge had been master of a ship that went around the Horn to San Francisco and the China ports. He had been lost at sea a good many years ago during a terrific gale.

" 'Twas always figured," Mother went on to say, "that Captain Elnathan was well fixed and that he'd left a tidy sum for Aunt Betsy Ann. I guess likely he did, for it's taken care of her real comfortable-like all these years. But Squire Nickerson says there's hardly any left in the Yarmouth Bank now."

"Golly, what'll she *do*?" asked Peter anxiously.

"Well," continued Mother, "some folks hereabouts have heard tell of vessels out San Francisco way, that Captain Eldridge owned shares in. The Squire came to see if Father knew anything about it."

"What's that got to do with the money running short in the Bank?" asked Eben, puzzled.

"Why, like enough Aunt Betsy Ann could get some money for his shares in the vessels, if it was certain sure he owned them," explained Mother. "I told him Father'd be home, come Friday, and would call over to the Bank to see him about it."

"Do you s'pose Father knows for sure about Captain Eldridge's business dealings?" questioned Peter.

"I'm dreadful afraid he doesn't know any more'n the rest of the folks. It appears like it's easy enough to recollect things hazy-like, but that won't help Aunt Betsy Ann a mite," said Mother with an anxious frown.

"Then *that's* why she wants to sell her hen!" exclaimed John, laying down his fork with emphasis, and then he told how he and Joe had been called in as they passed her house that afternoon.

When he had finished Mother said, "I'll just step over to see Mrs. Baker right after supper and tell her how things are so's she can fix it to give Aunt Betsy Ann an extra good sum. She can make out as how the hen's such a special fancy one it ought to fetch a big price."

"Gee, I wisht we could give her lots of money," sighed Eben, " 'cause I guess she needs it real bad. This noon when I was down't the store to get the lard and cinnamon for you, Mother, Aunt Betsy Ann was there getting some tea and corn-meal and sugar. When Mr. Kelly told her how much 'twas, she fished in her purse and then laughed kinda funny and said, 'My patience, what's come over me, orderin' sugar when I don't need it any more'n a cat needs two tails! I'll just take the tea and the meal, Ezra.' When she went out Mr. Kelly looked after her, puzzled-like, and I heard him say to himself, 'I wonder what's in the wind? It's quite a spell since Miz Eldridge got sugar. Like enough she must need it by now. Hmmmmm.' I couldn't make out what it meant then, but I see *now*," finished Eben soberly.

"Can't we *give* her some things, Mother?" suggested John eagerly.

"No, not just out bald and plain," answered Mother, shaking her head thoughtfully, " 'twould only hurt her feelings. She's real proud and has never been beholden to folks for things. Maybe Father and the Squire can fix up some way to help her."

"I'm sure they can and that'ud be better," agreed John with perfect confidence in Father's power to set things right.

In a few days John had slipped back so completely into the routine of home and school and chores that the weeks at sea seemed like a dream. On Friday Father came, as he had promised, but he had only two days to spend at home before he had to join the vessel again.

Nevertheless, he took time out of his brief stay to drive over to Yarmouth for a talk with Squire Nickerson. He had no exact knowledge of Captain Eldridge's affairs to offer the Squire, but the two men talked over ways of helping Aunt Betsy Ann. When Father got home he went down the lane to the little white cottage for a talk with her. He found that she knew the address of the lawyers who used to handle the captain's business and he suggested that she write them and ask them if he had owned any vessel on the west coast.

Before he left for Boston again Father made a careful inspection of the chicken house, sheds and garden. "I'm real pleased with the shipshape way things are looking," he told the boys. "You've done well and I can go to sea with an easy mind about things at home. See to it that Mother doesn't have any extra things to worry about. I know I can depend on you."

For all the glow of warmth that Father's praise and confidence gave the boys, they felt very dismal when he had to leave again after such a brief stay. John, especially, felt his departure keenly after having been with him so constantly during the weeks at sea.

The days moved along so monotonously for a while that they all welcomed the stir and activity that the sailing of Grandfather's fishing fleet always brought to the village at this time of year.

After the fishermen had put in weeks of work, carpentering, painting and tarring, the five little vessels were ready to set out for their summer on the Grand Banks where the crews would catch codfish, split them and pack them in salt until the holds of the vessels were full to the brim. Since most of the men who manned the fleet came from the village, nearly every family had someone getting ready for the trip and all were busy with the bustle of preparation. The lane outside Grandfather's Ship Chandlery was crowded with wagons loading supplies for the vessels, and the store itself was full of fishermen selecting their outfits and stocking up on knives and tobacco.

John loved to help Grandfather in the store. The Chandlery had always fascinated him and he would spend hours arranging the neatly labelled boxes on the shelves. He loved to pore over the assortment of hooks and sinkers, and handle the tarry-smelling coils of cod line, dreaming of the catches he would take if he could use some of this fine tackle. This year, with the sea-faring knowledge gained from his voyage aboard the *Good Fortune*, he found the work in the store more interesting than ever.

Hurrying home from school each afternoon he was glad to see the wagons hitched outside the store and hear the bursts of talk and laughter coming from within. Unnoticed, he would slip in among the groups of fishermen, drinking in their yarn-spinning and storing away in his memory their comments upon gear and equipment.

The last afternoon before the sailing day John was helping Grandfather tidy up the store and rearrange the depleted stock. Breaking a companionably busy silence John asked, "Grandfather, can the captain of the fleet go to the Banks and do the real fishing?"

"Certain sure, John, that's what I did in my younger days," replied Grandfather.

"But did you have the store then, too?" persisted John.

"Yes, sirree! Quick as I was made captain of the fleet I opened up the Chandlery so's I could outfit the boats right and proper for well-found vessels. I used to hire a man to tend store while I was at sea, but I did most of the ordering and outfitting during the season ashore," explained Grandfather.

"Then *that's* what I'm going to do when I grow up," stated John with decision. "Of course I want to go to sea. Doesn't seem like there's anything *else* a boy could rightly want to do, but I'd ruther fish than just sail 'round carryin' cargoes."

"Well, I presume likely I made up my mind to try the Banks when I was a shaver not much bigger'n you," said Grandfather. "Leastways, it won't do you a mite of harm. A man can learn a powerful lot from the sea and the ways of fish and it'll stand by him, no matter what he turns his mind to later on." These last words were wasted on John who was imagining what he would pick out if he were getting ready to sail the next day.

The sailing day dawned clear with a fresh breeze from the northwest and the fish wharf was crowded by the time John reached it. Grandfather had sent him on ahead with a logbook for the captain of each boat, in which he would keep the daily record of the navigation and fishing "take" of his craft. Feeling very important John wormed his way through the groups of people to the edge of the wharf and ran up the gangplank of the first vessel. From there he scrambled across from boat to boat, entrusting a logbook to each captain in turn.

Grandfather followed in a few moments with the vessels' papers. After his final words to the captains, the fishermen said good-bye to their families and leaped aboard to their stations at the hawsers and halyards. One after another the boats were warped away from the dock and edged out into the river where the tide carried them along while the flapping sails went creaking up the masts.

Joe had slipped through the crowd to stand by John on the extreme edge of the wharf. Watching the first vessel make sail and stand away down the river John said to him, a quiver of excitement in his voice, "Golly, it don't matter if it's a big vessel or a small one—settin' sail's awful kinda solemn and pretty-lookin', too!"

Joe nodded his agreement and then burst out, "Say, John, do you s'pose we c'ud race 'em down to the bridge and get there in time to see 'em go through the draw?"

"Come on!" was John's answer as he whirled around and dodged eel-like through the waving, shouting crowd on the wharf. Leaping over the clutter of discarded gear on the inner end of the wharf they gained the shore and raced along the path beside the river. When they were pounding down the final slope to the road John panted, "Lookit! Old Enoch Henry's just opening the draw!"

With a squealing and clanking of chains the draw-bridge was being cranked open by an old man, bending over the hand windlass. The boys dashed out on to the thumping planks of the bridge just as the leading boat slipped through the yawning draw. They elbowed their way to the rail among the crowd of boys and men already lining the bridge to watch the departure of the fleet. Climbing astride the rail they shouted and waved wildly as, one by one, the vessels passed, their crews waving in answer.

John and Joe stayed perched on the rail to watch the draw go clattering and groaning down again and the waiting buggies and lug-wagons drive across the clanking draw section and go their ways. Then they gazed after the gleaming sails of the five boats until they were out of sight down river.

"It seems like they've had a good kind of start and maybe that'll mean they'll have a lucky voyage," said John as they climbed down and turned homeward.

One day, a week later, John stopped at the Post Office on his way home from school and waited impatiently while the Post Mistress deliberately sorted over the mail. At last she handed out two letters to John. He grabbed them, darted out of the door and made for home as fast as he could, for one letter was from Father!

While no day of Captain Crosby's long absences from home passed without speculation as to where he was and how the weather was affecting him, the days on which letters arrived were marked with red chalk on the kitchen calendar. John burst into the kitchen, waving the letter. Mother sat down at once to read it and smiled as she read, so John knew everything was all right. Going to the calendar he drew a fat red circle around the date and then, figuring back to the blue line under the day of departure, realized that Father had been gone several days over a month. Just then Mother looked up to say, "Father will be home in a few days. This was written from Baltimore. He's bringing a cargo of coal to Boston. Here's a part of the letter for you boys: 'Tell the boys I have a present for them, something I found in Chesapeake Bay. I had the men take it aboard so's I could bring it home to them.'"

Mother laid down the letter and laughed at John's puzzled expression.

"Doesn't he say what it *is*?" asked John.

"Not another word than that," answered Mother.

"Where are Peter and Eben?" was the next question.

"Cleaning out the woodshed," replied Mother, and added, "don't forget you have to mend the slat fence back of the chicken house and paint it."

"I'll do it in a minute," called back John as he ran out to find the boys and tell them of the mysterious present.

Peter and Eben dropped their work at the first words and were as excited and puzzled as John.

"What in *time* do you s'pose 'tis?" questioned Eben.

"I bet it's some kind of a big fish," stated John with decision.

"A *fish*?" jeered Peter. "What'ud it *smell* like by the time Father got it here, I'd like to know!"

"No," said Eben thoughtfully, "it's got to be really alive—like a turtle'ud be—or not ever alive at all—like a ball or somethin'."

"*I* think it's prob'ly a new fish car for keeping fish fresh down at the Cove," said Peter with authority.

"Maybe it *is* a *turtle*," suggested John, clinging to his idea that it was something alive.

Neither Peter nor Eben seemed to take much stock in that suggestion but they had nothing to offer on which they could all agree so the present remained a complete mystery.

☼ 4 ☼

The Chesapeake Present

THE NEXT MORNING the boys wanted to stay home from school and watch for Father from the scuttle, but Mother felt sure it was too soon to expect him. She promised that they might begin the next day taking turns on watch so that only one of them need be away from school at a time. They went off reluctantly, feeling that the only bright spot in this day of impatient waiting was the prospect of telling the other boys about the mystery and having them share their curiosity and anticipation.

Joe, on hearing about it, decided without hesitation that it was something alive. For once he studied his geography very intently in an effort to learn what animals inhabited the shores of the Chesapeake. He could not make up his mind exactly what it would be but, by noontime, he and John had planned a circus to exhibit *it* as well as Joe's hen.

Mother was right and the day passed without a sight of the *Good Fortune,* but it passed more quickly than the boys had dared hope because it occurred to them that if they hustled around and got ahead with the garden work they would have more time in the next few days to devote to "the thing."

Another day dragged slowly by but it brought the assurance that the *next* one must surely end their vigil. Luckily that day was Saturday so all three boys could be at home. They had scarcely finished their extra, Saturday chores when Peter, who was on scuttle watch, gave the longed-for hail. Father's vessel was heading in to the breakwater! As the tide was going out, the ship's boat would land Father at the beach and not attempt the long row into the river against a strong head tide. The boys got permission from Mother to go and meet him and, though it was a mile to the beach, they started off on the run, for a short cut through the woods.

When they reached the lighthouse Father was just approaching the shore in the small boat. Shouting and waving, the boys raced down to the water's edge to lend a hand in beaching the boat and landing Father's luggage. Once ashore Father pointed back toward the *Good Fortune,* lying at anchor inside the breakwater, and said, "Do you see that, boys?"

Following the direction of his hand the boys saw something low in the water—a small craft of some kind—being paddled ashore by one of the sailors. They looked at each other, hardly daring to believe their eyes! Could it be a *BOAT*! Of their very *OWN*!

With devouring eyes they watched its approach to the shore. When the sailor beached the craft they swarmed around it. It was a dugout canoe. It had been skillfully hollowed out of a great log and was strong and smoothly finished. Seats had been built in it at the bow and stern, in addition to two seats amidships. The canoe was about fifteen feet in length and three feet wide. While the boys were examining it from every angle Father told them how he had discovered it adrift in the Chesapeake and, realizing what fun the boys could have with it in the Cove and river, had ordered the seamen to hoist it aboard the *Good Fortune*.

"Come on, Eb and John," said Peter excitedly, "get aboard and we'll paddle her up river and into the Cove."

Intent upon taking full possession of the craft all three boys pushed and shoved each other in their hurry to climb over the gunwale. John caught his toe and pitched headlong into the bottom of the dugout. He picked himself up hastily, rubbing his head, fearful that his mishap would somehow detract from his dignity as part owner of a real boat.

"Hold on a jiffy," cautioned Father. "Strikes me it's a mighty long pull up to the Cove with head tide and head wind. She's heavy and wouldn't move along so spry with three aboard."

"Aw, we c'n make it all right, Father," urged all three boys eagerly.

"No," said Father in the firm tone that allowed no further argument. "Peter, you may take her, and Reuben here," addressing the sailor who had brought the canoe ashore, "can go along to help you paddle."

Noticing Eben and John's disappointment as they climbed reluctantly out of the dugout, Father added, "You two boys can come along with me and borrow Captain Ed's blue lug-wagon to drive back here and fetch my dunnage."

On the return journey to the beach Eben and John made old Prince trot along at a pace very disturbing to his settled ways, for they wanted to run no risk of missing the arrival of the dugout in the Cove.

In record time Father's valise and sea bags were delivered at home and Prince, dazed by his own speed, was duly returned to Captain Ed. The boys running down through the fields to the Cove eagerly scanning the expanse of water, found that the dugout was not yet in sight around the wooded point. Relieved, they sat on the little dock swinging their feet and talking together, as they waited.

"Say, Eb, d'you know what?" burst out John excitedly. "Now we c'n go into the fishin' business and make us a lot of money. Havin' the canoe for our very *own*—to go out in whenever we've a mind to—we c'n go regular *every day* and supply folks steady." John's heart beat fast as his idea grew and he saw his chance to earn the money he needed to buy some of the longed-for tackle in Grandfather's store.

Eben, having weighed John's suggestion in his usual careful way, answered, "It looks like we could, right enough, and as the flat-fishing season's just commencing we c'n start off with something folks prize and are pretty certain to buy."

After a pause during which John's fancy was ranging over the shelves and drawers in the store, Eben asked, "What're you gonna do with the money you earn?"

Jealously guarding his new-found hopes and plans for a career as a fisherman, John said casually, "Oh, I dunno—get some new lines and things, I reckon. What're you?"

"Well," replied Eben seriously, "I've been thinking I'd just save mine—save it steady all this year and next, maybe—until I have a right smart sum of money. Then likely I could go clear to Boston on the cars and see around the city and visit Uncle Osborn's publishing business and all that. Seems like a big city would be a dandy thing to see!"

John was amazed that Eben's dream should have nothing to do with the sea and ships. He had always taken it for granted that all three of them would follow in Father's and Grandfather's footsteps. He was too astounded to make any comment. After a brief attempt to account for Eben's strange choice, he dismissed the matter with the thought that Eben always did set great store by books and studying, and turned his attention back to the thrilling prospect of being the founder of the Bass River Fishing Company.

When they sighted the dugout rounding the point they ran up to the house to bring Mother down for her first glimpse of their marvelous present. Proudly all three boys took a hand in tying the canoe securely to the dock and then, as they stood around admiring her, the question of a name was raised. They all thought hard for a few moments and then Mother suggested that, since the canoe had been on such a long voyage for a small boat, they call her the *Rambler*. Everyone was instantly satisfied that that was the right and proper name for her.

Since the next day was Sunday the boys had to content themselves with looking at the *Rambler* and gloating over their plans for using her. The idea of the Bass River Fishing Company had been unfolded to Peter and he had taken up with it enthusiastically, provided he could be at the head of the new enterprise. Eben and John consented without much protest, knowing full well that his age and experience would place him in that position anyway. But John, treasuring the thought that it was his idea in the first place, dreamed of the day when he would be such a capital fisherman that he could challenge Peter's right to command.

One of Father's first questions, when he had settled down after supper Sunday evening to catch up on the news of the village, was about Aunt Betsy Ann. "Has she had any word yet from the Boston lawyers, do you reckon, Susan?" he asked.

"Not as I know of," answered Mother, "and seems like she'd have told me first off if she *had*."

"She hasn't been to the Post Office or gotten any mail in a month of Sundays," offered John positively.

"Are you setting out to better the Post Mistress's record for knowing other folks's business, son?" laughed Father, and then turning to Mother he added, "Maybe we'd better step down the lane, Susan, and see if Betsy Ann's making any headway to windward. It's a pretty night and real mild feeling."

When they came home a little later Father answered the boys' eager questions in some exasperation, saying that Aunt Betsy Ann hadn't even written the letter yet. "She's about the hardest person to help I ever came across," he protested, "but there was *one* thing she allowed you boys *could* do for her some day soon, and that is to spade up her mite of a kitchen garden for her."

"Gee," grumbled Peter, "there's a terrible lot of work to be done, come this time of year, and we haven't even been out in the *Rambler* once yet!"

"As far as I could see her garden plot isn't bigger'n a spare topsail," commented Father. " 'Twon't take you but a little spell."

"All she's got in it is some pie plant," put in Mother. "Seems like 'twould be kind of nice to slip in a few of these extra seeds we've got such a store of around here."

Her suggestion roused an interest in Aunt Betsy Ann's meager garden and forgetting the *Rambler* for a moment, they started speculating how nice they could make it for her and how surprised she'd be when the unexpected seeds began coming up.

Fortunately for the boys' pent-up eagerness Monday

was a fine day and directly after school they set out flat-fishing. They had splendid luck to christen the new boat and came proudly home at supper time with a basket of gleaming flounders. Mother readily agreed to wait supper a while and cook some of the fresh fish that Father was willing to clean. Meanwhile the boys hastily divided up the surplus flounders and started out to secure customers for their new business. In half an hour they were back home, beaming—John and Eben with thirty-four cents apiece, and Peter with forty.

The boys' delight in the *Rambler* increased with every day of ownership but the trouble was that they never had enough time to spend in her. The garden was coming along so fast and the new raspberry canes and strawberry plants that Father had brought home from the south needed so much care that the days were not half long enough. In addition, they doggedly took turns putting in their spare moments on Aunt Betsy Ann's little vegetable garden. Hoeing weeds and transplanting tiny seedlings was hard work when all their thoughts were tugging them toward the *Rambler*. They cast many longing looks at the Cove which sparkled so invitingly. But when Father went away at the end of the week he pronounced everything up to the mark and promised the boys more freedom for their fishing business.

John was convinced that, with Joe's help, he could get in some extra fishing in the early mornings if he could only depend on waking up early enough. That meant he must have an alarm clock in his own room. So he decided that hooks and lines would have to wait a little while. As soon as his fish money amounted to two dollars he stuffed the hoard deep in his pocket and trudged across the bridge to the neighboring village where he bought himself a small wooden clock with a sturdy tick and a vigorous alarm bell. Showing it only to Mother, John installed it in his room. When, next morning, he and Joe made a successful fishing trip before breakfast and flaunted their catch under the noses of dumbfounded Peter and Eben, John felt well satisfied with his first investment.

After a time the boys began to think of adventuring up river, to the fresh-water ponds, where they might catch perch and pickerel and add variety to their stock. To solve the problem of going so far from home, Peter hit upon the idea of rigging a sail for the *Rambler*. Grandfather was consulted and gave his consent to the plan since the canoe was heavy and steady in the water. Peter cut, trimmed and stepped the mast, while Eben and John, with a little help from Mother, made a mutton-leg sail out of a discarded jib from the *Good Fortune*. Grandfather showed them how to set in brass grummets, to bind the holes in the sail through which the ropes passed, and when the sail was finished he pronounced it a very seaman-like job. It was a proud day when the *Rambler* made her maiden voyage under sail!

One afternoon after school John, whose class was dismissed first, waited on the steps for Peter and Eben. Their plan was to make a bee-line for home, grab the fishing gear and get out in the *Rambler* as fast as pos-

sible, since they had unusually large orders for floun-
ders. When Eben came out alone, wearing a long face,
John looked surprised and asked impatiently, "Where's
Peter?"

Eben jerked his head in the direction of the schoolroom and said in exasperation, "What d'you s'pose happened?"

In response to John's anxious headshake he went on,
"Peter went and made the composition class laugh jes'
now with one of his funny stories, only Mr. Parker didn't
think it was funny, so he's makin' Peter stay in and copy
some solemn ol' verses. Peter oughta had more sense'n
to do it on a day when we've got such big orders."

"What a dunce!" exploded John. "He oughta know
Mr. Parker never thinks anythin's funny—'cept his own
ol' jokes. What'd he hafta be so smart for? Now *what're*
we goin' to do?"

"We've *gotta* wait for him 'cause he's got the most
orders and we couldn't be sure of gettin' enough for all
hands, if we was to go alone," decided Eben.

"What say we sneak in and give a signal to Peter
and go on home and get the gear ready and maybe do
some chores ahead of time, while we're waiting?" suggested John.

"Good enough!" agreed Eben, brightening at the
prospect of making use of the dragging minutes. "But,
say! We'll have to be dreadful careful how we sneak in.
If Mr. Parker was ever to catch us he'd keep *us* in too,
and then we *would* be in a fix!"

John giggled and then clapped his hand to his mouth.

With the greatest caution the two boys tiptoed into the entry and crept over to the schoolroom door. Inch by inch they peered around the door frame. There sat Peter, facing them, doggedly copying verses. Luckily Mr. Parker had his back to the door as he sat at his desk, correcting papers, but even so, how were they to attract Peter's attention without giving themselves away to Mr. Parker? There was nothing to do but stand motionless and wait for Peter to glance up and see them. They could hear their own hearts beating in the silence broken only by the scratch of pens and the slow ticking of the big clock.

At last Peter looked up to cast a desperate glance at the time, and his attention was caught by the two pairs of eyes peering around the door frame. He looked quickly to see if Mr. Parker was watching and then glanced back to the door to get the message of silent, frantic gestures. With a tiny nod to show that he understood he turned back to his task, and Eben and John heaved an almost audible sigh of relief.

Just as they were about to start their stealthy retreat Mr. Parker suddenly cleared his throat and, shoving back his chair, rose from his desk. The boys stood frozen in their tracks! If he was coming to the entry for a drink of water, all was lost! They waited with bated breath. They heard him walk with firm tread—to the bookshelf in the far corner of the room! They were saved.

Under cover of the noise of his movements they slipped out of the entry and sank limply on the steps, only to leap up in a moment and make for home, eager to put a safe distance between themselves and the schoolhouse.

Once at home they did all the chores they could at that hour and then lugged the fishing gear down to the *Rambler,* giving frequent, anxious glances at the lengthening shadows. When they went into the house to get an apple apiece they saw Aunt Betsy Ann in the sitting room with Mother and heard her say, "Captain Crosby'd be real provoked if he was to know I'd been slower'n molasses 'bout gettin' that letter off to those lawyer folks. I know right enough I shoulda done it, but I'm not much of a hand to write letters and I couldn't seem to figure what to say. Now, if you was to write out what I'm s'posed to ask 'em, I could copy it off, like as not."

The boys could tell from her voice how flustered she was and they were glad to hear Mother say, in her quiet, kindly way, "Why, sure enough, I'll do it, Betsy Ann, and between us we'll get it so's they'll think you've got a right smart head for business."

With a relieved chuckle Aunt Betsy Ann settled back in her chair and rocked contentedly while Mother got paper and pencil to make up the letter.

Looking out the kitchen window for the hundredth time the boys saw Peter coming up the lane. They dashed out, grabbed him and hustled him down to the Cove. He was cross and grumpy over his unjust punishment and the wasted afternoon so, when John took him to task for his ill-timed prank, he retorted hotly, "Yes, and you two came *mighty* near getting caught sneaking in like that. Ninnies! Come on now, crowd on the canvas! We've gotta get a mess of fish 'fore dark."

They had fair wind and finally reached the fishing grounds about half past four but it seemed to be their unlucky day. The fish were not biting well and, though they kept shifting their grounds, the big basket in the center of the dugout filled very slowly.

"We'll never get enough at this rate," grumbled Peter.

Glancing over the side of the canoe John exclaimed, "Aw, gee! The tide's turned and it's running out. Now the fish'll quit biting altogether!"

"We've *gotta* keep on and catch a few more," said Eben doggedly. "Captain Ed and Uncle Aberdeen want theirs very special."

Once more they changed ground and tried every trick they knew to tempt the flounders, with little success. Presently they heard the mellow tones of the church clock striking six and they looked at each other in dismay.

"We'd oughta start home. Mother'll be watching out for us," suggested Eben.

"But we haven't got *half* enough fish," complained Peter.

"It doesn't look like it was doin' us much good to stay here and miss supper. I haven't caught a single fish in half an hour," grumbled John as he jerked in his line and wound it up.

"I haven't either," admitted Peter. "I s'pose we might as well go home, but this is going to hurt our trade something dreadful." Peter's face was very long as he pulled in the slack of the anchor rope.

Eben, glancing about at the darkening sky and water, muttered in disgust, "I declare if the wind hasn't hauled to the south'ard and it's dying out calm. We're gonna have a tough time getting home."

The boys hastily headed the *Rambler* about and hoisted the sail to catch the failing breeze. She made a little headway toward home, creeping past several small islands of marsh grass growing on the flats, and then she stopped and her sail hung limp while she began to drift down river again with the outgoing tide. In exasperation Peter and Eben dragged out the paddles from the bottom of the canoe and started to work her laboriously up river against the strong tide.

John was clearing up the mess of fishing gear underfoot when he happened to glance astern and ejaculated, "Well, I snum! If it isn't comin' in foggy!"

Peter and Eben turned sharply about to see a wall of soft, white mist creeping in from the Sound, and Peter said crossly, "Don't it beat all! It'll be on us directly and then how in time're we to keep our bearings around into the Cove?"

Even as he spoke the first wisps of fog drifted by, and almost before they knew it they were surrounded with grey whiteness.

"What say we don't try to get all the way home?" suggested Eben. "Why not tie up to the fish wharf and leave the *Rambler* there for the night?"

"I guess likely that's what we'll have to do," agreed

Peter, peering anxiously overside to get his direction from the way the tide was running.

"I took a look just before it shut down and if we bear off to starboard we oughta make it pretty nigh," said Eben paddling vigorously.

After a few moments of steady going they began to notice the dark mass of the wooded shore looming ahead of them. Moving forward cautiously they were tremendously relieved to make out the dim bulk of the black piles at the end of the fish wharf. They beached the canoe and climbed out, thankful to be safe on shore again. After unloading their fishing gear and the basket containing their meager catch they made the *Rambler* fast to one of the piles of the wharf. Loading up with their dunnage they started home, tired, hungry and disgusted with their afternoon.

This was a lonely stretch of lane and they passed only one fisherman's cottage whose lighted windows made patches of brightness in the grey gloom. Farther on they could see a dark bulk that must be Aunt Betsy Ann's house, but there was no gleam of light to be seen. They stumbled along in the chilly, clinging greyness until they suddenly overtook a small, dark figure that had been hurrying up the lane ahead of them. They were amazed to discover that it was Aunt Betsy Ann.

She gave a little gasp when the boys popped out of the fog beside her and then, recognizing them, said, "Land sakes, but you gave me a start! Seems like folks ought to carry foghorns, a night like this, same's vessels do."

"But what're you doing out on a thick night like this, Aunt Betsy Ann?" asked Peter.

"Well," explained the little old lady, "I got to worryin' about that letter your father wanted me to write a long while back. Your mother figured it all out for me this afternoon and, thinks I, I'd better get it all set down afore I forgit it. So I just finished writin' it all out real nice and I was aimin' to carry it to the Post Office and have it clear off my mind."

"I'll take it for you," offered John. "It's my turn to get the mail tonight so I'll be goin' down to the Office as quick as I get home."

"Now, I declare, that's real obligin' of you, John. I don't mind sayin' I'll be glad to get back to a warm kitchen and a lighted lamp such a night as this. I will so!" With that Aunt Betsy Ann handed over her letter and bobbed briskly away, disappearing quickly in the muffling whiteness.

They found that Mother had been watching anxiously for them and listening for the whistled signal that always told her of their approach. The moment she had heard it she had set about putting on the table the supper she had been keeping hot for them. When they told her their tale of woe they found that their troubles vanished to a point where they could giggle over their chapter of accidents.

All the boys' friends had been out in the *Rambler*, at one time or another, and quite frankly envied them their luck in having a boat of their own. However, it was a crowning satisfaction when the three Crosbys were asked to place the dugout on the entertainment program of the coming Sunday School picnic, an event eagerly anticipated for weeks beforehand. Sails in the *Rambler* were to be offered as a special treat and the buzz of excited chatter caused by this announcement gave the boys a pleasant feeling of importance. The picnic was to be held in the pine grove on Long Point and the boys would sail back and forth across the Big Cove. In preparation for the day the dugout was given a thorough scrubbing and the activities of the Bass River Fishing Company were temporarily suspended so that the skippers could practice sailing.

The boys were wondering if Father would get home in time for the picnic. For several years he had just happened to be home for the event and this year they were especially anxious for him to come because they wanted to surprise him with the sail in the *Rambler* and show their skill in handling her. Consequently, the house echoed with whoops of delight when, at dusk on the evening before the picnic, Father drove up with Ezra Hallett.

The next morning as soon as he had swallowed his breakfast he was hustled down to the Cove to see the *Rambler*. He inspected the mast, sail and rigging and gave them his approval. "You'll make sailormen yet, the lot of you, sure's I live!" he exclaimed as they shoved off on a trial trip to feel out the wind. They took a reach across the Big Cove and decided that while they were near by, they might as well land and see how things were going in the picnic grove.

Amos Cahoon, a master hand at clambakes, was in command of the preparations. When the boys strolled up he was tending the hot fire that he had lighted early that morning in a pit filled with a layer of stones. He was just about ready for the next step in the progress of the clambake and told the boys that if they wanted to help, they could go down to the little beach where they had left the dugout and bring up basket loads of the wet seaweed and rockweed they would find piled there. Delighted to share in the fun the boys worked diligently until they had the entire pile of seaweed transferred from the beach to the grove. By that time Captain Ed had arrived with the clams, sacks of potatoes, and chickens done up in cheesecloth bags.

Amos had let the fire die down to a bed of coals and red-hot rocks. Now came the fun! He piled everything around him so that he could work fast and then he seized a pitchfork. Masses of wet seaweed were tossed onto the red-hot rocks! Steam rose in such fierce, hissing clouds that the boy leaped back from the heat! Working at top speed Amos covered the seaweed with a big piece of chicken wire and on that he dumped the clams, potatoes and bags of chicken. They, in turn, were covered with more wire and then the rest of the seaweed was heaped on and spread so as to cover the pile completely. Amos then drew a heavy canvas over the entire heap and fastened the corners down securely. When all was finished only an occasional jet of steam escaped. Amos stayed to keep an eye on the bake and help the men set up the long picnic tables, but the boys hurried home to get dressed.

Just before noon Father and Mother started off in the surrey with Aunt Ruth and Uncle Aberdeen; each of the ladies carefully carrying a cake covered with a snowy napkin, and Uncle Aberdeen, the champion lemonade maker, sitting with a basket of lemons and a sack of sugar between his knees. After seeing them off the boys ran down to the Cove, sailed over in the *Rambler* and reached the picnic grove ahead of the surrey.

The opening of the bake was a ceremony that everyone gathered around to watch. Amos pulled off the canvas cover and began raking away the seaweed. The odor of the steamed clams rose deliciously! When the wire was tossed to one side and the fragrant, smoking food was revealed everyone made a dash for the tables, to find places and be ready when the steaming platters were passed around. Everything tasted good, but the steamed clams, with the wonderful flavor that only a good bake can give them, were the greatest treat of all. A silence of complete absorption and enjoyment reigned over the long tables and astonishing piles of shells mounted beside each plate.

When dinner was over everyone was too full and contented to move or even talk for a while but, gradually, the boys and girls and then the grown-ups bestirred themselves and set about clearing the tables and preparing for the games.

The potato race was won by Eben because he was

patient and deliberate. The other boys were so hurried in their movements that they were constantly dropping the potatoes out of their spoons and having to start all over again. Peter's chum, Link Evans, sent everyone into helpless laughter by his antics in the sack race. After the first few hampered steps he tripped on the sack that was tied securely around his waist, and fell headlong, as did all the other contestants in the race. But instead of giving up, as the others did, Link rolled and flopped himself the entire length of the course and fell over the finish line, red-faced and panting for breath, but grinning with triumph.

John and Joe entered the three-legged race as partners. They started off bravely enough with a firm and measured tread but when they saw some of the others getting ahead of them they tried to increase their speed and trouble began. They were so unequal in height and length of stride that they jerked each other this way and that. They lurched along the course, glaring at each other in anger and chagrin, until, in a final burst of frenzied effort, they landed in a tangled heap on the ground. They lay helpless until they were lifted up and set on their combined feet once more, to receive the booby prize.

When the sails in the *Rambler* were announced there was a rush for the beach where the girls and boys lined up, jostling and fooling, to await their turns. The breeze was steady and the *Rambler* dipped along, tipping just enough to win delighted squeals and shouts from her passengers. Back and forth across the Big Cove she went on innumerable trips, for they all wanted "just one more turn." But the failing breeze finally put an end to the sails and the *Rambler* crept slowly home with barely enough wind to take her to her dock.

☼ 5 ☼

A Narrow Escape

THE WEEK after the Sunday School picnic Father had to set sail for a voyage across the Atlantic and up the Mediterranean to Genoa, Italy. It sounded thrilling but the boys knew what a long, lonely time it would mean for them at home and how they would wait anxiously for word of his safety. Sensing their unspoken dread of such a long voyage, Father assured them that it was the best time of year to cross the ocean, so, heartened by his optimism, they sent him off in excellent spirits to join the vessel in Boston.

That first night after supper Mother went across the fields for a little visit with Aunt Ruth, leaving the three boys studying their lessons around the sitting-room lamp. Breaking a long silence Eben remarked, "It don't seem like we've made a whole lot of headway with our plan for Mother to go on a voyage aboard the *Good Fortune*."

"No, we haven't and it don't look like we ever *would*," agreed John dolefully.

"Well, it's no earthly use to think of her ever going a *foreign* voyage! It'ud be too far and too long a time away from home," stated Peter and the other two boys knew he was right.

"Father spends most of the summer crossing the Atlantic, to and fro," commented Eben.

"Yes, and fall's the gale season so we wouldn't *want* her to go then, or in the winter when it isn't pleasant and sightly on the sea," protested John.

"I guess there's nothing for it but to wait till the coastwise voyages Father usually makes in the spring. We'd come a consid'rable sight nigher getting her to go then than any other time, it seems to me," said Peter.

"Leastways we'll all be a year older by then and that oughta make it some easier," John suggested hopefully.

At last school was over and the vacation stretched before the boys, when, nearly every day, they sailed down to the sandy beach near the fish wharf for a swim and then went on from there for a fishing trip up to the ponds. After a morning's fishing they liked to go ashore and build a fire to cook some of their catch, before they turned homeward to peddle the rest of their perch and pickerel. The *Rambler* was certainly earning her way and helping to swell the three hoards of "fish money." The boys would stop now and then to wonder how they had ever gotten along without her!

It was a nightly exercise, when the boys went to their rooms, to count over their money and enter any expenditures in the little account books Father had given them just before he sailed on this last voyage. Eben's savings mounted the fastest of the three, because he seemed to get along without spending anything. Peter was naturally a spender and was very generous about treating so he usually just kept an even balance. John was making systematic purchases at the Ship Chandlery so that his surplus grew slowly. Grandfather was watching him with considerable interest and every time he made his selection of fishing gear Grandfather gave him the benefit of advice based on years of experience. Nowadays the hours they spent together in the store were devoted to "fish stories," and John never tired of hearing the experiences of the seasons on the Banks. Not realizing that John had a silent partner in Grandfather, Peter and Eben were a little surprised when they were forced to admit that John was getting to be a first-rate fisherman.

When Father had been gone about ten days they began to get reports of him from captains of homeward-bound vessels who had spoken the *Good Fortune* in passing. It was welcome news to hear that Father had been sighted sailing smartly eastward.

Another piece of good news came to them during the summer when one of the boats from the fishing fleet returned late in July to bring reports of the fisher-men and to get fresh supplies to take back to the fleet. At word of her coming everyone hastened anxiously down to the fish wharf. As quickly as possible, word was given out that all hands were well, the fishing good, and the weather, so far, favorable. Relieved and happy, everyone turned to the task of loading the little vessel with provisions and sending her back to the fleet, laden with messages and home-cooked food from the fisher-men's families.

One day near the middle of August Eben came home from the mail with a letter for Mother in Aunt Cynthia's writing and, at last! one that the Post Mistress had given him for Aunt Betsy Ann! They had been watching for this letter for so long that now it was here they passed it eagerly from hand to hand to assure themselves that it was a business letter from Boston. There was some argument as to which one should have the privilege of delivering it to her.

Since Eben had kindling to split, John jumped at the chance of taking it down to her right away, hoping in the bottom of his heart that he would be able to find out what news it contained. However, when he came back a few moments later, he could only report that Aunt Betsy Ann was all flustered at sight of the letter and he had left her hunting for her spectacles so that she could sit down by the window and figure it out.

After speculating about what the lawyers probably had to tell her, Mother picked up Aunt Cynthia's letter and read it to John:

Dear Sister Susan,

I trust this letter will find you well, as it leaves us. I make no doubt that Brother Benjamin is at sea and it is my fervent hope that God has him and his ship in His constant care.

I am writing to say that Thomas has set his heart upon journeying to the Cape for a little visit. The heat of the city is very trying and I have thought he was looking a little peaked these recent days. I feel certain the trip would benefit his health. However, if this proposed visit should not prove convenient for you I count upon you to so inform me.

Should it be agreeable to you to have Thomas come we could send him down on the cars, in the care of the conductor, a man who is known to Osborn. In a week's time Osborn and I would come down and take him back with us. I will await your reply before acquainting Thomas with the plans for the proposed outing. Not only on his behalf but on my own I look forward to seeing you and your boys.

Our Ladies Aid . . .

"She just goes on to tell of her church work," said Mother as she refolded the letter, and then, smiling at John, she went on, "Won't it be real delightsome to have Thomas here and to have Aunt Cynthia and Uncle Osborn come to see us. I do want to ask her how the church ladies made out with their quilts. I must write her straight off and tell her to plan for Thomas to come real soon."

Mother looked so happy that John had not the heart to express his own misgivings in the matter. As soon as he could he escaped from the kitchen and wandered around until he located Peter and Eben out by the chopping block. He joined them and having told them the news, admitted his doubts about the pleasure of the visit. The other two boys seemed to share his lack of enthusiasm.

"Well, you'll have to look after him, John. He's nearest your age," said Peter loftily, as he whittled at a little boat.

"Aw, but Joe and I have heaps of things we wanta do," protested John.

"You'll just hafta take Thomas along with you," stated Peter, dismissing the matter.

"But he's only *seven* and he can't do the things we fellers do," complained John from the superiority of his ninth birthday, just past.

"Seems like I remember he was pretty plucky," offered Eben cheerfully, "and anyway, I'll help you take care of him, John."

Feeling better after that John went to feed the chickens and gather the eggs before he went into the house to read his *Youth's Companion*.

When he entered the sitting room he discovered Aunt Betsy Ann there and heard Mother saying, "But you do call to mind, Betsy Ann, that Elnathan wrote you about buying a vessel?"

"Yes! Yes!" answered Aunt Betsy Ann impatiently. "I recollect it plain enough. Seems like that oughta be a plenty for those lawyer folks."

"But what did you do with the letters?" persisted Mother.

"I always put 'em away in Elnathan's desk. He was a great hand to keep all his papers stowed away," replied Aunt Betsy Ann.

"Do you recall what he did with them?" asked Mother.

"Land sakes, no!" retorted Aunt Betsy Ann. "I had a plenty to do without I should take notice of what he was forever doin' with his bundles of papers."

"They must be somewheres around," suggested Mother.

"I presume likely they *be,* and I'll take a look for 'em *sometime,* if those folks won't take a body's word for what she remembers as plain as day!" With these words Aunt Betsy Ann took her departure, very much ruffled.

As soon as she was gone John's questions tumbled over each other, so Mother explained that the lawyer's letter had told Aunt Betsy Ann that, according to the ship agents in San Francisco, Captain Eldridge had had interests in vessels there years before. They stated that if Aunt Betsy Ann would send them Captain Eldridge's papers and letters, proving his ownership, they felt sure they could establish his claim and get the money for her.

"Say, that's dandy," exclaimed John. "Now everything's all right for her."

" *'Twould* be," replied Mother, sighing, "if so be she could *find* those letters they need."

"Hasn't she got 'em?" asked John, aghast.

"I guess like enough she *has* them tucked away some-wheres but she's so provoked at the lawyers for asking for written proof when she's given them her word about it that she won't even *look* for them any."

"But—but she's jest *got* to," sputtered John. "We'll have to *make* her search an' search for 'em. Why'nt you go—"

"I presume she'll come to it right enough," inter-rupted Mother quietly, "when she's had a chance to simmer down a mite. But it may take her quite a spell and meanwhile we'd best not plague her about it."

Mother looked up smiling as she finished speaking and John had to admit grudgingly that he supposed she was right but it was awfully aggravating to have to sit and do nothing when they were all so eager to help solve Aunt Betsy Ann's problem.

When the day of Thomas's arrival came Eben and John waited somewhat apprehensively for the stage that would bring him from the train. "Wonder what he'll be like," muttered John gloomily, as he dug his boot toes in the sand outside the gate.

"It's funny, but I can't call to mind jes' what he looked like last year—'ceptin' he was kinda white and thin," said Eben.

"Well, we'll soon know! Here he comes," John re-marked grimly as he watched the stage swing around the corner and come up the lane. Before the driver could pull the horses to a stop, the door of the stage flew open and out leaned a freckled, grinning boy, yelling, "Hi, boys, I've come! C'n we go fishing?"

Eben and John were speechless with surprise and relief. Thomas jumped out of the stage and capered around to stretch his legs and, in a moment, the other two boys had collected their wits and were starting off to lead Thomas around the end of the house toward the woodshed and the Cove. They were all three sharply recalled by a hail from the stage driver bidding Thomas come back and fetch his valise.

Impatient at having to bother with such humdrum matters, they turned back, and Thomas, lugging his clumsy valise, staggered up the flagged walk to the west door. Mother was waiting there to welcome him and suddenly he remembered his manners and all Aunt Cynthia's careful instructions and messages. But once they were off his mind, Mother had hard work to detain Thomas long enough to make him change his good suit for his old one. Free at last of tiresome details, the three boys rushed out to start their tour of inspection.

The next afternoon John, Joe and Thomas were out in the woodshed getting ready to go fishing. John and Joe had been proudly showing Thomas how they kept their hooks, lines and lead sinkers neatly stowed in round wooden boxes with tight-fitting covers, when Mother called to them. She was standing by the back door holding a wooden tub.

"Will you boys go down to the salt works and get me some salt?" she asked, and then, as the boys came across the yard to get the tub she added, "Don't let Hiram Fisk fill the tub full. It 'ud be too heavy for you boys to carry. Just get it half full, that'll be plenty."

Casting a regretful glance at their fishing gear the three small boys went down the lane toward the river. When they came out of the pine grove they saw the windmills of the salt works on the high land along the shore. The sails were spread on the short, blunt arms of the mills, and they were whirling briskly in the breeze, reminding the boys of pictures they had seen of Holland.

As they drew near the drying field John explained to Thomas, "They only pump water when the tide's comin' in so's to get it just as salty as they can, comin' right in from the sea."

They stopped beside one of the vats that dotted the open field. It was made of wood and was about fifteen feet square and a foot deep. It had a wooden roof, or cover, that rose to a peak in the center and was fastened at one corner on a swivel so that it could be swung off on bright days, leaving the vat exposed to the full heat of the sun. At night or on rainy days the cover was swung over to protect the vat from moisture. The salt water, pumped by the windmills from the river into the vats, gradually evaporated, leaving the salt behind.

The boys walked about among the vats, peering in to see the level of the water and the crust of salt around the edge of each one. They each chose one at random and then investigated to see which of them had picked the one with the most salt. When they tired of that game they went to the edge of the bank, overlooking the river, and saw the salt house below. A wide, wooden chute led from the level of the drying field down into the salt house. The salt, when scraped out of the vats, was

trundled to the chute in wheelbarrows and dumped in.

At sight of the wide mouth of the chute Thomas exclaimed, "Say, come on, let's slide down into the salt house!"

"Wouldn't the men workin' in there be scared when we popped out at 'em so sudden," giggled Joe.

John's eyes sparkled at the thought of the fun but he looked doubtfully at Joe and said, "Gee, it'ud be a heap of fun but Hiram Fisk's *awful* cross and mean. Like as not he'd get dreadful mad and go'n tell Grandfather on us, same's he did when Peter and Link oiled the swivels of the vat covers till they moved real quiet and easy. They figured they was bein' helpful but the covers moved *so* easy the wind c'ud blow 'em on or off any time it had a mind to! Hiram's had it in for us boys ever since then."

Joe reluctantly agreed with John that the slide might not prove to be fun after all, and, thinking that the matter was settled, he and John started to clamber down the bank. Suddenly they heard Thomas say, "Well, I'm gonna try it anyway." And with that he disappeared into the chute!

John and Joe looked at each other, speechless, for a moment and then John scrambled madly up the bank, calling as he went, "Come on, Joe, we gotta do it too."

Joe followed obediently although he could not quite grasp what John meant. At the top of the chute John stopped and explained hastily, "If we let Thomas do it all alone, Hiram'll maybe hurt him or scare him real bad, but if *we* pop out at him, too, he'll likely be so mad and flustered we c'n get clear away before he c'n think of things bad enough to say to us."

Without another word Joe plunged into the chute. John waited a moment and then he, too, went hurtling, feet first, down the planks, polished smooth by the constant scraping of the coarse salt.

Below, in the salt house, two men had been patiently shoveling salt into big sacks. Suddenly their work was interrupted by the arrival, in their midst, of a flushed and wide-eyed small boy! While they were gazing at him in amazement, a second boy popped out at them! When still a *third* one, red of face and resolute of chin, was hurled at their feet, they collapsed on the heaps of salt and the air rang with their roars of laughter.

It was the boys' turn to look amazed. Wildly John's glance darted around the dim interior. He was all crinkled up inside, waiting for the harsh, angry voice of Hiram Fisk to lash out at them. But he heard nothing but laughter and the echoing giggles of Joe and Thomas. Finally John gasped breathlessly, "Where's Hiram?"

"Was *that* what you was all so plumb scared about?" asked one of the men, sitting up and wiping his eyes. "Well, you can rest easy, 'cause Hiram's at home with the rheumatiz. But, by fishhooks! I never see anythin' funnier in my days than you young'uns poppin' out here, lookin' scared out of your senses!"

"Strikes me they *showed* their sense, bein' scared, if they thought likely Hiram was here," chuckled the other man. "He'd a-been so mad he'd a-took a fit sure! But, say, did you young'uns want somethin' or did you jes' drop in, friendly-like?"

Reminded of his errand John fetched the tub which the men partially filled for him then, sure that they were safe, the boys slid down the chute to their hearts' content.

Suddenly realizing how late it was growing they grabbed up the tub, shouted good-bye to the men and hurried up the lane. John and Joe, carrying the tub between them, found that, even half full, it was heavy and bumped awkwardly against their legs at every step. Reaching home John thrust the tub at Thomas, to deliver to Mother, while he went out to do his belated chores. In the kitchen Mother gave Thomas the salt grinder that looked like a small coffee mill, and he sat by the stove grinding the coarse, sand-like grains into a fine, white powder to use on the table.

One bright August morning the boys came into the kitchen where Mother was busy and stood watching her. Smiling she looked up at them and said, "What is it, boys?"

"We'd like to go blueberrying up to the pond," Eben answered. "Do you s'pose we could take a lunch and stay all day?"

"I don't see why not," replied Mother, "as long as you ask Grandfather if you can use the skiff boat. I don't want you boys to take the dugout for such a long trip without Peter. The skiff's lighter and easier to handle.

John, you run into the store and ask Grandfather if you can borrow her, if you promise to be real careful."

John was back in a moment with the desired permission and Mother said, "Good enough! Now I'll fix a picnic for you and if you bring me home a nice lot of berries I'll make you a blueberry pie."

With whoops of delight the three were off to get ready. They collected berry pails, and got out the oars and oar-locks for the boat. Thomas insisted on finding a toy boat he had made the previous summer, to take along to play with. After a search in the workshop, a fascinating place where a bench, tools, paints and bits of wood suggested all sorts of carpentering exploits, the boat was found and equipped with a long piece of string. By that time Mother had the lunch all packed and she watched them as they loaded up with all their things and went down the hill to the Cove where the skiff boat, the *Gull*, was tied up alongside the *Rambler*.

Eben rowed and John steered with an oar while Thomas hung his feet over the side and trailed his little boat astern. It was a long row up river to Aunt Dinah's Pond but a fair tide helped them along. They took their time, playing along the way, for they had the whole day ahead of them.

"What're those men doing?" asked Thomas as they passed men in boats in the shallow water that bordered the channel.

"They're digging quahaugs," answered John and then added, as he saw Thomas's puzzled expression, "small, hard-shelled clams, you know."

"Are some of 'em lying down resting?" was the next question.

"No," laughed Eben, "those men lying on the stern seats of their boats are working in such shallow water that they can reach bottom and dig up the clams with their hands. In deeper water they have to use long rakes with wire baskets on 'em."

When they came to the upper bridge they rowed into the dusk beneath it and hung onto the mossy piles while they tried out the strange, hollow echoes. Where the river widened out into Aunt Dinah's Pond, the boys beached the skiff on a strip of sandy shore and climbed out.

"I'm hungry," announced John as soon as they had landed, "let's eat our lunch right away and then we c'n pick berries without stopping."

Eben and Thomas heartily agreed and Eben said, "I reckon I can find a spring along here somewheres while you fellers get out the food."

Sure enough, he came upon a spot near the edge of the bushes where a tiny spring trickled out. He scooped a little hollow in the sand and, after waiting a moment for the sediment to settle, had a pool of clear, cool water to fill their tin cups. When every crumb of the generous lunch had disappeared they lay back, hands under their heads, and lazily enjoyed the warm sunshine.

"We'll never get a blueberry pie at this rate," said Eben, at length, sitting up and stretching. The boys agreed and set to work fastening the berry pails to ropes around their waists in order to leave both hands free for picking. As they started up the sloping field to where the blueberry bushes grew thick and tall, John suggested, "Let's each take a patch and see who gets the most berries."

The picking was fine, for the berries were big and ripe and plentiful. The boys called back and forth, at first, reporting progress, but soon they became so absorbed that they drew farther and farther apart and pushed their way deep into the clumps of bushes. John, who had worked higher up the hill than the others, was just looking proudly at his two pails of luscious berries when he grew conscious of a deep rumbling in the distance. He glanced up quickly, thinking that a thunderstorm must have come up while they had been busy, but the sky was still cloudless and the afternoon sun lay warm and golden on the hillside. Turning his attention back to the berries John decided that he had earned the right to eat a few handfuls. He reached out for a tempting cluster—and the rumble and roar came again, nearer this time!

Rrrrrrrrrrrrrrrrrr!

John felt uneasy and stood hesitating, puzzling over what it could be. It came the third time—louder and nearer still! John ran out from the clump of bushes and saw, at the top of the field and coming toward him, an angry bull!

For an instant he was frozen in his tracks and could not move or think what to do. Then another bellow made him leap away down the hill. Eben and Thomas were nowhere in sight so John shouted their names as he ran. To his relief Eben popped out of a thicket right in front of him and stood dumbfounded when he saw the danger that threatened them.

The two boys looked at each other and gasped in the same breath, "Thomas!"

Just then they heard his voice answering John's frantic shout. It came from farther up the hill—nearer the bull! With one accord they turned and dashed in his direction. The bull, angered by their shouts and the sight of their darting figures, lowered his head and charged down upon them faster.

Rrrrrrrrrrrrrrrrrrr!

Reaching Thomas, Eben and John each seized one of his hands and, before he realized what was happening, were off down the hill, fairly dragging him between them. Berries flew in all directions as they raced along. The bull was gaining on them rapidly. They did not dare to look behind but sped on, hoping fervently that they would all keep their feet and not stumble and fall. The shore and the boat were in sight. One last spurt would make it!

They felt the hot breath of the bull on their backs as they dashed across the little beach and flung themselves into the boat. Eben shoved off and, grabbing an oar, pushed the skiff away from the shore with frantic jabs. The bull plunged through the bushes and splashed into the river after them. Standing in water up to his knees he shook his head and bellowed at them in baffled rage.

Once well out of his reach the boys sank down in the boat, exhausted, and looked at each other with round eyes. They were actually more frightened now that they realized what a narrow escape they had had than they had been while it was happening.

The tide was running out and now carried them slowly down river while they rested. Ruefully they inspected their berry pails. "I've lost every one of my nice, fat berries!" wailed Thomas.

"There're *some* in the bottom—of each of my pails— 'bout half a pail in all," reported John, still breathing hard.

"Mine's 'bout half full, I guess," said Eben disconsolately, "and I'd picked 'em so *specially* clean!"

"They were the biggest, juiciest berries I ever saw. I'd like to *wallop* that pesky o' bull!" said John, shaking his fist at the distant bull, still standing in the water, looking after them.

"Mean ol' thing to spoil all our fun. I jes' wish I could tie a knot in his tail to get even with him!" shouted Thomas excitedly.

Eben, meanwhile, was carefully pouring all the berries together into his pail which happened to be the largest and deepest. "There's just one good pailful left," he announced. "Just think of all those big, *blue* ones rolling around on the ground back there! It makes me so plumb mad I c'ud butcher him and eat him."

"Aw, he'd be so tough you couldn't chew him," grunted John in disgust.

The three boys lapsed into a tired and doleful silence as they rowed slowly down river. The sunlight was level and golden when they finally reached home and climbed the hill with lagging steps to offer their lone pail of berries to Mother. While they were telling her of their adventure she was busy making the promised pie out of the one pailful of berries. When supper time came and they cut through the flaky, brown crust and tasted the rich, purply juice they decided that nothing was ever so delicious as that hard-earned blueberry pie!

That evening Mother wrote to Aunt Cynthia suggesting that she delay coming for Thomas, since he and the boys were having such a good time together. Peter took the letter down to the Post Office and came racing back waving aloft the long-expected letter from Father! Mother took it and read with deep thankfulness that he was back in New York after a safe and very profitable voyage, and that he would be able to get home in about three days.

Those days flew by in a bustle of preparation and then, suddenly, Father was with them again, filling the house with his hearty laughter and brisk orders until they all wondered *how* they had gotten through the long weeks without him. The four boys sat for hours listening to his stories of the voyage and of foreign ports. And then the climax of the excitement came with the arrival of a huge packing case!

The entire family gathered around for the ceremony of unpacking, and exclaimed in wonder as Father drew forth the treasures he had brought from Italy. Two white marble vases, carved in delicate lacework, for the mantel in the best room; a number of little marble ornaments, each with its polished wooden base and domed glass cover to protect it from dust and harm; a new carpet for the best room—a present that made Mother gasp with amazement and delight—and from the bottom of the box, the best thing of all—a beautiful oil painting of the *Good Fortune*! For a moment they were all silent, gazing in wonder, and then they burst out with excited exclamations and questions.

"Why, it jes' looks *real*," John said in an awed tone.

"How in tunket did you ever get it done so *natural*, Father?" asked Peter.

"And look how every tiny line is done so clear and all," exclaimed Eben.

Father, beaming at their enthusiasm, explained, "I had it done in Genoa, Italy, like it says there on the bottom. The artist fellow first came aboard the vessel and took down all her measurements. Then he sat out in his little boat and sketched her as she lay at anchor in the harbor. Just once we had to hist the sails for him so's he could see the set of 'em."

"He *couldn't* of painted that big picture jes' sittin' in a little, tippy boat," interrupted John incredulously.

"No, son," laughed Father, "he didn't. He took his sketches and all the figures home to his little shop or whatever, and told me to call around for the picture in three days."

"I don't see how he could get it looking right jes' from *that*," said Eben.

"Well," admitted Father, "*I* was a mite anxious, too! It didn't seem likely he could make a real proper-looking vessel out of those numbers and scratchy drawings.

When I called around to his place on the day he'd set I was plumb flabbergasted to sēe her painted there so pretty."

"Where're we goin' to hang it?" demanded John.

Mother spoke up and said, "Don't you think 'twould be nice to put it in the best parlor? It's going to be so handsome in there with the new carpet and fancy ornaments."

"No, sirree!" protested Peter. "It's—"

"Now, Mother," put in Father, "it seems like it ought to be where we can set eyes on it any time we've a mind to—not just on Sundays and high days."

"Oh, yes, it *must* be where we can look at it *all* the time," said John fervently.

"How'd it be right here in the sitting room over the mantel?" suggested Eben.

"Well said! That's a first-rate place for it," approved Father. "We'll just move this colored picture of mountains—guess likely it's Switzerland—into the best parlor. How'll that be, Mother?"

"I declare that does seem more fitting, somehow. That picture's of foreign parts and the best room'll be our place for things that are brought from away," agreed Mother.

The painting was the first thing to be shown to Aunt Cynthia and Uncle Osborn when they arrived the next day, and they exclaimed over it almost as enthusiastically as they did over Thomas's tanned plumpness. When the Monday morning stagecoach bore all three visitors away on their journey back to Boston, Thomas hung out the window, waving to the boys and shouting, "See you't Thanksgiving! Pick plenty-a cranberries for the sauce."

When Aunt Betsy Ann came by the next afternoon Father, with a twinkle in his eye, asked her how her garden had made out. "My conscience!" she said. "I never saw the like of it, Captain! Everything came up so thick and sturdy I've had garden sass and to spare all summer long. I declare there was things growing in that patch I couldn't recollect planting at all! No, I couldn't!"

The boys had to turn away to hide their telltale grins, and Father, laughing heartily, said, "Looks like the boys must have given it a good deep spading last spring. That does the trick. Like enough you'll give 'em the job again, come next spring."

"I will so!" agreed Aunt Betsy Ann beaming at them. "They're first-rate workers, those boys are."

Four days later Father started off again, this time to sail for Cardiff, Wales. The boys knew how much Mother was hoping that this would be his last voyage across the Atlantic for this season. The shorter, coastwise voyages seemed safer in the stormy weather of fall and winter, and they did not mean such long weeks of anxious waiting without a word of news. Father was so hearty and strong that, as long as he was with them, it seemed absurd to be fearful of anything happening to him. But, once he was gone, they found themselves lonely and troubled over the changing weather, dreading what it might mean to the *Good Fortune*.

Fortunately the beginning of the harvest work kept

them all busy and took up their minds just at first. Mother and Grandmother were both preserving, and delicious, spicy smells greeted the boys every time they came to either of the two houses. They went scurrying back, very willingly, to the garden to gather more loads of grapes, pears, cucumbers and early apples. In their minds' eyes they saw the pantry shelves stocked with row after row of jars of pickles, jams, preserves and jellies for the long winter.

6

By Lantern Light

ON HIS WAY to the mail one evening in the middle of
September, Eben noticed an unusual number of people
gathered around the Post Office door. Wondering what
was going on he quickened his steps to a run. Just as he
reached the gate he was hailed by a shrill whistle and
Dave Sears came dashing up to join him. Seeing the
crowd Dave exclaimed, "Somethin's up! Wonder what
'tis?"

"Maybe there's news of some vessel that's been lost
in foreign parts," suggested Eben soberly.

When they reached the door and eeled their way in
among the men they soon caught snatches of the buzz-
ing conversation:

"Thinks I, it's nigh about time for cranberryin' to start
and—"

"—Weir Village bogs are kinda sheltered and the berries git ripe—"

"—if'n we don't git started pickin' right smart now the frost'll ketch us sure as preachin'!"

Eben and Dave grinned at each other. The signal for the cranberry picking had been given. They had better help spread the news.

"I hope the weather holds good till we get the crop in," said Eben.

With promises to see each other on the bogs the next day the boys hurried home. On his way up the lane Eben stopped at Uncle Abner Bangs's to leave his mail and tell him that the cranberry signal had been given.

"That's capital!" said Uncle Abner, "It'll be a good day, you mark my word. You boys fixin' to ride over along with me?"

"Yes, sir, you bet we are!" replied Eben, "and I guess likely Dave and Link and the rest are counting on you, too."

"Good enough! Good enough!" chuckled Uncle Abner, "Of course they be. You boys be over here along about eight o'clock. It don't do to be in too much of a hurry. Dew's so heavy these mornings you can't no ways get on the bogs so powerful early."

Reaching home Eben shouted, "Cranberry picking starts tomorrow and I've fixed it for us to go over with Uncle Abner."

Peter and John threw down their books shouting "Hurrah!" and began talking of preparations they ought to make for the morning's early start. John searched in the dark closet for the kneeling board he had made for himself the year before. He and Joe had worked out the idea of stuffing a small canvas pillow with straw and nailing it to a board, to protect their knees from dampness and prickers. He brought out the lunch basket but failed to find the board and decided it must be up in the attic and he would have to wait till morning to find it. Eben asked Mother for some old gloves to use for finger protectors, and together they hunted up a supply for all three boys.

Early the next morning Mother packed the lunch basket, while John hunted for his kneeling board. He found it at last behind one of the old sea chests in the attic.

A few minutes later the three boys were in front of Uncle Abner's barn, in time to see him driving out in his red wagon. "Didn't I tell you 'twould be a good, nice day?" he called as he caught sight of the three boys. "Climb up lively now, and we'll get under way."

Uncle Abner stopped on the way to pick up the waiting passengers, filling up every inch of space in the big wagon. Everyone was in the gayest spirits. They clattered across the bridge and turned into the sandy, wood road that led up along the river to Weir Village where some of the finest bogs were located. They were the first to arrive but the foreman of the bog was ready for them.

The bog was lined off with white string, in lanes about three feet wide, in order that the pickers might keep to their own sections. At the beginning of each row was a bushel crate into which the picker emptied his pail as soon as he had filled it.

John took one of the old gloves, to protect the fingers of his right hand from sharp sticks, and then he and Joe grabbed up a 6-quart tin pail apiece and chose rows next to each other. Everyone got to work without delay, for the longer and faster he worked the more he would have earned at the end of the day when all were paid at the rate of two cents a quart.

"I'm mighty glad we made these kneeling boards," said John with an air of importance, as he adjusted his at the beginning of a row.

"The ground *is* awful wet," agreed Joe, and added, "How many quarts d'you think you c'n pick?"

John studied the bog carefully and answered, " 'Bout forty, I reckon!"

"Aw, I wager I get fifty," boasted Joe.

They both bent to the task and were far too busy for any further talk. It was tedious work, leaning forward to lift the long runners from the ground and pick off the berries with flying fingers, but the large, plentiful cranberries made picking easy. John beat Joe filling the 6-quart pail the first time and jumped to his feet to run back and dump the crimson berries into his crate. It was a welcome chance to straighten his back and stretch his cramped legs. Before Joe got to his feet with his first load John was back again, hitching his kneeling board forward and starting in with renewed energy. The two boys kept along very evenly, first one and then the other getting just enough ahead to make the laggard redouble his efforts.

The noon signal was the pleasantest sound they had ever heard, for backs, hands and knees were aching from the strain of unaccustomed work. The boys left their pails just where they stood and hurried back to the wagon for their lunch basket. The Crosbys, Joe, Link and Dave went into the yard of one of the empty houses of the deserted village near the bog. The herring industry had once made it a prosperous settlement but for some reason the fish had left the waters of the upper river, and now the little houses stood forsaken in the midst of their tangled gardens. The boys enjoyed the cool shade of the overgrown yard after the hot glare of the noonday sun on the bog. They sniffed with delight at the air filled with the spicy smell of bayberry, tansy and sweet fern.

After lunch was eaten and they had rested a while in the soft grass, they began hunting for stray fruit and flowers in the old garden. Peter called to the others from the near-by meadow which he had started to explore, and, when they ran down to join him, he showed them a tangle of wild grapevines laden with small, sweet clusters of grapes.

"Say, Mother'd like it fine to have some of these to make jelly out of. Let's pick 'em for her," suggested Eben.

They soon had their lunch basket full but still there were quantities on the vines. Looking disdainfully at the meager supply they were able to take with them John said, "We'll hafta bring along a real big *extra* basket tomorrow and get a lot of 'em. These don't amount to nothing!"

Just then they heard the call that marked the end of the noon hour, so they stowed their basket of grapes in the wagon and hurried back to work. After their rest they picked with fresh vigor and the afternoon passed quickly. At five o'clock they all stopped and dropped wearily on the ground while the foreman figured up their records. Peter was in the lead among the older boys with eighty quarts, nearly a barrel, for his day's total and stepped up to receive his $1.60. Eben had sixty quarts to his credit, giving him $1.20. John had beaten the mark he set for himself by picking forty-two quarts, while Joe totaled forty-five which was not quite up to his expectations, but both boys grinned broadly as they jingled their money.

Mother was watching for the boys and had a good hot supper ready, for she knew how tired they would be after the first day's picking. She was delighted with the wild grapes and anxious for the boys to get her more the next day. "You might watch out for some beach plums, too," she suggested. "It seems like there's nothing quite so tasty, come wintertime, as beach plum sauce."

The boys began to grow drowsy in the warmth of the kitchen and dreaded the thought of moving, but they managed to drag themselves through their chores before they stumbled sleepily up to bed.

The good weather held day after day and every morn-

ing saw them start off with Uncle Abner. Each evening
they came home bringing some find from woods or
meadow: wild grapes, or beach plums, or branches of
thick-set waxy bayberries for candle-making. As the
boys grew accustomed to the work they felt less tired
each day. At the end of the first week Peter realized his
ambition and succeeded in picking one hundred quarts,
a full barrel, in a day.

Toward the end of the second week they spent a day
on their own small bog on the Cove road where they
harvested a fine crop of glossy, dark-red berries. When,
as a special treat, Mother made them cranberry sauce
for supper they all admired its glowing color and
smacked their lips over its sharp, bright flavor.

When supper was cleared away Mother said, "John,
I want you to take a basket of these cranberries down to
Aunt Betsy Ann. It's just the edge of the evening and
I've a mind to step down the road to borrow a hooked
rug pattern from Sadie K. and see if maybe there's a
letter from Father. Seems like it was time we were
hearing from him. Peter, you and Eben can tend to the
chores here."

Mother put on her bonnet and cape and went down
the lane and the boys separated on their various errands.
John, coming back a little later, set on the kitchen table
Aunt Betsy Ann's return gift of a jar of apple butter, and
joined Peter and Eben at a game of dallies in the sitting
room. They glanced enviously at the molasses cooky he
was munching and asked, "Did Aunt Betsy Ann say anything about finding the letters?"

John shook his head and then, swallowing the last big bite, said thickly, "She never said a *word* about 'em! I hung 'round quite a spell, figurin' that she might, and then I jes' up and ast her right out! She said—(John giggled at the recollection)—'Those trifling lawyer men haven't a proper notion how busy a body can be keeping her house red up. Daytimes I've work a plenty, and lamp-light's no account for figurin' out those old faded letters. They can just wait a piece and maybe they'll come to their senses.'"

"Those lawyers don't care if she *never* finds 'em," protested Peter in exasperation. "She's only keepin' herself from getting that money but you can't make her see that nohow!"

"Father'll be awful put out when he finds she isn't even *hunting* any!" said John.

"I wonder if 'twould do any good if Mother was to talk her into writing 'em again and telling 'em how clear she remembers it all and how *other* folks hereabouts recall his owning west-coast vessels, too," suggested Eben.

"It *might*," agreed Peter doubtfully, "and if it *wasn't* enough proof for 'em, like enough they could make it plain to her why she just *had* to search out those old papers."

"We'll ask Mother what she thinks about it anyway," concluded John.

In a few moments they heard Mother coming and knew from her quick, light step, before they saw her smiling face, that she had the letter from Father. She hastily laid off her wraps and sat down by the lamp to read it to them.

Beloved Wife,

I take pen in hand to write you from Bristol, England, that we arrived safely in Cardiff after a rough passage. We had one severe storm off the coast of Ireland. I think I never saw the glass lower in all my time at sea. We passed through some anxious and trying hours but God preserved our lives and brought the vessel through unscathed.

From Cardiff we came to this port for orders. I have this day learned that we are to proceed to Leith for a cargo of steel for New York. We depart on the morning tide. From Leith I purpose to sail north about Scotland on the homeward voyage. It will be a month, at the least, from the time that you will receive this letter before you can look for my return.

I think constantly of my loved ones at home and pray that God may watch over you all. I look forward to the time when I shall be with you once more.

Your loving husband
Benjamin

"Gee, I'm glad they got through that storm all right," said John in a hushed tone as his memory brought back, vividly, the storm off Hatteras.

"He doesn't say *how* low the barometer fell, does he?" commented Peter. "But it must have been dreadful wild weather if 'twas the lowest he'd ever seen."

"I kinda wish he wasn't coming home north-about,"

sighed Mother. "It sounds like it must be an awful cold, desolate journey, someways."

"But Father's well on his way by now and maybe he's having this spell of fine weather, too," offered Eben hopefully.

"It does seem like one storm to a voyage is plenty," said Mother, re-reading the letter.

Just before bedtime the boys suddenly remembered about Aunt Betsy Ann and explained to Mother their idea of a second letter to the lawyers. She agreed that it might help and, since it certainly couldn't do any harm, she would go down to Aunt Betsy Ann's the very next afternoon and help her get the second letter off promptly.

Driving home in Uncle Abner's wagon from the last day's picking on the Weir Village bogs the boys shivered in the chill of a grey afternoon.

"I declare, it feels almost like frost," said Eben.

"No," contradicted Peter, "it's just coming in thick and fixing for a spell of weather. But I'm glad it held off until now."

"You can see the fog comin' up river. I can hear the foghorn on Pollock Rip Lightship, can't you?" said John, as a distant, hoarse moan broke the stillness when they paused a moment to listen.

One afternoon a week later John was tugging and pulling at a great bundle of sail cloth, trying to spread it out on the ground in the sunny place in front of the woodshed. Once it was stretched out to his satisfaction he disappeared into the shed and came out carrying three, long flexible flails. These he propped up beside the door and then, catching up a bushel basket, he started down the hill to the garden. He inverted the basket and hung it on his head so that it swung behind his shoulders, and, with his hands deep in his pockets, went whistling on his way. Fall was a pretty good time of year, he was thinking, with the sunlight warm and golden, the air tingling, and the Cove a deep, sparkling blue; school didn't have to be thought of for another week, and his cranberry earnings more than made up for the lull in the activities of the Bass River Fishing Company.

Peter and Eben were at work in the garden harvesting the pole-beans, and John was on his way down to get a load of the dry, twisted vines and carry them up to the back yard. The two boys in the garden had been pulling up the dried vines, laden with full pods, tearing them loose from the supporting poles, and tossing them in tangled heaps. The grey tepees of bare poles showed John how fast they had been working. He hailed them and began stuffing the vines from one of the heaps into his basket. When full the basket was not heavy but it was clumsy to carry at arms' length. John walked a few steps with it and then set it down while he pondered an easier way to do the job. In a moment he called, "Hey, Peter, what say I bring down one of those big, ol' nets from the shed? We c'n spread it on the ground and heap the vines on it and then carry it up between us. We c'n get a lot more at a time than in this ol' basket."

"I say it's a good idea, boy," replied Peter, "only bring down two nets 'stead of one, and then the fellow left behind can be heaping up and packing down the second load and have it all ready."

"And *I* say, go easy on the packing," cautioned Eben. "These beans're so dry they'll fall right out of the pods if you joggle 'em much."

John did not wait to hear the warning but ran up the hill and was back in a minute, lugging two of the old nets. They spread one on the ground, heaped it high with the brittle, yellow vines and then Eben and John, gathering up the ends of the net and drawing them over their shoulders, bore the huge bag up the hill and dumped it on the waiting canvas by the woodshed. When they got back to the garden the next load was ready and so, taking turns loading and carrying, they soon had the entire crop piled in the back yard.

The boys sprawled on the ground to eat an apple apiece and rest a minute and just then Mother came up the lane from Aunt Betsy Ann's where she had been making an afternoon visit. John called out to her, "Look here, Mother, we've got the whole crop ready to thresh!"

"My conscience," exclaimed Mother, "I didn't know's you'd any more than get them pulled up today."

"Well, you see," explained Eben, "we—that is, mostly John—thought up a dandy scheme for carrying 'em up from the garden."

"If we was to get 'em 'most done before supper, do you s'pose we c'ud go out eeling with the lantern tonight?" asked John hopefully.

"I presume likely. A mess of eels would taste real good for dinner tomorrow," answered Mother.

The boys lost no time in getting back to their task. They grabbed the long flails and fell to beating the pile of vines so vigorously that the beans, released from the dry pods, hopped high in the air and bounced off into the grass in all directions. Noticing the results of their violent attack Peter suggested, "Let's beat in time to our counting-out rhyme and then maybe the beans won't scatter so like the mischief."

Accordingly they began to chant slowly in unison:

> *Intery, mintery, cutery, corn,*
> *Apple seed and apple thorn,*
> *Briar, briar, limber lock,*
> *Three geese in a flock,*
> *One flew east, one flew west,*
> *And one flew over the cuckoo's nest*

and their beating settled into a steady, even stroke.

After a while Eben interrupted the chant, fallen now into a muttered rhythm, to say, "Do y'know, these vines'ud make a bully bonfire. Let's save 'em and burn 'em in that sand patch in the north-west corner of the garden. It'ud be safe enough there."

"That'ud be dandy fun," agreed Peter," but we'll have to wait and do it tomorrow 'cause we won't have time for the picking over tonight."

In spite of the beating a few pods always clung to the vines and had to be picked off and shelled by hand. That would have to wait until another day since the sun was already setting. The clear, apple-green sky gave promise of a heavy dew so the boys dragged out another big piece of canvas and covered the heap of vines before they hustled around to do up their chores.

While they were eating steaming clam chowder and pilot biscuit, Eben hastened to question Mother about her afternoon's visit. "Has Aunt Betsy Ann found Captain Elnathan's letters?"

Mother laughed softly, shaking her head regretfully, and gave the boys an account of her visit.

"When I went in this afternoon Aunt Betsy Ann was braiding carpet rags and we talked quite a spell before I could get around to asking if she'd had any more encouraging word from the lawyer folks. When I did, her eyes just snapped and she said, short-like, 'They say my word ain't a mite of good without those letters.' When I asked her if she'd looked for them again real thorough, she said, 'No, and I'm not agoin' to!' She was just set on being real stubborn and provoked and it took me a right smart while to make her see 'twarn't their fault they had to be so partic'lar when it came to other folks' money. Finally she said, 'Well, I snum, if I didn't need that money dreadful bad I wouldn't calc'late to eat humble pie! No, I shouldn't.' "

They all burst out laughing at Mother's imitation of Aunt Betsy Ann's peppery indignation. As the beach plum sauce and cake was being passed around she continued, "But before I left I persuaded her to set about hunting right off and I helped her search through the old desk. We looked through every nook and cranny there was, seemed so, and nary a trace of those letters could we lay our hands on. Aunt Betsy Ann says there're old trunks and sea chests full of papers up attic and she's promised to search through them, real thorough, first chance she gets."

"Golly, I hope she finds 'em," mumbled John through a mouthful of cake.

"Seems like they must be there somewhere," said Peter thoughtfully. "It's kinda like a—"

"Yes, it's like you read about in story books," interrupted Eben eagerly, "hidden treasure and all like that! Wish we could do the hunting *for* her. It'ud be real exciting!"

"I don't figure Aunt Betsy Ann is one to let other folks put a hand to her things," laughed Mother, getting up to clear the table, "and she's slow enough about doing it herself, sakes knows!"

Supper over, the boys buttoned on their warm jackets and, lighting their lanterns, went out to get the eel spears and the paddles for the *Rambler*. It was a quiet night without a breath of wind. The air was keen and the grass felt cool and damp about their feet. As they went down through the field they noticed that the Cove was absolutely calm, mirroring the brilliant stars. They needed just such a night for eeling.

One of the lanterns they set on the end of the dock to mark its location for their return. The other they fastened into a socket in the stern of the dugout. They pushed off and paddled quietly through the glossy black water to a place along the north side of the Cove, that was considered good eeling ground. Only one boy at a time could stand in the eeling position in the stern, while the other two managed the paddles and moved the canoe in response to the directions of the eeler.

Peter took the first turn. He stood with eel spear poised, gazing down where the light penetrated the still water and revealed every sign of movement. Slowly, silently the canoe crept, stern first, over the eeling ground. John and Eben, with every muscle alert, watched Peter intently, for when Peter saw an eel he made a lunge with the spear, jabbing it into the muddy bottom to catch the eel between the tines, and the boys had to be quick to steady the dugout. Luck seemed to be with them for Peter caught two fat eels on his first two tries. But he was so elated that he grew careless and thereby missed a number of fine chances. In disgust he made a mighty lunge. The spear went to so deep into the mud that Peter could not pull it out in the quick recoil that usually maintained his balance. The force of his thrust pushed the boat away from the spear and there he hung over the water, both hands gripping the spear and his feet held firmly under the stern seat of the dugout.

It all happened so quickly that no one had a chance to say a word, but Eben and John snapped into instant action. With swift jabs of the paddles they held the *Rambler* from slipping any farther away from the spear. Then, inch by inch, they pushed her back, stern first, so that Peter was very gradually raised to a standing position once more. They took the greatest care to make their progress slow and steady, for they knew that a sudden jerk would break Peter's straining grasp on the spear handle and he would get a cold ducking that would end their eeling for that night.

At last Peter was standing upright again! He yanked the spear out of the mud and threw himself down on the stern seat to rest his aching arms. "Whew!" he exclaimed, "that *was* a close call! Another inch and I'd of been in the water. You fellers did good work."

He was quite ready to let Eben try his hand at the sport. Warned against being too violent, Eben took it easy and landed four good-sized eels with only two misses. Next it was John's turn and he caught one big eel and one small one in five tries. By this time they had enough for dinner and it was getting late. Eeling was slow work, for there were always long waits between catches when they watched the lighted patch of water patiently for the sight of an eel. And, too, it took time to maneuver the canoe into the right position for the thrust of the spear. When the church clock confirmed their suspicions that it must be about nine o'clock they were content to turn homeward.

Mother had set a lamp in the sitting-room window where it shone out like a beacon. Guided by that and the tiny point of light from the lantern on the end of the dock, the boys made straight for home. They liked to see the way their dipping paddles made the star reflections dance and scatter as the *Rambler* moved quietly over the smooth, black water.

The next morning was grey and chilly, threatening

rain, so the boys hastily picked over the bean vines and then stacked them in a corner of the woodshed where they would keep dry for a future bonfire. They gathered up the beans in big baskets and lugged them into the house just as the first drops of rain began to fall.

In the comfort of the kitchen, snug from the dismal weather, the boys settled to the task of sorting and separating the yellow-eye beans, the white pea beans, and the red kidney beans. They had brought down from the attic the wooden tubs in which the different kinds were stored for the winter and now each boy selected the variety that he thought made the most delicious baked beans, and set to work. In their minds' eyes they saw a whole procession of brown bean pots with their rich, steaming contents, marking the Saturdays across the winter calendar. As the smooth, brightly colored beans slipped rapidly through their fingers they talked of the *Good Fortune* on her far northern voyage.

"Do you reckon they'll see any icebergs?" asked John, his eyes wide at the thought.

" 'Tisn't likely at this time of year," answered Peter, "but I'll wager it'll seem awful queer to have it light all night long, like our geography says 'tis, way up north."

Eben and John were silent while they tried to imagine what that would be like, and Peter went on, "Sometimes it seems like I can't rightly wait till I'm old enough to go to sea with Father. Gee, it must be a *dandy* life!"

"When do you figure Father'll let you go?" asked Eben.

"His mind's set on having me finish school next spring but I'm plumb certain I know *plenty* right *now*," complained Peter.

"Chances are he's fixing to take you on a voyage soon's school's out, come June, and that's not such a dreadful spell to wait," consoled Eben.

"I mean to go to sea for *good and all,* not just a voyage like we took before. I've got to get started being a plain sailor so as to get to be a captain as quick as ever I can."

John had not been listening to their talk. He had always taken for granted that Peter would follow the sea, and his attention had wandered back to the fascinating problem of the midnight sun. Now he burst out with, "If it's light all night long, how do the people know when to go to bed?"

"They must get tired and sleepy same as other folks, and I s'pose they aim to get their rest, light or no light," stated Peter.

"It must be dreadful hard on the hens, havin' to lay eggs the whole time and no chance to go to roost! I declare, seems to me 'twould be plumb confusin'!" protested John so vehemently that Peter burst out laughing.

With a shake of his head Eben gave up all attempt to solve the problem and asked, "Isn't it 'most time Grandfather was looking for the fishing fleet?"

"Yes, 'tis," put in John, switching readily to the new interest, "he was sayin' today that along about the end of next week we ought to go on watch for 'em."

"Aw, gee! School begins next week," grumbled Peter, "and then we won't have a mite of time for real important things like that."

"We can go on scuttle watch afternoons," suggested Eben. "I wonder who'll be the first to see 'em this year? I saw 'em last year and the year before they slipped in, just night, and surprised everyone."

"If they've had good luck I wonder if Grandfather'll have a celebration for 'em?" questioned John.

"I guess likely," replied Peter. "He 'most always does, unless there's been someone hurt or drowned during the voyage."

"Golly, I hope all hands are all right," said John thoughtfully.

By midafternoon the beans were finished; two full tubs of each kind. The covers were fitted on snugly and the tubs carried up to the kitchen attic where they would keep dry. The boys helped themselves to doughnuts from the golden-brown pile that Mother had just fried, and went outside to inspect the weather.

"The wind's hauling to the north'ard. I think it'll clear off just night," offered Peter in close imitation of Father's weather wisdom.

"Gee, I hope so," was John's fervent wish, " 'cause it oughta be nice for the cornhusking tonight at Captain Ed's."

Peter's prophecy proved true and at sunset the clouds broke, letting through a flood of golden sunlight. The boys hustled around, doing their chores in short order, and noticing with relief, as they went from the house to the woodshed and chicken house, that the sky was clearing rapidly.

Just before eight the boys lighted their lantern and, calling good-bye to Mother, set off down the lane toward Captain Ed's barn. They could see other lanterns bobbing along as young people came from all directions to the husking bee. Inside the barn a dozen lanterns lighted the space in the center of the floor while the corners and lofts, from which came pleasant odors of hay and stored grain, were dim and shadowy. In the circle of light on the barn floor lay a great, golden heap of corn, surrounded by rough wooden benches. The Crosbys joined the group of boys and girls standing about waiting for the signal to start work. John saw Joe beckoning to him and together they sauntered around until they located a small bench, just right for the two of them.

At a word from Captain Ed there was a rush for the benches and the husking began. The ears of corn thudded into bushel baskets placed at intervals in front of the benches, while the husks swished to the floor to make a rustling carpet underfoot. The air was filled with the rasping and tearing of dry shucks, with an undercurrent of talk and laughter.

"Huh!" snorted Joe in disgust after he and John had been working and watching for a while. "All they do is *fool*! They're makin' mighty little headway with the huskin'."

"I bet we have more ears done than any of the others when time's up," predicted John.

"Come on," said Joe, giggling, "let's speed up!"

Suddenly there was a shout and all the boys and girls were pointing at Peter, who had uncovered a dark-red ear of corn. It was the custom at husking bees for the holder of a red ear to kiss any one of the girls whom he might choose, so now Peter was the center of excited interest. John nudged Joe and whispered his guess as to which girl Peter would pick out. With twinkling eyes Peter rose from his place and, stepping outside the circle of benches, walked very slowly around it, pausing an instant behind each person and then moving deliberately on again. There was a chorus of giggles and suppressed squeals from the girls as the suspense increased. When he had them all in a gale of merriment Peter, bending swiftly, pecked at the cheek of a demure girl with lowered head, and then darted back to his place again before half the boys and girls had seen what had happened.

John, grinning because his guess had been correct, snatched up an ear and husked it as fast as his hands could fly, to make up for lost time.

Someone started singing "Aunt Dinah's Quilting Party," changing "quilting" to "husking," and everyone joined in so lustily that the rafters rang. They sang on, choosing some of the favorites learned in the sessions of Singing School, held on winter evenings. Everyone liked rounds, so they began with:

> *Useful labor brings us health,*
> *Inward peace and outward wealth*

and continued with:

> *Let us sing merrily, lightly and cheerily,*
> > *Let us be gay!*
> *Careless of sorrow, lightly we borrow*
> > *Hopes from tomorrow*
> > *Gladden today.*

They got into such a jumble over that one that they broke off laughing and someone started a regular song:

> *When you've work to do, boys,*
> *Do it with a will.*
> *They who reach the top, boys,*
> *First must climb the hill.*
> *Standing at the foot, boys,*
> *Gazing at the sky,*
> *How can you get up, boys,*
> *If you never try?*

That went so well that they tried:

> *Keep working, 'tis wiser than sitting aside*
> *And dreaming and sighing and waiting the tide.*
> *In life's earnest battle those only prevail*
> *Who daily march onward and never say fail.*

Every now and then the singing was interrupted by the flurry of excitement over another red ear. The heap of corn was dwindling rapidly under the attack of so many hands and the husks were a rustling, yellow sea covering the floor. When the last ear had been dropped into a basket Captain Ed went around to estimate who had been the most diligent workers. Although John and Joe had prophesied their own victory, they were wide-eyed and open-mouthed with surprise when Captain Ed stopped beside them to say, "I calc'late the prize goes, this year, to our youngest workers, John Crosby and Joe Baker. Seems like they've done a sight more *working* and a sight less *chatting* than the rest of you!"

The announcement drew cheers for John and Joe from all the others, and good-natured laughter at their own expense. In the midst of the din Captain Ed presented the two grinning, red-faced boys with a big bag of "store" chocolate candies.

Aunt Sadie, Captain Ed's wife, and some of the other women had been busy for some time at a long, plank table at one side of the barn and now they called the young people to come and get their refreshments. There were piles of gleaming red apples, small kegs of cider and great platters of stir cake (molasses cake with raisins in it.)

Uncle Abner Bangs, who had not missed a husking bee since any of them could remember, looked closely at the table and then looked sternly at Aunt Sadie and said, "How come there isn't any plum porridge, Sadie? Didn't you forelay to have any on hand?"

With an exclamation Aunt Sadie disappeared into the shed connecting the barn with the house, and returned in a moment with a willow-ware tureen which she set upon the table. Uncle Abner beamed as Aunt Sadie served him with a big bowl of cornmeal mush thick with raisins. Smacking his lips over it he said,

"This is real delightsome. You always was a great hand to make plum porridge, Sadie, and I couldn't figure that you'd go and forget it at a time like this, nohow!"

Some of the older people shared Uncle Abner's enjoyment of the porridge, but the young folks quickly demolished the piles of stir cake. Then by twos and threes they began getting on their wraps and lighting their lanterns. After good-byes were said, they went off in groups, calling back and forth and singing, " 'Twas from Aunt Sadie's husking party."

John and Joe lingered a moment by the gate in the fence. "It feels like frost tonight!" said Joe, shivering at the sudden change from the warm, lighted barn to the crisp, tingling darkness.

"If there *is*, it'll loosen the nuts," stated John. "What say we go over to the woods in the morning and see'f we c'n get some?"

"All right," assented Joe, "I'll meet you down the road 'bout ten. G'-night."

"G'-night," called back John, running to catch up with Peter and Eben, who were racing and shouting up the lane ahead of him.

7

The Wash-Out
Dinner

SCHOOL BEGAN the following week and with the fall
fishing season in full swing the days were not half long
enough. The boys spent every spare moment in the
Rambler, for they had only about a month more to use
her before they must put her up for the winter.

The fishing fleet was due home any day now and in
the air was a feeling of expectancy and anxiety. The
boys were taking turns on scuttle watch, staying home
from school a half day at a time so that there might
always be someone on duty. It happened to be John's
turn this fine October morning. He had felt very important when he watched the other boys going off to
school, but now, by midmorning, he was finding it

sleepy work to sit still in the sunshine. He stood on the top step of the stairs that led up to the scuttle, and stretched himself and took a look around. Below him, in the front yard, Mother's flower garden was bright with the last marigolds and zinnias. To his left the Cove was blue under the cloudless sky, and the pines about the shores were a glossy green. In the garden the apple trees were bending with fruit and the pumpkins gleamed yellow among the corn stacks. Looking across the field John could see Grandmother, directing Deborah, the neighbor's girl who helped her about the house, as she picked quinces.

After the inspection of his surroundings John once more scanned the Sound for a sign of the expected sails. Something white caught his eye and he peered hopefully through the glass only to discover that it was a three-masted schooner instead of a two-masted "fisherman." Besides, he soon saw, she was beating down the Sound, not heading in for the river. He sat down, with a sigh, on the top step and, taking a nail from his pocket, fell to scratching on the wooden frame of the scuttle opening, first his initials and then a schooner under full sail.

Mother's voice came up to him from the front yard where she stood, shading her eyes against the strong sunlight, "I think you can safely come below long enough for a cup of milk and a molasses cooky, son!"

John needed no urging. He clattered down the attic stairs and then down the back stairs at top speed. In a short time he was back in the scuttle, with an extra cooky for good measure, but found only an empty expanse of blue water to greet him. He did wish the fleet would come in sight soon so that he could be the one to shout out the glad news.

Hardly had the thought crossed his mind when his eye was caught by a tiny spot of white far to seaward. He waited, not daring to hope and hardly wanting to look again for fear it would have vanished. He counted fifty slowly and then gathered courage for another quick look. It was still there and plainer now, with another spot near it. They gleamed in the sun. They must surely be sails! This time he counted 100 very slowly and then looked. There were three gleams now. Three

vessels and no mistake! There should be five vessels if all had gone well with the fleet. Of course, there were other fleets sailing from near-by harbors and it was far too soon to be confident that this was the fleet he so longed to see, but he kept hoping.

He continued his counting game, making himself look steadily away from the sea while he counted 200. He was rewarded by finding *five* boats strung out along the horizon and coming rapidly nearer. He snatched up the spy-glass from the step beside him and hastily adjusted it to the penciled mark which Peter had put on the brass barrel to save time in getting the proper focus. Balancing the long barrel on the edge of the scuttle frame, John trained the glass on the distant patches of white sail but found that he could not yet distinguish the owner's flag at the masthead. Another ten minutes at the speed they were sailing and he ought to be able to make out the mark on the flag. If it was a pine tree on a white ground it was Grandfather's fleet, all safe and sailing home smartly.

John counted out the ten minutes, keeping his head turned resolutely toward the garden. Then he raised the glass slowly for the deciding look. Yes! There was the pine tree flag! And the fleet was plainly heading straight for the river. He jumped to his feet and shouted, "The fleet! The fleet! Five boats sighted and heading in to the river!"

At his first hail Grandfather appeared at the door of the store and waved to the excited figure on the roof. "Hurrah!" he called. "That's capital news. Come below now and we'll go down to the fish wharf and meet them."

John closed the scuttle and pounded down the stairs. Grandfather, cane in hand, was waiting for him by the gate and together they strode down the lane toward the river.

Somehow the tidings of the returning fleet had already gotten about, for Grandfather and John saw, coming toward them along the path beside the river, some of the wives and children of the fishermen. They all reached the fish wharf long before they could expect to see the boats coming up the river and their impatience only made the time drag more slowly. Finally they heard the creak and groan of the drawbridge being laboriously raised for the approaching vessels. Everyone surged to the end of the wharf, watching expectantly, and one by one the five boats came in sight. Their rigging crowded with waving, shouting men, the vessels came sweeping up to their berths at the dock. The sails came slatting down on the run and the mooring lines were made fast. The men leaped ashore to greet their waiting families, and the captain of each schooner came to Grandfather to report all hands accounted for and a record catch in the holds. Laughter and high spirits swept the crowd at this welcome news, and excited voices rose in a clamor of talk. Word went about that the fishermen were to go home to dinner with their families and report at the wharf at two o'clock to commence unloading the salted fish.

Walking up the lane with one of the captains Grandfather and John learned that the nearest they had come to disaster was when two dory-loads of fishermen had been lost for two nights and a day in one of the thick fogs common to the Grand Banks. They had not been able to locate their "mother" vessel in spite of all efforts with foghorns and signals. When at last the fog lifted, the men rowed back to their vessel, exhausted with hunger and anxiety but otherwise unharmed.

The home-coming of the fleet meant a half-holiday from school, so after dinner John ran over to get Joe and soon all four boys were on their way down to the fish wharf to watch the men unload and wash out the fish in the river. John and Joe took up their positions by the rough, wooden racks, or flakes, on the field where the codfish were to be dried, waiting for the fishermen to bring up to them the dripping basket-loads.

"I don't see *why* they take time to souse 'em all in the river like they're doin'," exclaimed Joe in perplexity.

"Why, they do that to wash off the salt that's on 'em, a 'course," explained John, disgusted at Joe's ignorance.

"But that's salt water they're washin' 'em in, isn't it?" challenged Joe.

"Sure," agreed Joe, "but they hafta put such a *terrible* lot of salt on the fish to keep 'em from spoilin' when they split 'em and pack 'em in the holds out on the Banks that this water's nearly like fresh."

"Well, the salt don't do 'em any harm—why not leave it on?" questioned Joe persistently.

"If they were to dry 'em with all that salt on," laughed John, "you couldn't ever eat 'em to save you!"

Just at this moment the first of the fishermen came up the path lugging the brimming baskets of fish and the boys, jumping to the work of spreading the fish on the racks, had no more time for talk.

Toward sunset Grandfather came down to see how the work was progressing. He was pleased to see the rows upon rows of fish on the flakes, ready for drying. He summoned all the men and, looking around at the deeply-tanned faces, said, "You've got a record catch here and if this fine weather holds we'll have them dried and ready for shipment with very little loss. Tomorrow you can finish washing out and clean ship. The next day, at noon, I want you all to come, with your families, to a dinner at Captain Crosby's home, to celebrate the end of a mighty successful voyage. I reckon the women-folks will know how to handle their end of the entertainment and we'll bring along our appetites and good cheer."

When he finished speaking there was a cheer for the Captain of the fleet and then the men scattered to their homes.

The day of the "wash-out" dinner was perfect and everyone was astir bright and early. After breakfast the boys helped Amos Cahoon set up the long picnic tables in the sitting room, where the dinner was to be held, since it was the only room large enough to accommodate such a gathering. That job finished, the boys were banished from the house, but gathered in the woodshed to plan some entertainment for the children who would come with their fathers and mothers. They went first to the field to drive a stake for the ring-toss game and to mark off a level place for a potato race. Then John was sent up to the loft over the workshop to hunt up some burlap bags for a sack race. When he came back with an armload of these he found Peter and Eben consulting. "Do you s'pose that's enough for 'em to do?" asked Peter.

"I *guess* so," replied Eben a little doubtfully. " 'Course I've got my ball if they want to play catch, only I don't want anyone to lose it."

"We c'ud play hide-and-go-seek," proposed John and they all agreed that that ought to fill up the afternoon nicely.

While they had been working the boys had seen a steady stream of fishermen's wives coming to the back door with covered dishes and carefully balanced trays. A combination of curiosity and hunger made them realize that breakfast had been eaten a long time ago.

"Jingoes!" exclaimed John. "I'm like to starve afore dinner's ready."

"What say we waylay some of these vittles that're going by under our noses and take a snack to hearten us a mite?" suggested Peter with mischief in his eye.

"All right!" grinned John, edging toward the back gate. "I got my fingers crossed that the next one'll be fat, sugary doughnuts!"

With a worried frown on his forehead Eben followed them slowly. "Maybe the ladies wouldn't take it right and we wouldn't want anything to fluster Mother. She's looking kinda tuckered out with all the stir there is in the kitchen," he warned them soberly.

The day was saved by the appearance of Mother herself, at the kitchen door, beckoning to them. When they ran up to her she handed them each a fat molasses cooky and advised them to get washed and dressed as it was nearing noon and their guests would soon be arriving.

Brushed and clean, the boys took their places at the gate to welcome the company and show them to the front door, where Grandfather and Grandmother were waiting to greet them. They arrived in family groups: the fishermen looking strange and awkward in their Sunday suits, their wives smiling and happy in their best dresses, and the children shy and rigid with starched clothes and company manners. When all were accounted for, the door into the sitting room was thrown open. What a sight met their eyes! Two long tables whose white cloths were barely visible under the *abundance* of food spread out upon them! A whole roast pig held the place of honor on one table, while on the other were roast chickens and clove-dotted hams. Great platters of steaming corn, tureens of beans, and mounds of fluffy mashed potatoes were scattered the length of the tables, with plates of hot biscuits and dishes of pickles in between.

After Grandfather had given thanks for the safe and successful fishing voyage just finished, and asked a blessing on all those gathered around him, they took their places at the tables and fell upon the good things before them. When, at length, the heaped-up platters were emptied, doughnuts and cakes and pies of every sort took their places. Gradually, as appetites were satisfied, tongues began to loosen and, though it had started off as a very stiff and silent meal, it ended up sociably enough, with men of the different crews exchanging stories and poking fun at each other over the funny incidents of the voyage.

Peter, Eben and John ate until their waistbands were stretched tight and, though they could hardly walk when they got up from the table, they had to bestir themselves and coax the children outdoors to play games.

As the afternoon shadows lengthened, the women helped clear up after the feast, while the men inspected the garden and stood around talking and smoking their pipes. When the work indoors was finished, the women gathered their families together for the return home and the company began to scatter down the lane and across the fields. Suddenly a buzz of excited questions arose in the last group that lingered near the gate. The boys drawing near, in curiosity, learned that a small boy of four, the son of one of the crew captains, was missing! No one could remember having seen him since dinner and his mother was becoming worried. Everyone who remained set to work, at once, to make a thorough search. The women went into the house to hunt in every nook and corner, attic and cupboard. Some of the men went down to the garden, and others, looking serious, went to the Cove.

The boys were anxious and troubled, for the children

had been their responsibility and they could not recall when last they had seen little Hiram. They searched the workshop and woodshed, shouting his name repeatedly, but no trace of him could they find.

In a short time the various groups gathered again at the house to report their failure and consider what they could do next. They finally decided to make the rounds of all the fishermen's houses, hoping that Hiram might have tried to find his way home alone, or gone along with some of the other children.

Since there was nothing more the boys could do, they turned away to gather up the scattered playthings before it grew too dark to see them. Tired and troubled by Hiram's disappearance, John went, with lagging feet, to pick up the pile of bags thrown aside after the sack races. As he stooped for an armful of bags his foot struck an obstacle and, losing his balance, he plumped down on top of something solid in the midst of the pile. He was so surprised that he sat still an instant, wondering what he had landed on. Suddenly the obstacle moved and grunted, and John tumbled backwards. He found himself gazing in amazement at a small boy with a red face and tousled hair, who sat up in the midst of the bags. It was a moment before John could collect his wits and shout toward the house that Hiram was found!

The good news was taken up and called by Peter, Eben and Grandfather to the groups separating for further search. Greatly relieved, they all hurried back to find out just what had happened. By the time John, secretly feeling very important, had guided them all out to the field, Hiram was wide awake and quite bewildered at finding himself the center of so much attention. It turned out that he had grown sleepy while watching the older boys and girls play games, and had curled up on the bags to rest. When the races were over, the children had tossed their sacks on the pile without noticing the small sleeper. So he had been covered up, and because his nest was so snug and cosy none of the shouting had roused him from his sound sleep. He was led away home by a relieved mother and father. The Crosbys were so tired that they could only look at each other, as they stood out by the gate, and heave sighs of relief that the day was safely over.

When their thoughts were no longer taken up with the excitement over the return of the fleet and the "wash-out" dinner, the Crosbys had to face the fact that the month Father had mentioned in his letter from Bristol was more than gone. They should have had word of his arrival in New York long before this. There had been no reports of severe storms at sea, so they were puzzled as well as worried by the continued silence. Each morning they were hopeful that the day would surely bring the longed-for letter, and each evening found them a little more sober and anxious. The boys haunted the Post Office at every mail and they began to notice that groups of older captains would gather in serious talk, shaking their heads dubiously, but would change abruptly to bluff and hearty greetings at the approach of the boys. They did not tell Mother these things. They did not even acknowledge them to each other, but their hearts grew heavy as the days dragged by.

Mother was calm and went about her work quietly, but they could not help seeing how worn and tired she looked. Unknown to her, the boys often met in the attic, when they had slipped up to the scuttle to see if by *any* chance there was a sail in sight, and talked over what more they could do to help her.

They would never forget the day that the *Good Fortune* was listed as overdue in the shipping column of the Boston paper! They tried to hide the paper, but Mother found it and saw the notice. After reading it she laid the paper down and said quietly, "There's something happened that I don't rightly understand, but the vessel is *not* lost! I feel certain in my mind that Father's all right and will get home safe, somehow."

In spite of her faith the boys felt pretty gloomy and went about their tasks with slow steps. Everyone was very kind to them during these trying days. In school the boys' inattention and poorly-prepared lessons were overlooked and the other boys and girls tried to brighten things up by suggesting new games. At home Aunt Betsy Ann, Aunt Ruth and other neighbors kept running in to see Mother, bringing her a piece of fresh cake or some crisp doughnuts, and stopping to chat a-while. So many of the people had been through the same experience themselves, at some time, that their sympathy and understanding were very deep.

Another four days dragged wearily by and at the end

of the fifth, a day of grey November rain and fog, the boys lingered listlessly by the fence after their chores were done. They dreaded having to go into the house and appear cheerful for Mother's sake.

Peter broke a long silence by saying, "I jes' *can't* make it out any way I figure it! Here we've had a long spell of bully weather and not a single bad storm. 'Tain't the season for icebergs, and steel's not a dangerous cargo that'd cause a fire or anything."

"Father's such a dandy captain I don't see how anythin' *could* happen," mused John, thinking out loud.

"There aren't any new hands in the crew that'ud likely make trouble. It jes' don't make sense, *no* way!" sighed Eben.

"Gee, I wisht I was with him!" said Peter fervently.

"What good'ud *that* do?" asked Eben indignantly. "If you was there, Mother'd have *two* to worry about!"

"Maybe so," reluctantly admitted Peter, "but I'd *know* what was happening and I'd be there *with* Father and not here jes' waitin' and thinkin'!"

Deep in his heart John knew just how Peter felt. He remembered the storm on his voyage—Father's confidence and wisdom and the sustaining vigor of his presence. He echoed Peter's revolt against inaction, and his longing to be face to face with the dangers of the sea and pit himself against them. He sighed heavily when he thought how many years nearer that goal Peter was than he!

After a long silence the boys could only shake their heads and turn reluctantly to the house. They sat around the sitting-room lamp for a while, making a brave attempt to seem absorbed in the stories they were reading. When Peter threw down his book and suggested a game of dallies, the other two boys agreed briskly, welcoming any diversion, but it proved to be such a half-hearted game that they finally gave it up and went to bed early.

John lay awake a long time, peering into the darkness and seeing in his mind's eye countless pictures of the *Good Fortune.* Vivid recollections came to him of every little incident of his voyage with Father. In spite of his efforts to keep his thoughts on pleasant things he felt fear mounting in his heart and he tried to quiet it by assuring himself that the longed-for letter would come tomorrow without fail.

Suddenly he started up in bed, certain that he had heard a step on the east porch, directly under his window! There was silence for a moment. He sat rigid, listening intently. All at once the stillness of the night was broken by a man's deep voice singing quietly:

> *So let the wide world wag as it will,*
> *We'll be gay and happy still,*
> *Gay and happy, free and easy,*
> *We'll be gay and happy still.*

The voice grew stronger and heartier as it went along, and before the song was ended the house resounded to glad shouts and a scrambling rush for the sitting room. Mother, wrapped in a warm flannel robe, was the first to reach the east door, which she flung open with a cry of, "Benjamin! I *knew* you'd come!"

There stood Father, well and strong and beaming with joy at being home. Such a hubbub followed as he strode into the room! They all talked and exclaimed at once while they bustled around, lighting the lamp, opening the drafts in the air-tight stove to encourage the fire, and helping him off with his heavy seaman's jacket. The boys were sent upstairs to hustle into some warm clothes and raced down again to pour such a flood of questions upon Father that he held up his hands, laughing, and said, "Belay there! Come up into the wind a jiffy till we all catch a breath and then I'll heave ahead with the yarn."

When they were all gathered close about him he told his story. "As I wrote in that letter from Bristol, we set out to come north-about Scotland. I'm willing to say I was a mite uneasy about that part of the passage, for there's more islands and rocks than you can shake a stick at, and the winds and currents are likely to be mighty ornery. But, sure's I live, we had fair winds and clear weather the whole way and come around as smart as you please. I kinda sat back and felt like I was 'most home, but that's just where the trouble began!"

"Did you see any icebergs?" questioned John.

"Nary an iceberg," replied Father. "I almost wish we had—'twould have been plumb diverting! As 'twas we didn't see *anything* for days on end. We struck the longest spell of fog and calm that ever I saw. We just stuck there, rocking and rolling in the easy swells, with the sails flapping and the booms creaking, and fretted and fumed day in and day out. The crew put in so much time whistling for a wind that when *at last* it came—it blew great guns from the wrong quarter!"

"I should think *any* wind woulda been better'n none," said Peter.

"Well, 'twas kind of a pleasant change just at first," admitted Father, "and we certainly worked ship for all we were worth. But tack as we might, each noon when I took a sight of the sun and figured our position on the chart, I'd find we were traveling to the east'ard again; kinda hankering to get back to Ireland, seemed like."

"You must have been dreadful anxious, knowing how the delay would seem to us at home," said Mother, thinking of those long, weary days of waiting.

"I *was*, Susan," replied Father soberly; "times I'd get pretty nigh frenzied thinking of all at home and feeling helpless to make any headway. On top of that worriment I began to see that our water and provisions were running powerful low. Mr. Gibson and I put all hands on short rations as a precaution. The men were getting edgy and grumbled about it, and they commenced whispering about the luck of the ship—but we came down hard on 'em and gave 'em plenty of work to take up their minds."

"Wasn't you afraid of *mutiny*, Father?" asked John with bated breath.

"Well, son, I've seen it happen for less reason," admitted Father grimly, "but just as I was getting about *desperate* the wind swung all of a sudden into the northeast and drove us home so fast we pretty nigh lost our whiskers! I laid my course to come through Vineyard Sound so's to stop ashore long enough to let all hands know we were still alive and well. We didn't make the breakwater till way after dark and the ebb was running strong, so I landed at the beach and walked up, figuring how I was going to wake you up without frightening you worse'n if I'd stayed at sea! All at once that song come to me and I calc'lated that singing— even *my* singing—would wake you up kind of easy and pleasant."

When he had finished his story, questions began pouring out again and they talked and talked until after midnight. Then they all trooped out to the kitchen where Mother fixed them a snack before they tumbled into bed for a few hours' sleep.

Father had to be aboard the vessel again at sunrise in order to reach New York with his cargo as soon as possible, so they were all up at daylight, to have breakfast with him before he started back to the beach. Peter and Eben went with him to help carry the hastily assembled provisions that Mother was sending aboard, but John ran across the field to waken Grandfather and Grandmother and tell them the glad tidings. Everyone was so happy that the grey November day seemed as bright as a summer day, and every little thing they did seemed important and interesting.

In a few days a letter came from Father in New York saying that the *Good Fortune* must sail at once for Baltimore. Since she was so long overdue she had to make up for lost time, but Father said that he would surely be home for Thanksgiving. Mother and the boys had hoped that he would be able to come directly back from New York, for the few hours he had been at home were short and tantalizing. They were disappointed at this further delay but nothing really mattered now that the long anxiety was over and they had the holiday to look forward to.

Thanksgiving was the most important holiday of the year to the Cape folks. It was a day of home-coming and a gathering of relatives from far and near. Often it was the one time in the whole year when the entire family was together. Great preparations were made for days beforehand in the Cape homes, and the Crosbys were no exception to the rule. Both Mother's and Grandmother's kitchens were scenes of activity and wonderful smells! In spite of growing appetites the boys didn't see how they were ever going to eat up the array of pies, cakes, doughnuts, baked hams and cranberry sauce that was accumulating in the buttery.

The Tuesday before Thanksgiving Father arrived home, bringing with him a barrel of Chesapeake oysters, and announcing that he could stay nearly a week. That first afternoon he helped the boys haul the *Rambler* up on shore, above the reach of winter tides, and showed them how to turn her bottom-side up and cover her with a thick mat of dry seaweed. They had been reluctant to give up using her but knew they must make her safe and secure against the winter storms.

At supper that night Father asked for the news of

Aunt Betsy Ann, and Mother told him of the difficult time they had had trying to make her understand business ways.

"But *has* she found the records and letters?" questioned Father.

"No, and she isn't hunting," answered Mother. "Leastways she hasn't said anything about it lately. *I* don't know if she rightly senses how *much* she needs that money."

"It seems kind of hard lines to get her all worked up, telling her how poorly off she is and all, but I reckon *something's* got to be done," said Father seriously.

"It's perplexing work, trying to help her! She wouldn't take it kindly for folks to give her things, she's so proud and peppery-like," explained Mother, and then, as an idea come to her, she went on quickly, "I've a good mind to ask her to have Thanksgiving dinner with us! She hasn't any folks of her own and I think she'd be real pleased to come. What do you think, Benjamin?"

"It's a first-rate idea, Susan," replied Father, "and maybe 'twill give me a chance to ask her about the lawyers and urge her a mite to hunt for those papers."

The next day Aunt Cynthia, Uncle Osborn and Thomas arrived for their holiday visit and the boys began their fun just where they had left off last summer.

Thanksgiving dinner was held at the Crosbys' and the entire family, with the addition of Aunt Betsy Ann, in her best black silk, gathered around the long table in the sitting room and did full justice to oysters, turkey, cranberry sauce and golden pumpkin pies. Talk did not lag far behind appetites with all the events of the past year to be shared and discussed.

Father found a chance, after dinner, to question Aunt Betsy Ann about the papers, and she said, "It's real kind of you to plague yourself about those provokin' lawyers' actions, Cap'n Crosby. I can't seem to lay my hands on those old letters, no way, but it comes to my mind there's an old hair-trunk up attic that Elnathan might of poked 'em in. First chance I get I'll search through it."

There the matter had to be left for the time, but Father was sure that Aunt Betsy Ann failed to realize how important it was for her to get that money if she wanted to keep her little house and have something to live on. She was so deeply offended by the lawyers' insistence on actual proofs, instead of accepting her word in the matter, that she could not bring herself to try to satisfy them.

At every opportunity during the visit Eben plied Thomas with questions about Boston, but Thomas was short and vague in his answers. He was much more interested in the Cape and all the fun that living in the country had to offer and for these few days did not want even to *think* of the city. Finally Eben was forced to seek out Uncle Osborn and, in him, he found a completely satisfying source of information. Uncle Osborn, in his turn, was so impressed with Eben's alert interest that, on the last night of the visit, he said to Father, "Look here, you ought to let this boy come up to Boston some time to stay with us a spell. It's high time he was getting a notion about city ways. You can't expect to keep them *all* doused with salt water the *whole* time, Ben!"

Father laughed and said, "Right enough, Os. 'Tisn't likely they'll all follow the sea, and I presume Eben, here, would set great store by a look around Boston. Come to think of it, *you* were kind of like Eben, years back, always sorta partial to book learning, and taking to business ways. Maybe, come this time next year, we could fix it so's he could go back with you for a visit and you could help him get his bearings."

"Well, we'll be mighty pleased to have him," said Uncle Osborn, and added as he looked at Eben with a twinkle in his eye, "and I've a notion, Ben, you might's well make up your mind that one of your crew's going to turn into a business man!"

John marveled that there should be anything in just the prospect of a visit to Boston that would make Eben look so excited and glowing.

That night at bed time John, poking his head in at Eben's door, found the latter busily counting his fish and cranberry money. Looking up at John with an expression of intense satisfaction on his face Eben said, "By this time next year I'll have a good, nice sum for my trip and enough to bring home a real dandy present to Mother. It must be awful interesting to be in charge of a big business concern, like Uncle Osborn is, and have stacks of books made and get 'em sold to folks who want 'em. I guess I'll be kinda lucky, visiting someone who's running things up city-way!"

Eben's absorption in his dream was so great that he failed to notice John's puzzled expression and lack of enthusiasm.

Monday morning saw the stagecoach crowded as the host of visiting relatives returned to their own homes. Father and Grandfather went away with Aunt Cynthia, Uncle Osborn and Thomas, and the boys followed the lumbering coach down the lane to give them a proper send-off. Grandfather was going to visit Aunt Cynthia and Uncle Osborn for a few days while he went to the sail lofts and rope walks in Boston to order the gear the fishing fleet would need for its spring refitting. Father went to take charge of the *Good Fortune* while she was towed to the dry dock in East Boston, where she would be scraped clear of weed and barnacles, and recoppered to protect her hull against the action of worms and water. When that had been done the sails, standing rigging and running gear would come in for their share of inspection and replacement. Father was very particular about this annual refitting so that the *Good Fortune* would have the best chance possible to weather stormy voyages. He always planned the overhauling for this time of year, for that gave him an uninterrupted stay at home for the holidays.

This year he had a slight change that he wanted made in the rigging of the jibs and topsails. As he had watched the *Good Fortune* he had come to feel that she was capable of more speed than he was getting out of her and so he had worked out a plan of alterations. Poring over the diagrams that Father had made, the boys had decided that the change was going to work like a charm, but Grandfather had only shaken his head dubiously, thinking that the old ways were the best ways. Father had laughingly admitted that his idea might be wrong and, in any case, the advantage would only show on a long haul such as the European voyages offered.

Father was home again at the end of ten days, bringing with him two big, mysterious-looking boxes which had been stored for him in the Boston warehouse. The boys were fairly bursting with curiosity but Father only laughed at them and stowed the boxes away out of sight. Then he settled down to enjoy his longest stay at home for the entire year.

8

The Fight in the Snow

JOHN WOKE UP one morning to find it snowing. The first snowstorm of the season! The whirling flakes, driven by the northeast wind, made such a thick curtain that John could barely see the Cove from his window under the eaves. It was too cold to stand watching the storm, even though the first one was always especially exciting, so John scrambled into his warm clothes and hurried down to the kitchen where the crackling fire in the stove and the steaming teakettle seemed very cosy.

Eben joined him by the south window where they could look down the lane and see by the fences that the snow was not yet very deep. They were glad to find that they would be able to get to school, for they were eager to get out into this first snow. As they watched the whirling flakes John asked, "Do you s'pose we'll have a white Christmas?"

"Gee, I hope so," was Eben's reply. "We could have a lot of fun coasting and skating in vacation."

"I wish 'twas vacation right now, without having the last day of school," sighed John.

"Why, what's the matter with Exhibition Day?" asked Eben, surprised. "I think it's fun."

"Our class has got to speak pieces," grumbled John.

"Aw, that's nothing!" said Eben loftily.

John did not say anything more just then, for Mother called them to breakfast, but inwardly he was thinking that it certainly wasn't *nothing*. He was shy about things like that and it made him very miserable to recite before people. Having discovered that Eben was not going to be any comfort to him, he kept his troubles to himself and dreaded the approach of that "last day." He had not yet found a piece to say and did not want to find one! He fixed his mind resolutely on Christmas and vacation and felt a little more cheerful.

After breakfast, the boys bundled up in their warm coats with knitted scarves tied about their throats and the earlaps of their caps pulled down, and went out to dig a narrow track from the west door to the gate. Uncle Elijah Howes had driven by with his sleigh so, once in the lane, they could follow the tracks of the runners down to the main road. The narrow path finished, they dumped the shovels in the woodshed, stumped into the house to grab their books and started off to school early so that they might have time to play along the way.

The snow was too dry and soft to pack but they tossed it at each other in handfuls and pushed each other down in the feathery drifts. On the main road several groups of girls and boys passed in sleighs and they greeted them with flying blobs of snow.

On the doorstep of the school the three Crosbys stamped vigorously and shook off the snow as best they could and then hurried inside to help Mr. Parker get the fire started. He was working there alone, banging clumsily at the stove with hands stiff with cold. Together the four got a good fire going. Then, glancing up, the boys discovered Caleb Wixon hanging around in the back of the room, unnoticed by Mr. Parker because of his preoccupation with the stove. The boys thought it queer that Caleb, who must have been there when they arrived, had not offered to help with the fire. He was one of the older boys and was supposed to do his share of the janitor work with the rest of Peter's class.

The big room was as cold as a barn so they all stood around for a while with their coats on, alternately stamping their feet and holding their hands close to the stove. Gradually the roaring fire began to have its effect on the chill and the boys could take off their wraps. For once John was content to be in the lower class, for their benches were in the front of the room and they would get the most warmth.

The children worked two at a desk, sitting on wooden benches slightly hollowed out to make them more comfortable. One long bench, for the class that was reciting, stood directly in front of the teacher's desk. Back of that were the low desks for the younger children while the higher ones for the older boys and girls were toward the back of the room.

The rest of the pupils were arriving now, in laughing groups, all red-cheeked and panting from their tussle with the storm. Mr. Parker rang his hand bell and silence fell as they all hurried to their seats. Suddenly the subdued rustling in the room was interrupted by a scream from one of the older girls, followed by a chorus of gasps and suppressed giggles from the others in the back row. Instantly all necks were craned to see what had happened.

Mr. Parker looked up with a deep frown, fixed his eye upon the excited girl who stood hesitating by her desk, and asked in forbidding tones, "What is the meaning of this unseemly behavior, Experience?"

"Oh, Mr. Parker," stammered Experience Baker, blushing a rosy red, "someone spilled water on my bench and I—and I *sat* in it, and—it was *cold*!"

In spite of Mr. Parker's deepening frown, a wave of tittering swept over the room but everyone looked at Experience with sympathy because it was icy cold in that last row, farthest from the fire.

"*Spilled water*, you say?" thundered Mr. Parker in such a tone that everyone sat up straight, eyes front, and began to feel solemn and uneasy. "I was not aware that water was used in that part of the room. The drinking pail is located in the cloakroom. I greatly fear the water was deliberately poured upon your bench. I will consider this disgraceful conduct later."

With that Mr. Parker swept the faces of the boys and girls with such a piercing glance that they all shifted guiltily in their places. Then, realizing that Experience was still standing by her desk, shame-faced and confused, he added less sternly, "You may come to the front, Experience, and may stand with your back to the stove while you study your geography lesson. The first class in arithmetic will recite."

Relieved from the tension, the scholars ducked their heads to get their books out of their desks and set to work with feverish energy. But John simply could not keep his mind on his spelling lesson. Glancing up once he had caught Mr. Parker's eyes resting upon Peter with a speculative look. With a sinking heart John realized that they were bound to be suspected because they had been such early arrivals at school that morning.

Even the dancing snowflakes lost their charm for John as he thought how unhappy it would be, just at Christmas time, if any of them should be under a cloud of suspicion. Father had no patience with school pranks and always upheld Mr. Parker, even though his methods were rather stern and harsh. Eben, John felt, was not likely to be suspected because he was so quiet and serious-minded, but Peter was full of fun and loved to tease. It might easily be thought that he, John, had aided and abetted Peter in carrying out the practical joke.

Suddenly John remembered that Caleb Wixon had been there, hanging around the back of the room, when they had arrived that morning! It was all plain enough now, and it was a relief to know who had played the unkind trick, but how was that going to help them? John knew he could not tell on Caleb and *how* could they make him own up? John glanced covertly around and caught the big boy grinning slyly behind his geography. He was inclined to be mean and the other boys didn't like him at all. John vividly recalled the day last spring when Caleb had put a grass snake in the teacher's desk and then had let little Luther Nickerson be blamed and severely punished for the prank. That wasn't an encouraging thought!

Just then the spelling class was called and John made so many mistakes, even on the easy words, that the other children began to snicker and Mr. Parker smiled unpleasantly.

The hours of the morning dragged slowly by. The storm increased steadily until the wind was howling around the schoolhouse. After studying the weather Mr. Parker stated that there would be no afternoon session of school. Ordinarily that would have been cause for great rejoicing, but John could only think of the hour of reckoning ahead of them.

When noontime came Mr. Parker said, "The girls are dismissed. The boys will remain."

After the girls had bustled out, giggling nervously,

an awful stillness fell upon the room. Mr. Parker fixed the boys with his stern and accusing glance and let the heavy silence make them thoroughly uncomfortable. John stole a glance at Caleb. He looked very bland and innocent! John saw that Peter and Eben shared his realization of their unpleasant position, for they both looked worried.

After studying all the faces, Mr. Parker began questioning each boy closely. One by one he dismissed those who were free from suspicion. When Caleb's name was called Peter, Eben and John held their breath. Caleb lounged up to the desk and stood boldly confronting the teacher.

"Did you have anything to do with pouring that water, Caleb?"

"No, sir," came the gruff answer.

"Did you arrive at school early this morning?"

"No, sir."

Mr. Parker hesitated a moment. It was easy to suspect Caleb of such a prank for he was sullen and unpopular with the other boys and girls. But he did not know that Caleb had been there early that morning and so he allowed the boy's tone and innocent expression to convince him.

"You may go," said the schoolmaster, and John's heart sank to his boots. What *could* they do now?

At length the three Crosbys were the only ones left in the room. With growing irritation and impatience Mr. Parker questioned them and received identical answers from all three:

"Did you pour that water?"

"No, sir."

"Do you know who did?"

"Yes, sir."

"Will you tell me who it was?"

"No, sir."

Baffled by the solid front they presented and angered by the thought that one of them might be lying and the other two protecting him, Mr. Parker frowned heavily and finally pronounced judgment, "You three boys were the first ones here this morning. You must be considered the culprits until such time as you can get a confession from this other person whom you accuse. You may have no part in the program on Exhibition Day unless you can clear this matter up by then."

The boys silently got into their wraps and filed out into the storm. Even the unexpected respite from the dreaded piece-speaking on Friday afternoon failed to lift the gloom from John. All the mothers and fathers came to Exhibition Day and the School Committee was always present in all its dignity. If the three Crosby boys had no part in the program, their disgrace would be plain to everyone in the village. John wished fervently that he might speak a dozen hated pieces rather than have Father and Mother so shamed on their account.

They plodded along through the deep snow, buffeted by the wind and floundering in the drifts. Each one was trying to find some way out of their unfair position but, so far, not one of them could think of anything that would help. They talked only enough to agree not to say a word about their trouble at home.

After a good hot dinner their spirits rose a little. Not seeming to notice their unusual silence, Mother suggested some extra jobs to fill the long, stormy afternoon. John's task was to pick over a half-barrel of apples, taking out the bruised ones to prevent their spoiling the good ones. She directed that the ones he took out he might cut up for apple sauce, while the soundest and reddest ones he came across in the barrel might be polished up for use at Christmas. John's thoughts were busy as he examined and sorted, and set aside the prettiest apples in a little basket.

Suddenly an idea came to him and he hurried through the final polishing so that he could carry it out right away. He put his red apples in a cool place where they would keep well until next week, and went quietly into the entry to get his wraps. Luck was with him, for no one was around and it was only the work of a few minutes to get into his warm things and slip out before anyone could question him.

Once outside, he noticed that the storm was letting up and showed signs of clearing by sunset. He was tempted to cut straight across the fields to Caleb Wixon's house but he knew it would be hard going on account of drifts, so he decided he would save time in the end by sticking to the lane and the main road. As John trudged along he hadn't much idea of what he was going to say when he got there, but the conviction had come to him that it was up to him to make some attempt to bring Caleb to time. He knew that neither Peter nor Eben could be hired to appeal to the boy who had deliberately gotten them into trouble.

When John came in sight of the small grey house where Caleb lived alone with his father, he walked more slowly, trying to decide how best to find Caleb alone. Luck favored him again and by cautiously following the sounds from the woodshed, he came upon the lanky, freckled-face boy chopping wood. When Caleb glanced up and saw John standing watching him, he looked thoroughly scared for a moment. To hide his guilt and fear he put on a great show of bellowing bluster. "*What* you doin' here, kid? Ha! Ha! Your fine brothers sent you—knowin' you're too little fer me to lick!"

"They did *not*!" burst out John hotly, his anger at the taunt helping him to find his voice which had threatened to desert him. "They don't even *know* I'm *here*! I jes' came to tell you that I *know* you poured that water and if you don't own up—I'll tell your father!"

"You wouldn't dare to," sneered Caleb, alarmed in spite of himself by that threat, because his father was a rough, hard man, easily aroused to violent anger by his son's waywardness.

"I *would too*!" retorted John staunchly, with more courage than he really felt at the moment.

The fact that John had actually come, alone, to face the bigger boy gave weight to his threat and Caleb's face grew dark with fear and anger. Raising a stick of wood above his head he shouted at John, "You git *outta* here before I let fly with this. Now, *git!*"

John turned and departed with all the dignity he could command, though he longed to break into a run. All the rest of the afternoon and evening he was alternately hopeful and discouraged over the probable result of his attempt.

The storm cleared in the late afternoon and the sun came out to turn the unbroken stretches of fresh snow to sparkling beauty. The dark pines stood out sharply against the dazzling whiteness. When John reached home he found Peter and Eben shoveling paths and set to work at once to help them. They thought that he had been over at Joe's so they did not question him, much to John's relief. They finished the paths to the gate, the woodshed and the chicken house, before supper and did their chores in the gathering dusk.

The next morning when school was called to order Mr. Parker cleared his throat with great solemnity and said he had an announcement to make: "It gives me great satisfaction to be able to tell you that the real culprit in the unfortunate episode of yesterday has come forward and confessed so that I can now clear Peter, Eben and John Crosby of the unfair suspicion that rested upon them. I feel that it will be sufficient punishment if the culprit makes public confession of his wrongdoing. Caleb!"

Everyone turned with eager interest but with very little surprise to face the boy who rose slowly in his place. With sullen face and feet that shuffled restlessly, he mumbled, "I did it and I know I shouldn't of," and slumped into his seat again.

Peter and Eben looked at each other in amazement and relief, while John wanted to jump up and shout for joy! To think that his scheme had worked and he had saved the situation!

When they all came out of the schoolhouse at noon, Caleb waited near the steps until Peter passed him and then jeered, "Had to hide behind your kid brother, didn't you!"

Peter turned on him, his eyes flashing with anger, and said, "I don't know what you're talking about but if you mean I've ever asked John to do anything I was scared to do myself, it's a *lie* and I'll wash your face in the snow to prove it!"

"Aw, you *will*, will you?" yelled Caleb.

Flinging his books into a snowbank, Peter was upon him before he could move and the fight was on!

The boys and girls gathered around in an excited circle. They were all on Peter's side, cheering him on. Though Caleb was the larger and heavier of the two, Peter was quicker and more wiry. The fight was fierce while it lasted. Legs and arms were a whirling mass in the midst of a cloud of flying snow. John found himself jumping up and down and yelling wildly. In one of his leaps he landed on something hard and feeling around with his feet he uncovered Peter's discarded books. Brandishing these in the air he cheered the fighters on to the final struggle.

At length Caleb's face was thoroughly scrubbed with snow and Peter stood up, panting and grinning broadly through scratches and reddening snow-scrapes. In his joy John was pounding him on the back with the bundle of books while the others helped him remove wads of snow from up his sleeves and down his neck.

The shouting circle quickly broke up into scattered groups that snowballed their way home. As the three Crosbys set out together Peter demanded, "Look here, John! *What* did Caleb mean, saying I was hiding behind you? The mean sneak!"

"Aw, gee," said John, "I didn't mean you to know. 'Twasn't anything, but I jes' went over to his place yesterday afternoon and told him we knew, for sure, he did it and he'd better own up. That's all!"

"But how'd you ever think of doing *that*?" pressed Peter.

"Oh, I figured *you'd* never go and beg him to, so it seemed like *I'd* better do *something*!" replied John casually, thankful that Peter and Eben couldn't guess how scared he had been.

"Well, you keep away from him after this, *I'll* 'tend to *him*!" insisted Peter.

"Well, I'm *terrible* relieved," admitted Eben. " 'Twould of been just *awful* for Mother and Father on Exhibition Day!"

The next few days passed very quickly with all the preparations for Friday's program in school and with the thrill of Christmas in the air. Some of the older girls and boys went on a sleigh ride and gathered hemlock boughs and groundpine to decorate the schoolroom. They made it look very festive and it smelled deliciously of the woods.

Exhibition Day dawned clear and crisp and two o'clock found the schoolhouse crowded. The boys and girls, in their Sunday clothes, occupied their usual benches, while all around the walls of the room sat a sedate row of mothers and fathers. In the front of the room, behind Mr. Parker's desk, sat the School Committee—three dignified, elderly gentlemen wearing frock coats and holding their beaver hats carefully on their knees.

The parents exchanged low-voiced comments and beamed with pride as they talked about their children. The subdued hum of conversation was suddenly hushed as the Chairman of the School Committee rose from his place, cleared his throat with great solemnity and addressed a few slow and solemn words of greeting to the gathering. The moment he finished, Abigail Baxter bounced onto the bench in front of the little parlor organ and dashed into the opening bars of "America." She pumped so vigorously with her feet that the two red roses in the front of her bonnet bobbed and wagged to and fro rakishly. Her face grew pink with exertion but she led the singing with enthusiasm, throwing her head back until her roses waved more wildly than ever.

Following the singing the program started off with a spelling bee for Eben's class in which Eben's victory was greeted with such hearty applause that he sat down hastily in great confusion. Next came the recitations by members of John's class. Several of them had been too ambitious and had attempted long, hard pieces. They had to have constant whispered prompting, in order to get through, which was embarrassing for the children and trying for the parents. When John was called, Mother clasped her hands tight in her lap, wondering *what* he would do.

He clumped to the front of the room, looking very resolute, and made his brief bow. He swallowed hard, paused and then said, in a loud, firm voice:

> *Speaking pieces is hard and tough,*
> *I've said two lines and that's enough.*

With another stiff bow he stalked back to his seat, inwardly trembling at his own daring.

Everyone was so taken by surprise that there was a moment's silence, and then shouts of laughter filled the room. The Chairman of the School Committee tried to look very stern and disapproving, but his lips twitched in spite of himself and he finally burst out laughing with the rest.

After that, there could be no traces of stiffness left. Everybody joined in the singing and seemed ready to enjoy everything that happened. Peter's composition on the subject of "Lighthouses" set some of the sea captains among the fathers to nodding their heads and exchanging approving glances.

The December dusk was drawing in when the townsfolk at length started homeward, afoot or in sleighs, over the crisp snow. More than one family group stopped to speak to the Crosbys and tell John that his was the best part of the program. He was surprised and somewhat abashed to find himself the center of so much laughter and comment. He had found the little jingle in his *Youth's Companion* and had taken it, in desperation, at the last moment, fully expecting to get a scolding for it when the entertainment was over.

"It does beat all how our most cherished hopes get blasted!" remarked Father as they walked up the snowy lane together. His voice sounded very mournful but, glancing up at him in the half-light, the boys caught a twinkle in his eyes and waited expectantly for the explanation of his mock sadness. He went on, "Here I've always been figuring on the proud moment that'ud come when one of my sons turned into an orator and kept us all a-listening for hours on end while he made long and weighty speeches. Now it don't look to me like John would be a candidate, after all!"

At the burst of laughter that greeted this remark John hung his head and grinned sheepishly, but he determined, none the less, to be on the watch for another jingle to help him out of a future piece-speaking dilemma, *if* he was ever asked *again*! At the thought that maybe, after today, he *wouldn't* be, he let out his shout of laughter when all the others had fallen silent. That was enough to set them all off again and they laughed so heartily that they saw Janey Ellis, across the way, peeping out between her kitchen curtains to see what all the noise could be about.

✺ 9 ✺

Christmas

AS THEY SAT around the supper table that night, still talking over the afternoon's program, Father suddenly changed the subject to ask, "How would you boys like to pop some corn this evening? I hear the Sunday School's going to need extra strings for the tree and, like enough, we'd better see about fixing some for them."

"Hurrah!" shouted all three and John added, "And can we make some m'lasses candy and corn balls, too?"

"I wouldn't wonder," agreed Mother, smiling. "Grandfather sets such store by corn balls we mustn't fail to have some to carry to him on Christmas day."

Everyone bustled around getting the supper dishes out of the way and the kitchen cleared for action. Eben went clattering up to the attic to get some ears of popcorn they had raised in the garden last summer and hung in the attic to dry. Father, Peter and Eben shelled the corn by rubbing the hard, rough ears together, while John rummaged in the pantry cupboard for the corn poppers. When they were found and dusted off, a layer of the hard red and yellow kernels was scattered in the bottom of each one and they were placed on the stove. Meanwhile Mother had been measuring out the molasses and now set it to simmer in the big iron pot.

The corn poppers shuffled back and forth over the hot stove lids and soon the little wire cages were bursting with snowy puff-balls. By the time there were two big bowls heaping full of fluffy popcorn, in the middle of the kitchen table, Mother said that the molasses was ready for the corn balls and suggested that they make them while the rest of the molasses cooled for the taffy-pulling.

While Mother poured the brown syrup in a dribbling stream over the platter filled with snowy corn, the boys washed their hands and greased them liberally with butter so that the molasses would not stick to them. Then they seized the sticky mass in handfuls and shaped it quickly into balls. They whooped and danced first on one foot and then on the other when occasionally the hot syrup stuck and burned their hands. No sooner would one of them laugh at another's distress than he himself would get a burn and join the yelping chorus. The trick was to squeeze and toss the balls swiftly from hand to hand. In spite of some mishaps they soon had a great mound of nubbly, golden-brown balls that grew glazed and crisp as the film of molasses cooled and hardened.

Testing the remainder of the candy, cooling in shallow pans, Father gave his opinion that they would have just time to eat a corn ball apiece before it was ready to pull. How good those corn balls tasted!

More butter had to be applied to their hands before they could start to pull the taffy. At first they had to work very rapidly to keep the candy from sticking, but, as it hardened, they took longer and longer stretches. It was fun to see it grow whiter and silkier as they pulled it. Finally they got it to the stage where they could twist and braid it and try all sorts of fancy stunts.

"There!" exclaimed John with satisfaction. "I've tied a bowline knot in taffy! That's the hardest one to do. All my candy's going to be made in knots but the rest're easy." So saying he went on working fast, to shape the rest of his taffy before it grew too hard to twist.

"Well, mine're loops and coils of rope," said Peter, "and maybe I can fix this last piece into a little dory to go along with 'em!"

Mother had fixed each of them a big buttered plate on which to arrange the finished candy, and when John and Peter had admired each other's nautical displays, they began to wonder what Eben was making with his taffy. He had been working quietly and intently at the other side of the table. They crowded around him to find that he had spelled out all their names in fine, silvery ropes of taffy! Laughing, Father presented him with an extra corn ball as a prize for the most original idea in their display of Christmas candy.

The next day a little more snow fell, sifting slowly from a grey sky. Joe came over early with his sled and he and John went out back of the woodshed to try the coasting on the hill toward the Cove. The snow needed more packing down to be really good, but it was so much fun to be flying along on their sleds once more that John and Joe were not very critical.

After dinner Peter beckoned Eben and John up to his room and, after closing the door with elaborate care, they held a conference over the contents of their banks. Later they all three got into their wraps and went out together, coins jingling importantly in their pockets. Down at the general store there was more debate and uncertainty but they finally made their purchases and returned home with their arms full of lumpy bundles. They spread the presents out on Peter's bed to examine them again. There were—embroidered handkerchiefs and a bottle of "scent" for Mother, a pair of heavy woolen gloves for Father, a rose-decorated sugar bowl and cream pitcher for Grandmother, and a pipe rack and a plug of his favorite tobacco for Grandfather.

When the boys had tied up their gifts John looked at the array thoughtfully for a long time and then said, "I can think of another sort of present for Mother that I wish we c'ud give her."

"What is it?" demanded Peter and Eben.

John went on thinking out loud while the other boys listened, puzzled and curious. "It really could be called a *present*," he asserted, " 'cause we'd have to *give* it to her, and she'll never get it 'less we *make* her take it!"

"*What is* it?" roared Peter and Eben, pouncing on John so that they all went down in a tussling heap.

"Get *off* and maybe I'll tell you," gasped John.

When they untangled themselves and could stop laughing John explained, "I mean about that voyage with Father that we want Mother to go on. Unless we keep urgin' her she'll jes' *never* go and leave us here alone. I wish we c'ud *some* way give her the present that we're old enough now to look after things all right so she can go off for a good, long trip."

"Say, John, that's a bully idea, but *how* can we give her *that* kind of a present? I don't see that there's any way at all!" objected Eben.

They all sat deep in thought for a while and then Peter said, "How would it be if I was to write out on a paper what we want to say, and then put it in her little old traveling satchel and hand it to her on Christmas morning?"

John and Eben slapped their knees and howled with delight at the suggestion, and promptly set about carrying it out. John, tiptoeing into the attic, got the little satchel and brought it back to Peter's room. Meanwhile Peter had gotten out a sheet of his school paper and was setting down in his best writing the wording that Eben had worked out for their present.

Peter, Eben and John Crosby do hereby give to Mother one voyage aboard the *Good Fortune* with

Father. They do solemnly declare that they can manage things at home during her absence.

When it was finished they read it through with satisfaction and admired the fine flourishes of the writing. They placed the paper in the satchel and put it among the other presents to await Christmas morning.

Early Monday morning Peter's Sunday School class went off to the woods in Captain Ed's big sleigh to cut and drag home the tree for the Christmas entertainment at the church that night, while Eben and John gathered a crowd of boys for coasting on the Cove hill. Finding that the snow was just right for packing they quickly abandoned their sleds and built a mammoth fort in preparation for a battle royal. As soon as sides had been chosen they went at it hot and heavy, but so evenly were they matched that for a long while it was a tie.

Then suddenly Eben's side, the attackers, withdrew to a clump of pines near by, and were quiet so long that the defenders grew bold and ventured outside the fort to get more snow for ammunition. When that failed to draw the enemies' fire the defenders gleefully claimed the victory. But just at that moment one of the boys standing within the fort, was hit in the back with a big snowball. He turned upon John to accuse him, indignantly, of playing a mean trick when John got a ball in the back of *his* neck. The two boys gazed at each other, stupefied, and then something prompted them to look around at the big hemlock tree growing

behind the fort. Just then a storm of snowballs fell upon
the fort and the attacking party, bursting from the
shelter of the low-sweeping hemlock branches, cap-
tured the fort by a surprise attack from the rear!

Peter came in late for dinner, hungry as a bear and
bubbling over with high spirits. "Golly, but we've got
a monster tree!" he burst out between mouthfuls. "It's
the biggest one we've *ever* had! We had a tough old
time cutting it down and making it fast to the sleigh
but we got it hauled to the church. We boys went in
and set it up for 'em so's the Ladies Aid could get to
work trimming it right off."

Peter ended with such a chuckle that John pricked
up his ears and eyed him questioningly. A wink from
Peter indicated that he would tell the joke later on.
Meanwhile Eben was asking anxiously, "Do you s'pose
the Ladies Aid'll have enough trimmings to fix it up
pretty?"

"Maybe they'll have to spread 'em around kind of
sparse but I presume likely it will look sightly," said
Father reassuringly.

John gulped down the last of his Indian pudding and
dashed out to the woodshed as soon as Peter left the
table. Eben, perplexed by the furtive signals he had
received, followed more deliberately. Peter joined them
and further tantalized them by collapsing on the saw-
horse in fits of helpless laughter.

"Aw, come on! Tell us what's so all-fired funny!" demanded John.

"Well," said Peter finally, "you know Aunt Mercy

'n' Uncle Abijah Snow and how she's real stout and hearty-looking while he's kinda poor and scrawny? And you've seen her at church always hauling down the pew cushion (it's an awful small cushion anyhow)—so's she can set on it while *he* has to set on the hard pew?"

Eben nodded assent to all this while John burst out, "But what's so comical 'bout that? They've been doin' it ever since I c'n remember."

"That's jes' it!" laughed Peter. "Link and I figured this'ud be one time when she *wouldn't* do it! We took and nailed that cushion fast to *Uncle Abijah's* end of the pew. Now tonight you fix it to sit behind 'em and you'll see some fun!"

Chortling over the prank, the boys hustled to gather the wood and kindlings for supper. When they came into the kitchen Mother told Eben and John to get ready to take a basket of Christmas good things down to Aunt Betsy Ann. As she packed it she said to Father, who sat reading in the rocker by the south window, "I don't see as Betsy Ann could be put out about my sending her these things. Near Christmas, like it is, folks are always aiming to give presents."

"I'm glad you're doing it, Susan," replied Father, "because like enough she really needs them but would never let on to anybody. I saw Squire Nickerson when I was coming down in the cars, a while back, and he was asking about her. I told him what she'd heard from the lawyers and how she'd got plumb becalmed as far as finding the letters was concerned."

"Did you let on she was considerable put out with

the lawyers for demanding written proof of Captain Elnathan's ownership, and maybe hadn't spent a whole lot of time hunting?" questioned Mother.

"I did, for certain," chuckled Father, "and the Squire laughed hearty, but he allowed as how he'd have to write her just how she's fixed. Something's *got* to be done or, sure as preaching, she'll lose her home, come June. I told him we'd be mighty glad to help out any way we could figure."

"It's just too aggravating that she can't find those letters," said Mother vehemently. "That money belongs to her in all conscience and it's shameful that she can't get it! It is so! I don't hold with these lawyers' doings, no way."

"You'd better not let Betsy Ann hear you talking that way or she'd never lift a finger to search," laughed Father.

By the time the boys were bundled up against the sharp wind, Mother had the basket ready. Carrying it between them they ran out of the gate and followed the snowy ruts down the hill. The wind buffeted them and took their breath away until, halfway down the hill, Eben called a halt saying, "Hey, let's set this thing down a minute and rest our arms. What in tunket did Mother put in it? It's terrible heavy."

Filled with curiosity the boys lifted a corner of the red and white tablecloth spread neatly over the basket, and peeked in.

"No wonder it's so heavy!" exclaimed John. "Look at the apples and turnips and nuts and cranberry sauce and pickles—two kinds—and—and a *whole pie.* Gee, she's lucky, gettin' all these things to eat all by *herself*."

Tucking the cover in again carefully, the boys picked up the basket and plodded on through the snow. Aunt Betsy Ann met them at the door and beamed with pleasure at being remembered with a Christmas basket. She insisted that John and Eben come in and sit by the stove to warm their cold fingers. She handed each of them an apple turnover and while they were enjoying the crisp little pies Aunt Betsy Ann stepped briskly to and fro putting away her gifts with many exclamations of pleasure. When she was out of the kitchen on one of her trips to the buttery John nudged Eben. "Say, Eb," he whispered, "do you see any places where those lost letters might be stowed?"

They looked quickly around the room and Eben answered in disgust, "Naw, she must have looked everywheres *here*, but I'd like to get up in her attic. I wager they must be up there *somewhere*. Wish she'd let *us* hunt."

They stopped whispering and sat straight in their chairs when they heard her quick steps returning. A moment later she disappeared into her tiny parlor and came back with a braided table mat which she wrapped up and placed in the bottom of the empty basket.

"You tell your mother that I made that partic'ler for her, seeing as how she's getting her best room all fixed up pretty. I kinda thought she'd admire those colors. Looked real handsome to me, they did," said Aunt Betsy Ann, nodding her head brightly.

The boys assured her that Mother would like it. Pulling on their woolen caps they took up the basket and wished her a "Merry Christmas" as they went out. On the way home they chased each other and swung the light basket in such wide circles that the little mat nearly landed in the snow.

"We'd better take care," warned Eben, "Mother'd be real worked up if anything was to happen to that little jimcrack. She'll set store by it 'cause Aunt Betsy Ann made it for her special."

"Say, this wind's blowin' half a gale," complained John as he was whirled around. "Do you s'pose it'll be a good night for the Christmas Tree?"

"Sure, it'll be all right," said Eben cheerfully. "The wind'll go down with the sun and it'll be a fine night, certain sure."

"I was thinkin' Aunt Mercy and Uncle Abijah mightn't come out if 'twas too blustery or anythin'," explained John, and both boys had a fit of giggling in anticipation of the evening.

When the Crosbys arrived at the church that evening what a sight met their eyes! Peter had not exaggerated. It was a magnificent tree towering, straight and tall, at the front of the church, its branches laden with gifts, strings of snowy popcorn, rosy apples, golden oranges and pink and white candy bags.

By dint of much jostling and nudging John, Joe and Eben managed to get into the pew just behind the one in which Uncle Abijah and his wife usually sat. Leaning forward to peer over the back of the pew, they saw

the cushion lying at the aisle end of the seat just as Peter had said. Settling back with stifled giggles they craned their necks to watch for the Snows to come in. People were arriving in family groups and the church was filling rapidly.

"You don't s'pose they *aren't coming,* do you?" whispered John fearfully.

"If they don't come pretty quick, someone else'll take that pew, as sure as preaching," predicted Eben darkly.

"Here they be!" announced Joe with a stifled whoop.

Sure enough—Aunt Mercy came sailing up the aisle, majestic in her best black taffeta and jet-trimmed bonnet, and behind her trotted a thin, grey-haired man, nervously turning his well-worn beaver in his hands. Aunt Mercy swept into the pew and seated herself with dignity and then looked down sharply for the explanation of the unexpected hardness of the bench. Seeing the position of the cushion she reached over and gave it a tug toward her. It did not move. Exasperated, she gave it a harder pull. It remained in its place. With a little snort of anger she leaned over and gave it a good strong yank. Still it did not budge. Suddenly realizing that she was attracting the amused attention of her neighbors, she sat up, very red of face, and gazed straight ahead of her with stony dignity.

Uncle Abijah, who had been hovering in the pew entrance during these maneuvers, now stepped in and sat down, with a sigh of content, on the cushion's softness.

By this time John had his handkerchief stuffed in his

mouth while Joe and Eben were doubled over with pains under their ribs from their suppressed laughter. Gasping weakly they all finally sat up and mopped their streaming eyes. They dared not look at each other, for one glance would have sent them off again.

Fortunately, at this moment, the minister opened the exercises, and by fixing their attention on the business of finding and singing the first hymn, they managed to sober down a little.

John fidgeted restlessly during the recitations. His inner rejoicing that he had not been asked to speak a piece was not enough to curb his impatience. He wondered if they would *ever* get to the important part of the evening and begin unburdening the tree! During the hymns he raced along a word ahead of the congregation, hoping vainly that he could hurry them up, but he only won snickers from the boys and disapproving frowns from the nearest grown-ups.

At long last the climax of the evening was reached and the classes were called up, one at a time, to the front of the church, where each scholar received a muslin bag of candy (pink bags for the girls, and white ones for the boys) and a gift, usually a story book, from the teacher.

On reaching home the boys eagerly examined each other's books and traded the striped and twisted hard candies from their bags until Father called a halt. After hanging their stockings, from the sitting-room mantel, the boys went up to bed still laughing and calling remarks back and forth between their rooms.

John was the first to waken next morning but his shout of "Merry Christmas!" brought an instant whoop and scramble from Peter and Eben. Downstairs they raced to look at their stockings, transformed from limpness to prodigious lumps and bulges. Stuffed in the top of each stocking was a pair of mittens and a knitted scarf from Grandmother—blue for Peter, green for Eben, and red for John. After trying on the mittens and pronouncing them a perfect fit, they dug out a handful of nuts and an orange apiece. The orange was a rare treat and must have come, along with those on the Christmas tree at the church, out of one of the mysterious boxes Father had brought home from the south.

Now they each came upon a flat package that proved to be a small, leather-covered diary with a note from Mother on the fly-leaf saying that she hoped the daily record would be neatly and regularly kept.

Next their reaching hands brought out paper sacks of candied fruits and sugared nuts, another treat from Father's southern boxes. In the toe of each stocking was a hard lump—a jackknife apiece from Grandfather.

Out of the corners of their eyes they had been noticing three bundles, too large for the stockings, that stood beneath them, on the hearth. Now they fell upon them and opened them with fingers made clumsy by eagerness. Peter was the first to get his undone and revealed a set of tools and pieces of wood for making brackets and ornaments of scroll-saw work. His eyes shone, for he had been longing for such a set. Eben's gift was a new pair of skates. The body of the skate was made of wood in the shape of a thick wooden sole. To that was fastened a steel runner with a graceful, up-curving tip, hand-wrought by the blacksmith. A screw set in the heel-plate of the skate screwed directly into the boot heel, while the toe of the skate was held in place by a leather strap fastened around the foot. In his delight Eben said to John, "Now you can have my old ones for keeps, and they're good and speedy, too!" That was like another present for John because, previously, he could only use them when Eben did not want them.

Now they all turned their attention to John, who was opening his bundle last and finally disclosed from its many wrappings a small brass lantern with a chain and ring to carry it by. He was speechless with surprise but his face beamed with joy, not only over the gleaming little lantern itself, but because it meant that now he was old enough to go to writing school and singing school at night. He had longed for it but had not expected this symbol of his growing-up for another year at least.

When they had admired their gifts all over again the boys exchanged signals and Peter hurried to the dark closet under the stairs and brought out their presents for Mother and Father. Last of all John offered Mother the satchel. She looked puzzled at being handed her own little traveling bag and held it at arm's length, looking from one boy to another in bewilderment. The boys were bursting with excitement and laughter but they managed to say, "Open it, Mother. Open it!"

She opened it cautiously and pulled out the paper. Father went to lean over her shoulder to look at it with her. He shouted with laughter when he read the message. Mother laughed, too, and said, "Well, I declare that's the best present ever a body got! Any boys who could think of giving their mother a present like that must be pretty nigh grown-up. I'll have to set my mind on using it, come nice weather next spring."

Father added, smiling at the boys and then at Mother, "Seems like it's a present to me, too! Nothing could be nicer, thinks I the other day, than to have Mother aboard the vessel once more." And the boys felt that their last present had been the best of all.

Before they knew it, it was time to dress for Christmas dinner at Grandfather's. Promptly at one o'clock the Crosbys went in single file through the narrow path across the field. Each one carried a package and Father, coming last, bore aloft a big platter of glossy brown popcorn balls. Grandfather shouted with delight at sight of them and ushered them in to a bountiful dinner of roast goose and mince pie.

During the night it rained and then turned colder so that morning revealed a coating of ice over everything.

"This ought to make the skating just *dandy*," exclaimed John as he slipped and slid on the crust in the back yard.

"What do you say we get some of the boys and girls and go skating up the river right off—before it c'n melt or anything," suggested Peter.

The idea met with instant approval and all three

boys set off to spread the news of their plan. Shortly after dinner the crowd began to assemble on the shore of the Cove. Skates were adjusted and away they all went, keeping to the solid ice near shore because the saltiness of the water and the force of the tide made the ice in mid-channel treacherous. Peter, who was far in the lead, was just turning back to warn them of air-holes when Joe caught the tip of his skate in one and fell with a resounding whack, flat on the ice. He lay there motionless for a moment and John's heart stood still with dread. Joe stirred and groaned just as the others came hurrying anxiously back to see what had happened. They helped him to his feet and found that the fall had knocked his wind out completely! But, save for a few moments of painful gasping to get it back again, he was unhurt and was soon able to follow slowly along with John. When the two boys finally came up with the rest they found them on the shore at the edge of a pine grove, gathered around a crackling fire, warming themselves and resting after the long skate against the keen wind. When fingers and toes were glowing once more they pulled out the sandwiches and apples that had been hastily crammed into their pockets. After they had eaten and sung a while, they got to their feet reluctantly, put out the fire, and fastened on their skates for the homeward trip. John and Joe tagged along in the wake of the others, doing their own private racing and exploring, while the shadows lengthened out across the ice and the winter sun sank behind the dark pines on the bank of the river.

10

The Rescue

"GREAT DAY!" exclaimed Eben, looking up from the Atlas the evening after Father had received a letter from his agents saying that the *Good Fortune* was ready and that he was to sail the following week for Rio de Janeiro. "I never knew Rio was so *awful* far away. Why, it's further'n going to England!"

"Is it *honest*?" questioned John, coming to lean over Eben's shoulder and peer at the map, too. "It don't *sound* so but, by golly, it *is*! That seems a terrible far voyage for *winter* time."

"But you forget that I'm going clear *away* from winter and plumb into *summer* down there," said Father, laughing at their anxiety.

"Gee, I never can remember that. It's all topsy-turvy down there," complained Eben. "Is it honest-to-goodness warm summer weather there *now*?"

Before Father could answer him Peter burst out, "But you've a whole piece of winter to go through before you get nigh to the warm parts."

"True enough, son," replied Father, "but you must call to mind that the *Good Fortune*'s in prime condition. I'd lay my course, in her, to any place on the globe in any kind of weather, the way she is now!"

The way Father's eyes kindled when he spoke of setting sail again made the boys realize how he loved the sea, and Peter and John knew they would feel just that way when they had vessels of their own. Catching Father's enthusiasm Peter asked, "Don't you figure that new rigging's going to make her a whole lot faster?"

"Well, I wouldn't go so far as to say that," Father replied, "and the way I look at it I'm not likely to see any powerful difference on these coastwise voyages. The set of the currents and winds is such that you can't make very long reaches."

"But you *do* think she'll sail *some* better, don't you?" questioned John anxiously.

"Yes, I do figure her tops'll set better but like enough I'll have to bide. my time till I take a run across the Atlantic to prove my point," said Father smiling.

"Well, I'll warrant she'll show every other vessel a clean pair of heels, beginning right now on this voyage!" stated Peter confidently.

When the day came and Father had actually gone, the house felt dreadfully quiet and lonesome. Everything seemed dull and pointless, for Father's presence always lent a zest to all that they did. It was some comfort, during the first week or so, to get reports of his safety from other captains returning to the Cape. But after that, the anxious period set in when every storm meant days of wondering and worrying.

Following one terrific gale that strewed the outer beaches of the Cape with wrecks and left everyone heavy-hearted with sympathy and dread, Grandfather came striding in one evening, in a state of excitement very unusual for his quiet dignity. For an instant Mother and the boys felt their hearts stop in sudden fear, and then they saw that it was *good* news that he was bringing.

"Have you seen the paper?" he cried. "How Benjamin went to the rescue of a fishing vessel in distress and saved all hands! By cracky! A capital job and daring, too! He's a first-rate seaman, Ben is, if he is my boy!" Grandfather was pacing up and down the sitting room in his excitement, flourishing the newspaper to emphasize his exclamations.

After the first rush of intense relief had passed, Mother and the boys began to clamor for the story. At length they got Grandfather's attention and he stopped in his tracks, looking bewildered a moment, and then burst into a hearty laugh at his own expense.

"By mighty!" he exclaimed. "I must be daft. Here I go pacing the deck and ranting like a good one and you folks all the while hankering to hear tell of this daring rescue. Well, it's a story worth reading. It is so!"

With that he handed the paper to Mother, and the

boys crowded around, hanging over her chair, while she read aloud the account which said:

> *The storm struck the West Indies with hurricane force and caused many wrecks.*
>
> *Captain Crosby in the three-masted schooner,* Good Fortune, *of Boston, was scudding along under storm tri-sails when he sighted a small fishing vessel with her ensign up-side down in signal of distress. In spite of the howling gale and huge waves, Captain Crosby came about and headed for her. As he approached he could see that the fishing vessel had struck a reef, bow on, and was held fast on the jagged rocks. The sea was pounding her to pieces.*
>
> *The storm having obscured the sun for three days, Captain Crosby had figured by dead reckoning that he was off the Guadeloupe Islands, and he now studied his charts to estimate the risks he incurred in running in so close. In spite of the treacherous nature of the waters he was navigating, he did not hesitate a moment in his errand of mercy.*
>
> *When the* Good Fortune *drew nearer it could be seen through the glass that the crew of the "fisherman" had taken to the rigging. Captain Crosby called all hands aft and asked for volunteers to attempt the rescue of the doomed men. The mate and three of the seamen offered to go.*
>
> *Captain Crosby brought his vessel as close as he dared to the treacherous reefs and ran up signals to hearten the men in the rigging. Then the ship's boat was*

lowered away over the stern and all hands watched anxiously to see if any boat could live in such a sea. Yard by yard the seamen, rowing with powerful strokes, fought their way through the mountainous waves toward the wreck. Captain Crosby, watching through the glass, saw them draw near the little vessel and he waited anxiously to see how the ship-wrecked men would act. So much now depended on their keeping their heads and helping their rescuers.

With immense relief he saw them climbing down out of the rigging and struggling along the tilted deck to the stern of the "fisherman" where they managed to fasten lines that hung overside. The mate maneuvered the ship's boat as close under the stern of the small vessel as he could without running the risk of having the little boat dashed against the hull of the larger boat and crushed.

The fishermen, with splendid coolness and courage, clung to their ropes and watched for the moment when they could drop into the ship's boat as it tossed about in the angry sea. All on board the Good Fortune watched the rescue with bated breath. Twice muffled groans went up from the watchers as two of the fishermen fell short of the boat and plunged into the foaming water. But willing hands were reached out from the tossing boat and they were dragged to safety. At last all hands were off the wreck, and then began the perilous return trip of the heavily-laden boat.

Captain Crosby with fine seamanship and daring brought the Good Fortune about so as to shorten

*the row for the nearly exhausted seamen. Eager hands
threw them a line and helped the weary men onto the
deck of the schooner where hot coffee, dry clothing and
blankets awaited them.*

*Captain Crosby had nothing but praise for his
mate and crew, saying that they alone made the rescue
possible. We are glad to join in his tribute to these
strong, courageous men, but we feel that much credit
is due the captain for his splendid seamanship and the
discipline which enabled him to have vessel and crew
ready to carry through such a dangerous enterprise.*

*Captain Crosby made port at Bridgetown in
the Barbados in order to land the rescued fishermen
and take on fresh supplies for the continuation of his
voyage to Rio de Janeiro.*

The boys' hearts beat fast and their eyes sparkled as
they listened to the exciting account. When Mother
finished reading and laid down the paper her eyes were
shining with pride and thankfulness. Then how they
all talked at once, exclaiming and marveling over the
wonderful adventure!

"If there was any homeward-bound vessel touching
at the islands after the storm we'll get a letter from
Father in a few weeks, like as not," said Mother hopefully, anxious to be reassured by hearing directly from
him after such a dangerous experience.

The boys were too full of pride and admiration to
have any room in their minds for worry over the risks
Father had run.

"Gee, I wish I'd been with Father!" said John long-ingly.

"Think of working the *Good Fortune* close onto those reefs and holding her there while the ship's boat made the rescue, and then getting her away again safely! I declare Father's the *best* captain afloat!" exulted Peter.

Mother had been right and two weeks later a letter came from Father from Bridgetown, telling briefly of the rescue. He gave the highest praise to the mate and the seamen who rowed the ship's boat, and he expressed deep thankfulness that they had been able to save the fishermen. Of his own part in the dangerous exploit he said not one word, so they were profoundly thankful that they had seen the newspaper story first, and they laughed over Father's dislike of praise.

They were to have another month of bitter, stormy weather before the gala day of Father's return. He came over in the stagecoach from the morning train and luckily it was Saturday so the entire family was home to give him enthusiastic welcome. Word of his home-coming spread rapidly through the village and the result was that all afternoon and evening friends and neighbors came in to see him and shake his hand. He laughed heartily at their attempts to make a hero out of him, but willingly told about the rescue, praising his own crew and the fishermen in the highest terms.

After the last visitor had gone Father unpacked his sea chest and brought out a group of stuffed birds of brilliant plumage, arranged among leaves and grasses, and covered with a glass dome. They were rare South

American birds of such gorgeous coloring that Father had not been able to resist them when he spied them in a shop window in Rio. John took a great fancy to them, walking round and round them to gaze at their beautiful colors and natural positions from every angle. Seeing how they fascinated him, Mother said they might belong to him but they must be kept on the mantel in the best room.

Next, Father unwrapped a pair of shell pictures which he had gotten in Bridgetown. They were intricate designs made of tiny shells in lovely colors. They all marveled over the time and patience it must have taken to make them. Peter and Eben admired them so much that they asked if they might each have one as a souvenir of the rescue voyage. It was agreed with the understanding that they also be hung in the best room.

In the very bottom of the chest was a flat package that Father took out and laid in Mother's lap.

"My gracious, Benjamin," exclaimed Mother, "seems like we'd had a plenty of presents. What *can* this be?" She unwrapped it slowly and disclosed a beautiful shawl of soft, fine wool, woven in deep, rich colors.

Mother drew it around her shoulders, saying in amazement, "Why, it's as light as a feather, but it's as *warm* as *toast!*"

John, capering around in his excitement, remarked, "Well, there's *one* present that can't be kept in the best room, no way!"

"Why, I don't know about that," said Mother thoughtfully as she admired and stroked the folds of the shawl,

"I was just figuring it would look real handsome laid over the sofa—"

"No, sirree!" burst out Father and the boys in chorus. "It's for you to wear!"

During Father's brief stay at home the boys never tired of hearing of the storm and the rescue and Peter's impatience to go to sea was raised to fever heat by all the talk. One evening, as they all sat around the sitting-room lamp, he flung down the school book he had been studying and demanded vehemently, "Father, *when* can I go to sea?"

Looking grave at the violence of Peter's tone and action, Father asked quietly, "When do you reckon you'll be *ready* to go, Peter?"

"Right now!" answered Peter instantly. "I've had plenty of schooling and I want to be *doing* things!"

Father studied his flushed face and flashing eyes for a moment before he said, "It's been my observation that a hot head and an empty one usually lands a man in the fo'c'sle for keeps. I take it you kind of hanker to be master of your own ship one of these days?"

"Yes, sir, I do," replied Peter a little more soberly but still with an air of confidence.

"What was that lesson you were just worrying the end of your pencil over?" asked Father, seeming to change the subject abruptly.

"Oh, that was just 'rithmetic and I won't need to be doing any more of those dull old problems," explained Peter, hastily dismissing the matter.

"Hmmmmmm," mused Father, "now just how do you

reckon you're going to take a sight of the sun and calc'-late your latitude and longitude on the chart if you don't know considerable arithmetic?"

Crest-fallen at the turn of the conversation, Peter hesitated over the words as he answered in a low tone, "I—I—I guess I—clean forgot about navigation."

"Kind of an unhandy thing to forget when you're out of sight of land," commented Father dryly, and then he continued earnestly, "if so be you've set your heart on going to sea, Peter, and I'm proud that you have, and if you aim to hold the place some day that a Crosby ought to hold aboard his own vessel, you prove it to me by finishing your schooling this year with a good record and by studying a course in navigation that I'll lay out for you. Come June, if I'm satisfied with results, I'll see about signing you on as able seaman aboard the *Good Fortune* for a trip across the Atlantic."

"I'll be ready to go that voyage, Father," said Peter solemnly, and there was a new light of determination in his eyes as he picked up his arithmetic book and bent to his work again.

John shared Peter's dislike of arithmetic but he felt very comfortable as he thought that, luckily, you did not have to know a lot of problems and troublesome numbers to be a crackerjack fisherman!

The next day Father heard from his agent that his coming voyage would take him only as far as Phila-delphia. Since March was certainly coming in like a lion, Father was not sorry to learn the news and Mother and the boys heaved a mighty sigh of relief. They saw him off on a morning of pouring rain and howling wind. It had been such a long, severe winter that, save for the discomfort and dreariness of Father's departing in a storm, they were glad to see the pelting rain carry away the snow and ice. They all found themselves watching longingly for the first signs of spring.

11

Mittens

JOHN AND JOE came trudging along the main road one afternoon in late March. The trees were just beginning to show a mist of swelling buds although the air was decidedly chilly as the sun went down. It was well that the boys were still wearing their winter jackets, caps, and copper-toed boots. Each of them had a small round basket in his hand. They had been to Old Field Woods hunting for mayflowers under the protecting carpet of pine needles. They kept sniffing at the fragrant bunches of tiny, pink and white blossoms in their baskets.

"Gee, we got a lot, didn't we!" said John, with satisfaction, as they clumped along.

"I guess likely we're the first to find 'em, too," agreed Joe.

"They're real sweet-smellin' and all, but I like 'em best 'cause they tell you, sure for certain, that it's *spring*," remarked John.

"I didn't know that I ever could get enough coastin' and skatin' but now it seems like I don't want to see any more snow for years and years!" said Joe earnestly.

"I guess Peter and Eben'll launch the dugout come Saturday," said John. "I've a mind to make some new eel pots to set out as soon as we have the *Rambler* to go out in."

The boys were standing at the foot of the path that led up to Joe's house. Agreeing to work on the eel pots after school the next day, they separated and John went on his way alone, deep in plans for the spring fishing. When he reached the corner of the lane he stopped short in surprise. There was a carryall standing before the Crosby gate and two men were unloading a sea chest.

In a flash John understood—Father had come home from his voyage sooner than they had dared look for him! John ran up the lane at top speed, noticing as he drew nearer the house that it was Ezra Hallett's carryall from the mouth of the river, which meant that Father must have driven along the main road just before he and Joe came out of the path from Old Field Woods.

Dashing in through the gate shouting, "Father!" John bounded into the sitting room and found the whole family gathered there rejoicing over this unexpected return. After the first moment of excitement John re-

membered his basket and presented the mayflowers to
Mother.

With a smile Father said, "I have another basket for
you, in exchange, son," and held up a closely-woven,
covered basket. John's eyes fairly popped with surprise
and curiosity as he took the basket and, finding it un-
expectedly heavy, set it hastily on the floor. Kneeling
beside it he unfastened and lifted the lid. There, on
a bed of old canvas, lay a grey and white kitten, looking
up at John with big eyes! John grabbed him up and
hugged him tight, and the kitten, instead of struggling
and scratching, nestled against John's coat, perfectly
content.

Father explained that the kitten was a present to John
from Alec, the cook aboard the *Good Fortune.*

"Oh," cried John, "then it's *Stowie's* kitten! I'm so
glad! I'm so glad."

It was indeed Stowie's kitten, Father said, and as
Stowie herself was Alec's inseparable companion and
the tiny galley could hardly hold two cats, Alec had
sent the kitten home to John. It was a pretty, blue-eyed
kitten with unusual markings of white and grey and
John was so proud of it and so happy he could hardly
speak.

Mother interrupted the chorus of admiration to say,
"Like enough the poor little thing's hungry by this time,
after being joggled around in the ship's boat and Ezra's
carryall. Why don't you fix him some milk, John? Get
an old saucer out of the cupboard in the pantry."

John hurried out to the kitchen to carry out Mother's

suggestion. Lifting the kitten gently from the basket he set it beside the saucer of milk and watched while it lapped up every drop, then curled itself up with its paws tucked under it and went to sleep.

John's next thought was about a bed for it. Since Mother was not willing to let it sleep in his room, he decided to fix a soft bed for it close to the warm chimney in the kitchen attic.

When the kitten woke from its nap it explored every inch of its new home with usual kitten curiosity. After supper it played with the boys, chasing dangling strings and rolling balls, to the amusement of the entire family.

Suddenly, in the midst of the fun, Eben asked, "What're we going to call him, John?"

John studied the kitten very intently, and then announced solemnly, "Mittens!"

When the rest of the family looked closely they saw that all four of the kitten's paws were neatly covered with grey while its legs were white, so, although other names were suggsted, none seemed as apt as Mittens.

During the days that followed Mittens became so much a part of the family it seemed he must always have lived with them. John hurried home from school each afternoon to romp with him and, as Mittens grew accustomed to his surroundings, John would take him out to the woodshed and workshop while he did his chores. Mittens liked the workshop best of all, for there he could find countless shaving curls and bits of wood to play with.

Father spent his week at home getting the spring

garden work started. He had Alonzo Small do the plow-ing and harrowing so that by the end of the week the garden was ready for planting. They would use some of their own seeds, saved from the most successful crops of last summer, but they had to get new ones, too, from the seed stores in the city. After they had all spent hours poring over seed catalogues and gazing at pictures of mammoth vegetables, they sat down together, the last night of Father's stay, to make up the order so that he could take it with him to Boston. Each boy was allowed one specialty in addition to the general garden which they all cared for. Peter decided to try melons; Eben wanted fancy varieties of cucumbers to sell to Grand-mother and Aunt Ruth for pickles; John chose beets be-cause he liked them so well he could never get enough of them. Mother had her flower seeds to add to the list so that by the time it was finished it was a very imposing order.

With a deep sigh John sat back and said, "Gee, it makes me so terrible *hungry*, lookin' at those pictures and thinkin' about the garden! It seems dreadful to think we haven't even got the seeds in the *ground* when it takes 'em such an everlastin' time to grow anyway!"

He spoke so earnestly and mournfully that the others burst out laughing, and Mother looked up from her mending to say, "If John's so nigh to starvation I pre-sume likely you'd better fetch some doughnuts from the buttery, Peter, and see if we can't manage to keep body and soul together, leastways till the seeds get here."

The next morning when Father went away in the

stagecoach Grandfather and Grandmother went too, to make their yearly visit to Uncle Collin, Grandmother's brother who lived in Providence. Grandfather had started the fishermen to work on some of the repairs necessary in the cabins and holds of the fishing vessels and could leave the work in their hands for a few weeks while he went on this visit which was the treat of the year for Grandmother. The boys had promised to feed the chickens and keep everything shipshape around their house while they were gone.

To John's unbounded delight Grandfather left *him* in charge of the store! All questions of materials and equipment for the fishing vessels were to be referred to Captain Berry who was in charge of the repair work, but, nevertheless, it was John's proud privilege to stand behind the counter and give out whatever gear was bought. He busied himself in the store for hours at a time and, though business was very light, he never tired of going over the orderly stock or leaning in the doorway with an air of great importance, surveying the empty lane.

About the third day of his proprietorship Mother noticed that he looked troubled and, fearing he had met with some complication over a purchase, she asked, "Everything shipshape in the store, John?"

"Y-yes," replied John slowly.

Puzzled by his gloomy expression Mother persisted, "If something's bothering you I might be able to set your mind at rest."

"Well," said John reluctantly, "you see, Captain

Berry came in to see 'bout some paint for the woodwork in the cabins and we had to look up in Grandfather's big book and—and—I *never* saw so much arithmetic before—not in all the school books put together."

Still not understanding his difficulty, Mother went on, "You must have known it took a powerful lot of figuring to keep all those orders and bills and shipments straight, didn't you, John?"

"I guess I never paid much attention to what Grandfather was doin' at the desk—I was so taken up with the gear and all. But it's dreadful discouragin'," answered John dolefully.

Divided between amusement and bewilderment Mother continued, "But Grandfather didn't look for you to have any care of the books, son. You needn't to pester yourself about them."

"But I'll *have* to some day, 'cause I'm going to be captain of the fleet like Grandfather, with the store and all. When Father was talking to Peter 'bout learnin' arithmetic I was thinkin' *I* wouldn't have to bother with the ol' stuff—just get to be a first-rate fisherman—but I guess likely I was *wrong*," finished John with a profound sigh.

"The captain of a fishing fleet has to know navigation, too, John," reminded Mother quietly. "Seems like it's kind of fortunate you've found out what studies you'll be needing, while you've plenty of time ahead of you."

"I s'pose so," agreed John somberly, not looking as though he felt especially fortunate at the moment.

One rainy afternoon, since there was no business in the store, John was up in his room, looking over old magazines and cutting out pictures for the panorama that he and Joe were making. Mother had stitched together a long strip of muslin on which they could paste the pictures. The boys had fixed two rollers in a wooden box so that they would wind the strip from one roller to the other and keep a slowly-moving procession of pictures passing in front of their audience. They had quite a collection of interesting views and planned to give short explanations of them as they were shown. John was trimming the pictures neatly and laying aside the printed matter to use in making up their speeches. Meanwhile Mittens was having a glorious time playing with the scraps of paper as they fell from John's scissors. He chased them under the bed and under the bureau and was doing his best to make the task of cleaning up the room as hard as possible.

Suddenly John heard a loud knocking at the kitchen door, Mother's step as she went to the door, and then her voice urging someone to come in. His first thought was that it was Aunt Betsy Ann and it flashed through his mind that the only thing that would bring her out on such an afternoon was to announce that she'd found Captain Elnathan's lost letters! He drew in his breath sharply and listened intently only to decide, disappointedly, that it wasn't Aunt Betsy Ann after all. Then who could it be? Curiosity got the better of him and he laid aside his pictures, grabbed up Mittens under one arm, and went downstairs to see for himself. He

stopped short in the sitting-room doorway, amazed to
see Mother ushering into the room an Indian woman!

Mittens clawed wildly and, escaping from John's
arms, scooted into the dark closet under the stairs. The
sight of the short, fat figure clad in a purple calico
dress, topped by a wrinkled brown face framed in long,
black braids, came near daunting John, as well. However, he was fascinated by the outlandish figure and
stood his ground in the doorway. Gradually it came
to him that he had seen her before and that she must
be old Nancy Pomp of the Gay Head tribe of Indians
who sometimes traveled through the Cape villages in
the spring, selling baskets. As he watched she dumped
her wares on the floor at Mother's feet and nodded and
pointed to them expectantly. John understood the slight
nervousness of Mother's manner, for everyone was a
little afraid of the Indians. If they were displeased with
their treatment they were likely to help themselves to
anything that took their fancy, so it was wise to be
polite to them and buy some of their wares. Fortunately the baskets were strong and well-made and it
seemed impossible to have too many of them for use
in the house and garden.

Mother motioned Nancy to sit on the sofa while she,
herself, drew up a straight chair beside the heap of
Indian handiwork. Nancy backed up to the sofa and
lowered herself to its surface. As she felt the springs
giving beneath her weight she jumped to her feet with
a gasp of fright and stood eying first Mother and then
the queer-acting seat. She did not quite know whether

to be frightened or angry. Her little black eyes flashed dangerously at the thought that it might be a trick played upon her.

Mother shot a glance at John, warning him to stifle his laughter and keep a straight face, and hurried over to explain the sofa to Nancy. She placed her hand on the seat and showed Nancy how it gave when she pressed on it. Then Mother seated herself and bounced solemnly up and down. She motioned to Nancy to sit beside her and enjoy it, too. Still looking uncertain, Nancy sidled up to the sofa and *very* cautiously lowered herself to it once more. When she found that it would really support her in spite of its softness, a broad grin spread over her wrinkled face and she bounced with childish glee. The sight of Mother and Nancy beaming at each other and bobbing up and down, side by side, on the sofa, made John nearly choke with laughter.

After a moment Mother rose with an expression of relief and went back to her inspection of the baskets. Nancy, all smiles and friendliness now, gazed around the room and, seeing John in the doorway, pointed at him and said to Mother, "You—papoose?"

Mother nodded, smiling at John's look of disgust at being called a papoose, and asked him to come and help her take from the bunch the baskets she was going to buy. The bargaining was quickly accomplished and Nancy Pomp, after a final series of bounces, gathered up her wares and took her departure, smiling broadly. When she was safely out of the gate, Mother sank into

her chair and joined weakly in John's gales of laughter.

After a time he went to the dark closet and coaxed Mittens out of his hiding place. Lugging the cat upstairs again he continued work on the panorama, still chuckling to himself and wishing that Peter and Eben would hurry up and come home so that he could tell them about Nancy and the sofa.

The next afternoon Peter borrowed Captain Ed's horse and blue lug-wagon and the three boys went to the cedar swamp to cut brush for the young pea vines and Mother's sweet peas to clamber upon. Laughing at each other's scratched and tousled appearance they drove home in the gathering dusk and dumped their load of brush behind the woodshed. Peter slapped the reins on the horse's back and rattled off down the lane on the way back to Captain Ed's barn, John made for the chicken house to do his chores and Eben went in to fix the kitchen fire for Mother. She had just come in from an afternoon with Aunt Betsy Ann and, at supper, told the boys about her visit.

"I feel real troubled about her! She's heard from Squire Nickerson and she's dreadful afraid she's going to lose her home if she can't pay up the mortgage," said Mother gravely.

"*Can't* she find the letters *any* place?" asked Peter.

"No, she can't seem to," said Mother, shaking her head. "She's just about used up, hunting the house high and low, and there's never a sight of them! If she *could* get that money from San Francisco she'd be real well fixed. The next time Father's in Boston I want him to see those lawyer folks for her. She's kind of helpless, down here, all alone like she is."

"Do you s'pose there's any secret closets or anything, that she don't know about?" suggested Eben.

" 'Tisn't likely," answered Mother, and then she smiled as she asked, "What kind of stories have you been reading, Eben?'

"There's a dandy story about secret cupboards in the *Youth's Companion*," grinned Eben.

"But those things do happen really and truly, sometimes!" burst out John earnestly.

"Maybe so," assented Mother, "but I don't figure that'll be the way out of Aunt Betsy Ann's troubles."

The eel pots that John and Joe had planned to make, had been long delayed on account of the spring garden work that demanded attention at both their homes. But they had reached a point, at last, where they could take some time for their own plans. Since launching the dugout was the first and most important step in their spring fishing program, the four boys lost no time in getting down to the Cove to tackle the job as soon as school was out.

With some anxiety they pulled away the thick mat of seaweed that had covered the *Rambler* all winter, as she lay under masses of snow and ice. She was as dry as a bone! They had often worried about her during the winter and wondered if she could possibly come through such a siege, sound and strong. Now that they found their fears had been groundless they were jubilant. The next step was to turn her over and they pried and lifted and pushed with all their combined strength until finally she rolled over, right side up.

The biggest problem of all was to get her down to the water's edge for she was a long way up on the grass. She would not budge an inch in spite of all their tugging and pushing. When they sat down to rest a moment Peter said, "No use talking, we'll have to use rollers to get her down. Seems like we had some 'round here somewheres."

After a search Eben and Joe discovered the smooth logs under a pile of seaweed near the garden fence. Even with the rollers it was not an easy task! By dint of much heaving they managed to lift the bow of the dugout onto the first roller and then by prying and lifting they got the others under her. At last she began to move in response to their vigorous shoving. When she lumbered off of a roller at the stern they had to hustle it around to the box and push it under her again. After a tedious, clumsy trip she reached the water's edge. All four boys heaved together and she rocked and splashed into the water. They made her fast to the dock and gathered the rollers into a pile, ready for future use.

Leaving the *Rambler* to soak a while, after her winter's dryness, the boys separated. John and Joe went off across the fields toward the main road and the general store, John explaining as he went along, "I'm goin' to ask Mr. Kelly if he has any ol' empty nail kegs he'll let us have. Seems like they'd make good eel pots."

"Say, that's a dandy idea," agreed Joe enthusiastically, "and we can bore some holes in 'em so's the water c'n get in and out easy, and then fix the traps in one end. They'll be bully!"

When the boys entered the store Ezra Kelly was waiting on Miss Maria Trippett, and Alonzo Small was waiting to get some chicken wire and a new garden spade. But when he had gone out Mr. Kelly had time to attend to the two boys. They were in no hurry to be waited on, however, for they were perfectly happy looking over the tools, toys and candy, and picking out the things they would buy with their eel money.

At the boys' request Mr. Kelly rummaged about in the cluttered back room of the store and found two empty nail kegs for them. He beamed at them kindly, over the top of his little steel-rimmed spectacles, as they went out, each lugging a keg.

It was hard to have to wait until after school the following day to find out what luck their new pots had brought them. When they raced down to the Cove, Mittens scampered after them, guessing that their new activity held special interest for him. The boys paddled out in the *Rambler* to the buoys that marked the position of their pots, pulled them up and found that they had a good mess of eels, enough for their own families and some left over to sell. Jubilantly they reset the pots and hurried back to shore and up the hill to the wooden bench where they could dress their catch. Mittens followed close at their heels and sat patiently behind them as they worked at the bench. Dressing the eels expertly, John and Joe tossed the heads and skins to him and what a feast he had!

After that, Mittens always knew when the boys were going fishing and would follow them down the hill and even out onto the little dock. Once or twice John coaxed him into the dugout, but the moment he felt it tipping he leaped back to the solid planks of the dock and there he sat watching their departure. The boys never could find out whether he sat on the dock all the while they were gone, waiting for them, or whether he prowled off through the lower garden on hunting trips of his own. Whichever he did, he never failed to be sitting on the dock when they came in sight on the homeward trip.

Setting their eel pots, going flat-fishing in the river, and "perching" up in the ponds kept the boys busy every moment they had to spare from school and chores. Once more the three hoards of fish money grew steadily and nightly entries were made in the little red account books. In addition to supplying their regular customers Peter, Eben and John took turns seeing that a basket of the choicest fish was always left, as a gift, at Aunt Betsy Ann's back door. It seemed that nothing else could be done to help her until Father could see the lawyer in Boston.

In the midst of this busy time came a letter from Father from Philadelphia, saying that the *Good Fortune* was due in Boston at the end of the week and that he would come down by train and stagecoach and have a few days at home. The boys planned a special treat of fried eels for supper the night he got home and when Father laid down his knife and fork at the end of the meal, he said with a sigh of satisfaction, "Now that's what I call capital eating!"

When the boys had finished telling him of their fishing luck—Father said that he could be at home for five days and then he must return to Boston to sail for Alexandria, Virginia. Mother's face lighted up at that news and she exclaimed, "Oh, Benjamin, then you can see Cousin Samuel Bassett and Dorcas and maybe stay with them and go up to Washington!"

"I shouldn't wonder a mite," replied Father and the boys noticed that he looked long and thoughtfully at Mother as she rose to clear the table. Soon the talk turned to Aunt Betsy Ann's trouble and the boys, after exchanging glances, slipped away to their rooms.

Once upstairs, the boys gathered in Peter's room and closed the door. Eben was the first to speak, "*This* is our chance to give Mother our Christmas present! This'll be *just* the voyage for her to take with Father."

John broke in eagerly with, "Did you see how happy she looked when she spoke of Cousin Samuel and Cousin Dorcas and Washington? She'd like to visit there."

"I think Father was thinking about her going with him, too, the way he looked," commented Peter. "We've just got to make her see that we'll be all right here by ourselves!"

"If only Grandmother and Grandfather were home from Providence it would be better," said Eben thoughtfully. "Of course we wouldn't need them to take *care* of us, but Mother'd be some easier in her mind about us."

"Well, they will be home pretty soon," argued Peter, "and we've got to make her go anyway."

Long after the boys were supposed to be in bed and asleep they were still planning in whispers the arguments they would use to persuade Mother. And downstairs, by the sitting-room lamp, Father was saying, "Couldn't you see your way clear to come with me this voyage, Susan? Dorcas and Samuel would like to have you visit them and 'twould be a real nice trip for you. You haven't been aboard the vessel since Peter was small."

"I'd like to go, Benjamin," answered Mother slowly. "I've never seen Washington and 'twould be real delight to see Samuel and Dorcas again, but it doesn't seem as if I could rightly leave the boys alone!"

"Pshaw! They're great, strong boys now. They'd make out first-rate for that short time. Ruth and Aberdeen and Betsy Ann are all at hand, and they'll keep an eye on them. You think it over, Mother," said Father, turning back to his newspaper.

The next morning at breakfast, Peter, who had been chosen spokesman, said, "Mother, we boys think it's high time you used that special Christmas present we gave you. It seems like this is an A-1 chance for you to go on a good, nice voyage with Father. Of course we'll be all right here 'cause we're all grown-up now and can take care of things fine and dandy."

Father's eyes twinkled and Mother smiled as she looked around at the four eager faces. "It looks like you have it all settled between you," she said, "but I'll have to think it over a mite. I can't bring my mind to it so sudden-like."

The boys had to be content with that but the thought of the plan was in the back of their minds all through the day. At supper that night there was an air of expectancy and finally Mother said, "Today I've been talking to Aunt Ruth and Aunt Betsy Ann and Janey Ellis, just over the way, and they agree to watch out for you boys. They all think I should make the trip, so I guess—I guess likely I'll go."

Her last word was drowned in a chorus of shouts and the three boys pranced around the kitchen like anything but the grown-ups they had claimed to be. Father clapped his hands and cheered, adding to the general commotion, until Mother laughed and covered her ears with her hands.

How those remaining four days flew! Father and the boys were busy in the garden while Mother cleaned the house, so as to have everything in apple-pie order for the boys' housekeeping, and cooked up enough food to last them at least a week. As she thought it over she realized that they were so accustomed to helping her about the house that they really were capable of managing by themselves for a short time.

In the afternoons Aunt Ruth came over to help Mother fix over her best black silk dress and retrim a bonnet according to the fashion plates that they studied together, and they selected and packed Mother's nicest things for the visit. The boys were glad to see that she was taking her South American shawl to wrap around her aboard the vessel, when it blew up chilly or damp.

And then the day of departure came and with it a bustle of last-minute preparations, and warnings and instructions for the boys. Before they knew it the stagecoach was at the gate, Father was helping Mother in, the luggage was piled on top, and away they drove, leaving the three boys waving by the fence. They watched until the coach swung into the main road and disappeared, before they turned silently back to the house, hoping to hide from each other their sudden sense of desolation. John picked up Mittens, who had been sitting on the fence solemnly watching all the excitement, and carried him into the kitchen, finding comfort in his lusty purring.

For once the boys were thankful for school since it would occupy their minds and take them away from the silent, empty house. They carefully fixed the kitchen fire, locked the doors and started down the lane, subdued and thoughtful. At length John broke the silence and voiced their feelings when he said hopefully, "Maybe they'll have fair winds the whole time and make the passage inside of three weeks!"

12

The Secret of the Old House

AS THE first two days crawled slowly by the boys agreed that, while they were glad Mother had gone on the voyage, they probably would never have had the courage to urge her to go if they had had any idea how they would miss her! They had thought they would have their hands full with all their own work to do in addition to school, but actually time hung heavy on their hands. The house was so spick and span and Mother had left so much food cooked up for them that there seemed very little to do. The continuation of the fine spring weather that must be speeding the *Good Fortune* on her way was their only source of satisfaction.

Friday night at supper time John came back from an

errand down at the fish wharf, looking very sober. Peter, pausing in his determined whistling, questioned him, "What's plaguing you, boy? Got a notion it's smurring up for rain?"

"No, it's clear enough, I guess," replied John, absent-mindedly. "Say, as I was comin' by Aunt Betsy Ann's she hollered at me and said she wanted us boys to come to her house for dinner on Sunday!"

"I don't see's that's anything to pull a long face about," grinned Peter. "You said we *would*, didn't you?"

"Yes—I did," said John hesitating, "but I don't know that I should have. I figured she might be real hurt and put out if I was to say no—but I—"

Noticing Peter's puzzled expression Eben broke in on John's slow speech to say, " 'Twas 'cause you thought she might not have enough vittles to get up a dinner for us, wasn't it?"

"Yes," said John with a sigh, "we do eat a powerful lot!"

Peter, stopped his whistling and exclaimed, "Say, you're right! We ought not to go! What we'd eat for just one dinner would do Aunt Betsy Ann for a week or more."

"But I said we *would*," reminded John, in distress.

"She gets hurt so awful easy, 'twouldn't do to try to get out of it now," said Eben positively.

"No, I s'pose 'twouldn't," agreed Peter, "but we'll have to get around it some way or other."

Supper preparations went on silently for a while as the boys pondered over the problem.

"What say we take our own dinner!" suggested Peter suddenly.

"Huh, how c'ud we do that?" scoffed John, while in the same breath Eben said, "No, sirree! She'd be *awful* mad at that, and besides, she'd have all her fixing and cooking done ahead."

"I don't mean we'd cook our own dinner and show up at her house lugging our plates in our hands, you ninnies!" protested Peter indignantly. "I mean we'll get together the *makings* of a dinner and fix up some way to ask her to cook it for us."

"Oh, I see," said John, brightening as he caught the idea, "like as if I was to catch some fish and ask her to fry 'em for me. Say, that's a bully idea!"

"We'd have to put it to her kind of pleading-like, and make out we hankered for her special cooking, but I dunno if it would work," assented Eben.

"Well, seems like you'd better think up the pleading part," ordered Peter, "and then dig a bucket of clams tomorrow morning. John, you go off fishing, like you said, and I'll do the chores and fix up a basket of apples and potatoes and turnips. Like as not that'll be plenty for a bang-up dinner and leave a considerable mess for her to use up afterwards."

Saturday noon when the boys arrived at Aunt Betsy Ann's door with the provisions and she said, at sight of the things, "You hadn't any call to fetch all those things!" their hearts sank and they felt that their plan had failed. Shifting their feet uneasily and cramming their hands deeper in their pockets, in their worry and embarrassment, they managed to get out the speech Eben had planned, "Do you s'pose you *could* make us clam chowder and apple pie? 'Twouldn't be too much trouble, would it? You see, we're awful fond of 'em and we can't seem to make 'em ourselves."

Aunt Betsy Ann's face cleared as she listened to their plea and, thinking it was prompted entirely by boyish hunger for good things to eat, she accepted their gifts with good-natured chuckles and allowed as how she might try her hand at a chowder. The boys went away, chasing each other up the hill for sheer relief that the difficulty had been settled.

Sunday dinner was a real treat, for Aunt Betsy Ann was a good cook and the boys ate so heartily that she beamed with satisfaction. During the meal they started her talking about old times by asking if she had always lived in this little cottage near the fish wharf.

"Sakes, no!" she replied with spirit. "When Elnathan was alive we lived in that house beyond the salt works and had things real nice. The house really belonged to his two sisters but they went off, long years ago, to live in Ohio somewheres and wanted him to live in it. Since he's been gone they've let the old place go to rack and ruin. Kind of shameful, seems like to me. The Cape's not good enough for them after city ways, I s'pose. A pity 'bout them!" Aunt Betsy Ann's eyes snapped with indignation.

Anxious to get away from the subject that seemed so disturbing to her Peter began telling of their school work and that set Aunt Betsy Ann off.

"I call to mind the time your father was about as big as John, here. He was as full of mischief as a blackberry is of seeds. None of you boys take after him the least mite, of course."

The boys exchanged delighted glances. This was going to be fun! It was a side of Father they had never even guessed at. Fearful of distracting Aunt Betsy Ann from her story they ate very quietly and deliberately as she went on, "That winter there was a young school-master named Paxton, sorta lean and hard-grained, he was. He was put to it to find a boarding place, so Elna-than and I figured we could put him up for a spell. He used to come home from the schoolhouse, nights, greatly upset over the dreadful way the boys acted and like as not 'twould be Ben Crosby was at the bottom of the mischief."

Aunt Betsy Ann chuckled over her recollections as she got up to clear away the chowder tureen and fetch the pie and cheese. As she cut the glistening brown crust she continued, "One time it seemed Ben and the other boys had somehow rosined the bottom edges of the drawers of the teacher's desk so that every time he went to open or shut one of 'em, it sounded like someone had trod on the cat's tail!"

The boys burst out laughing as they imagined the sound and its effect on the whole school. "Tell us some more!" begged all three as Aunt Betsy Ann showed signs of rising from the table. Settling back in her chair she went on, with twinkling eyes, "Those days there was an old man down South Village way, used to try out skunk oil for his rheumatics and Ben and the boys heard tell of his little shanty. Nothing would do but they must go down and see him and after some dickering they came away again with a bottle of skunk oil."

Exclamations of amazement and disgust interrupted the story and, laughing, Aunt Betsy Ann said, "I presume likely they hadn't gone far before they realized that they had a strange kind of cargo! No one wanted to carry it and not a one of 'em dared to take it home with him. Passing by the schoolhouse Ben suggested they leave it there. I mind Ben, himself, telling Elnathan the whole story, years back, and I can hear 'em laugh now!

"Next morning when school was called, everyone sat sniffing and whispering how a skunk must have been around in the night. The girls held their handkerchiefs to their noses and pretended they was awful distressed but Mr. Paxton didn't take any notice. Then he told one of the boys to light up the fire in the air-tight stove to take the chill off the room. Well! My stars! When the fire began to burn the wood that was laid so carefully in the stove, the smell got so *dreadful* that all hands had to pick up and *run* out of the schoolhouse as fast as they could go! And there wasn't any more school *that* day."

"Did Father get punished for that one?" gasped John.

"No, Mr. Paxton thought 'twas just an accident to the woodpile. He never figured on boys *pouring skunk oil* on the firewood! Poor young man! Those young ones plagued him something dreadful," and Aunt Betsy Ann's laugh ended in a little "ho-hum" of recollection.

The question of the lost letters had become such a

hopeless and discouraging one that the boys, by tacit consent, avoided referring to them, but they couldn't resist curious glances all around the room and they wondered again how such a tiny, neat little house could so persistently keep an important secret.

On Monday morning the boys eyed the house a little doubtfully and decided that they had better spend the time after school tidying up. The day was grey and chilly and when it began to rain in the early afternoon it was easier to carry out their good resolution. Eben and John agreed to tackle the stack of dishes in the kitchen sink if Peter would sweep and dust the sitting room. The work in the kitchen progressed slowly because John used the cup towel for a romp with Mittens, while Eben tried a juggling act with some dishes, until both boys were sobered by the splintering crash of one of the good plates. After that the dishwashing went forward more sedately while loud whistling and vigorous sweeping sounded from the sitting room. The kitchen was in very good order when Peter came to the door and demanded, "Who wound the sitting-room clock on Saturday?"

"I did," replied John.

"Well, what in tunket did you do with the key?" continued Peter. "I can't find it."

John looked blank for a moment and then he said rather soberly, "Oh, I know. It's up in my room. I had to use it to wind my clock. Joe and I took *my* key out in the workshop the other day to start some of the little bolts on his scroll saw, and we lost it." John was halfway upstairs when he finished his explanation.

Peter and Eben followed him to his room and there, sure enough, was the key still on the winding post of John's clock. There it was and there it meant to stay! The post was evidently a shade too big for it and John had somehow jammed it on tightly. They all took turns trying to work it off but it refused to move. Finally, in spite of all their care, the slender brass key snapped in two! Since the part still on the winding post was the important part, Peter worked and worked with all sorts of tools until he succeeded in getting it off. They went slowly downstairs and stood in front of the sitting-room clock, John holding the broken key sorrowfully in his hand.

"Well," said Eben, "we've got to get it fixed somehow. Mother sets great store by that clock because Father brought it to her from England. She always says it makes her feel real spry, it strikes so brisk and smart."

"I wonder if the blacksmith could fix it for us?" questioned Peter.

"I'll go and see," said John, starting toward the entry. "It's my fault so I ought to get it fixed." He put the broken key into his pocket and pulled his cap down over his eyes.

Eben, anxious to cheer him up, said, "And I'll make some sponge cake for supper. I've watched Mother and I think I can do it."

"That would be dandy," answered John, halfheartedly as he started out into the rain. He felt pretty blue as he clumped along through the puddles in the lane;

what with a plate and a key broken, and a storm making up, it was a dreary day.

The roaring blaze of the blacksmith's fire was heartening to John as he stepped in out of the storm. Sylvanus Thatcher was making an iron tire for a cart wheel. While John watched, he took the glowing hoop out of the fire, fitted it swiftly over the wooden rim of the wheel and then plunged the whole wheel, hissing, into his great tub of water, to shrink and cool the hot metal. When he had set the wheel aside to dry, he turned to John with a broad smile and said, "What can I do for you, boy?"

John took the broken key from his pocket and told Sylvanus the story. When he saw the trifling bit of brass in the smith's broad hand and glanced around at his massive tools, it seemed to John that he had come on a foolish errand. Sylvanus, himself, chuckled and said, "I can't make you any such fancy bit as this, but I calc'late I can rig up a little piece of iron that'll wind the clock so that your mother needn't miss its pert sound, when she's home again."

John was relieved and grateful. He watched with intense interest while the smith chose a small piece of iron, heated it in the fire and shaped it on the anvil with painstaking care. Heating it again he deftly reamed out the proper size hole for the winding post. He plunged it into the water to cool it off and then handed it to John. It was as large as the palm of his hand and had a flaring scroll on either side of the main post. Sylvanus was proud of his handiwork but John was a little dismayed by the difference in the two keys. However, if the new one would fit and wind the clock that was all that mattered!

John dug his hands into his pocket and pulled out some of his eel money to pay the blacksmith but, with a hearty laugh, Sylvanus pushed the money away and bade John run home and try his great iron key.

He hurried along through the storm, noticing anxiously that the wind was rising and driving the rain before it in stinging gusts. He burst into the kitchen with a swirl of wind and rain and had to slam the door behind him. Peter and Eben looked astonished when John produced the big iron key, but when it fitted to perfection and wound the clock easily, they were delighted.

By the time John had changed his wet clothes Eben had supper ready and proudly exhibited his sponge cake. It *looked* all right, and when they sampled it Peter exclaimed, "Say, Eb, this is real light and tasty! I guess we'll sign you on as cook for this craft." When supper was over every crumb of cake was gone!

All evening, as the boys tried to study around the sitting-room lamp, they would look up anxiously when the wind tore and wailed around the house. They wished they could think that the *Good Fortune* was safely in port by now, but they knew that was really impossible. The gale continued through the night and was still raging the next morning. The boys fought their way to school with heavy hearts, and found their anxiety shared by the other boys and girls who had fathers or brothers away at sea.

On their way home at noon they could not resist stopping at the Post Office although it was much too soon to look for a letter from Alexandria. They could not believe their eyes when they were handed a letter in Mother's handwriting—from Philadelphia! They tore off the wafer that sealed it and crumpled the paper clumsily in their haste to get it spread out. Crowding together they read:

My dear Sons,—

> *It is my earnest hope and prayer that this letter will find you all well and ever mindful of your health and the precautions relating to the stove and lamps about which I spoke to you particularly. Your father and I have thought and spoken of you often and wished you might be sharing this pleasant voyage with us.*

> *I make no doubt you will be surprised to notice that this letter comes from Philadelphia. Your father had a little business to attend to in this city and, being warned by the falling barometer that unpleasant weather might be ahead, he put in here for a day or so on the way south. It is a pleasure to me to see this great city and to miss the rough seas that we might otherwise have encountered.*

> *If you should have stormy weather at home, John, do not neglect to wear your overshoes. Eben, be sure you draw up close to the sitting-room lamp when you study your lessons or read a story book. I have*

noticed that you are a little inclined to read in poor light. Peter, if any of you get a sore throat remember that the red flannel and camphor are in the chimney cupboard in our sleeping-room.

> *Your father and I have you constantly in our thoughts.*

> > *Your loving Mother*

So they had been safe in port during the storm after all! The boys whooped and capered around the little Post Office while the Post Mistress peered at them with shocked disapproval from behind the row of letter boxes. They slammed out the door and raced up the road, unmindful now of wind and rain. That afternoon they finished up their house cleaning so that, when the storm was over and the sun shone brightly the next morning, they could turn to garden work and fishing again.

On Friday they had a letter telling of the *Good Fortune's* safe arrival in Alexandria, and of the plans for seeing all the points of interest in Washington. It was plain that Mother was enjoying every minute of her trip and the boys felt so good about it that they decided to celebrate by having company for supper Saturday night. After school that afternoon John invited Joe, Eben asked Dave Sears, and Peter, Link Evans. All three of them accepted the invitation with enthusiasm, so that evening the Crosbys were faced with the problem of what to give their company to eat. Peter thought he could manage a chowder, John wanted to try his hand at soda biscuits, and Eben promised another sponge cake, hoping that his success with the first one had not been just beginner's luck!

Going to the kitchen, a little later, to get a drink of water at the pump, John stopped short and stood gazing out the north window in surprise. After a moment's pause he called out to the boys in the sitting room, "Hey, Eb and Peter, Grandfather and Grandmother must of gotten home!"

At his words the other two came hurrying into the kitchen to look out the window. "Sure enough!" exclaimed Eben. "There's a light in the kitchen."

"They weren't s'posed to come back till next week," said Peter in a puzzled tone. "Wonder what fetched 'em home sooner?"

"Suppose we go over and take them the eggs we gathered tonight, and find out," suggested John.

"And let's take over the letter from Mother, too," added Eben. "Seems like they'll be real glad to hear she's having such a dandy time."

As the boys stepped out of the back door of the wood-shed they saw a patch of lantern light bobbing toward them across the field. It was Grandfather coming over to see how the boys had gotten along alone. They ran to meet him and, turning, they all hurried back to Grandfather's house where they could see Grandmother standing in the lighted doorway, listening and waiting for them. She was glad to find them all well and said, as she studied each one in turn through her sparkling, steel-rimmed spectacles, "It don't look as if you have pined away under your own cooking, not a mite! Howsoever, I reckon you might be able to sample some of this chocolate cake they set such store by up city-way. To my mind it's kinda rich, seems so, but Collin and Phoebe wouldn't hear of anything but that I should bring some home. I figured I'd be able to get it eaten, if I was to coax you boys."

The boys' mouths watered as they watched Grandmother cut three fat slices out of the rich, brown-frosted cake, and when they tasted it they decided rapturously that it was the finest thing they had ever eaten. Grandfather, who had been watching the boys' enjoyment, suddenly realized that Grandmother was putting the cake away and he shouted in alarm, "Why are you stowing that away, Thankful? I was aiming to have a piece just a wee mite bigger than the boys'."

"Land sakes, you know it's powerful rich for you this time o' night, David," sputtered Grandmother, but the boys grinned at each other when they noticed that she was cutting him a big piece all the while she talked.

"We weren't looking for you back so soon," said Peter, when his last mouthful of cake was gone.

"No," admitted Grandfather, "we did make port a mite ahead of time, but, you see, your grandmother, here, got to thinking of you boys cruising along alone and nothing would do but we must crowd on the canvas and speed up our homeward voyage."

"Now, David Crosby," said Grandmother indignantly, "you aren't agoing to shove all the blame onto me. You were as uneasy as a fish out of water, wonder-

ing about the boys, let alone hankering for news of
Ben and Susan."

Reminded of the letter Eben produced it from his
pocket and Grandfather read it aloud. When he had finished he said with a chuckle, "Well, whatever it was that
fetched us back, I must say that three faces trimmed
up with grins and chocolate cake, and that letter from
Alexandria stack up to a pretty good welcome home."

John, who had been waiting impatiently for a break
in the conversation, put in hastily, "Say, Grandfather,
everything's jes' fine at the store—I mean—I hereby report that matters at the store are all shipshape and I'd
like for you to go over the stock with me tomorrow
just to make sure."

"Now, that's what I call real smart and business-
like," answered Grandfather with a pleased twinkle in
his eyes, "and I'll be on deck tomorrow to take account
of stock. Now you've been proprietor of the store seems
like you ought to be all fixed to be my right-hand man
this spring."

John fairly swelled with pride as he answered in a
voice he tried to keep unconcerned, "Yes, I guess I'll
be quite a help to you this year, knowin' the business
like I do."

Peter laughed and Grandfather put in quickly,
"Come the busy season, a mite later on, I'll be needing
three helpers, let alone *one*—can I count on you and
Eben, Peter?"

"Yes, sir!" came the prompt answer from both, and
Peter added, grinning, "'Course we'll just be green-

horns but maybe we'll make out to help a mite, too."

Going home across the fields Eben remarked, "It seems sort of more homey with Grandfather and Grandmother back—next best to having Mother and Father home again!"

Saturday was a fine spring day and the boys imagined that Mother and Father were seeing the White House and the Capitol in the bright sunshine. They worked in the garden all morning and then went clam-digging in the afternoon and by the time they had peddled all the clams they didn't need, it was pretty close to suppertime.

When they burst into the kitchen and looked at the clock they were overcome with surprise! They all started rushing around at top speed, colliding with each other and the furniture and accomplishing nothing. When they were on the verge of an exasperated squabble, Peter burst out laughing at the ridiculousness of their flurry, and then took command in proper quarter-deck manner. "Eben, seeing as how you made your cake this morning—we won't say a word if *'tis* a mite sad in the middle—you open the clams and then set the table. John, if you don't set those plates down afore you *drop* 'em and hustle those biscuits together we won't have 'em till tomorrow! I'll turn to on the chowder, hoping I don't get the proceedings hind side to!"

After that, things went a little better but there was still considerable stir and confusion in the big kitchen. Eben's muffled voice came from the pantry demand-

ing, "Where does Mother keep napkins? As we are to
have company I s'pose we gotta use 'em." And later,
"Have we gone and used every single tumbler? There
isn't a clean one on the shelf. Oh, well, so long's it's
only water I'll just rinse 'em out."

In his hurry John had forgotten to take off his jacket
so he was working at fever heat, beside the long dresser
strewn with a clutter of bowls and pans. Without warning the flour sifter slipped from his hands and thudded
to the floor in a cloud of white dust. John picked up the
sifter and emerged from the cloud, well-powdered and
sneezing lustily. Without taking time to brush himself
off he doggedly finished the biscuits, thanking his lucky
stars that he had so often watched Alec make them in
the galley of the *Good Fortune*.

Peter, red-faced and weeping onion tears, stirred the
beginnings of the chowder in the big kettle. When he
turned away to chop the clams Eben took advantage
of the moment to add a generous supply of seasoning
to the bubbling contents of the pot, knowing that Peter
was apt to skimp on it. Peter, returning to the stove,
bethought himself that most folks liked more pepper
and salt than he did so he'd better put in extra. A few
moments later John, going to the oven to peek at his
biscuits and remembering Peter's failing, took that
opportunity to season the chowder according to his own
ideas.

Peter had kept cramming wood into the stove in
order to cook the chowder fast and furiously, with the
result that he triumphantly pronounced it done just as

they heard Joe, Link and Dave, clattering up to the kitchen door. In the midst of the noisy greetings John suddenly sniffed suspiciously and, with a wail of anguish, made a dive for the oven door. The biscuits were certainly *amply* brown, but they had risen enormously and looked like muddied snowballs.

The boys scuffled to their places at the table and Peter ladled out the steaming chowder. Joe, too hungry to stand on ceremony, took a large and hasty spoonful. Instantly pain and horror were stamped on his features and he choked mightily. They pounded him vigorously on the back and he tried feebly to fend them off as he gasped and the tears rolled down his cheeks. After he had gulped down a whole tumbler of water, he eyed Peter reproachfully and sputtered, "What in *time*'d you put in that chowder? It's hotter'n *tophet* and *salty* as *brine!*"

Curious, the others tasted their portions cautiously and all hastily grabbed their tumblers. Bit by bit the explanation was pieced together and the blame divided equally. Then Peter suggested that they might try adding a lot more milk to dilute the excess seasoning. With plenty of pilot crackers the resulting chowder was relished by appetites sharpened by the delay. John's dark-brown biscuits disappeared like magic and Eben's down-cast cake had not one crumb remaining.

Turning their backs on the array of dirty dishes the boys trooped into the sitting room and played games until they were hungry again. Returning to the kitchen they shoved enough pots and pans out of their way to pop corn and end the evening by eating the batch of doughnuts that Mrs. Sears had sent over by Dave.

When their company had finally gone the boys stood surveying the wild disorder. "It sure does look like fury," exclaimed Peter, "and I don't see how we can clean up any till after school Monday."

"Mother'd be upset if she was to see her kitchen right now!" giggled Eben. "It don't seem exactly proper to leave it looking so, yet she wouldn't want us to do any cleaning on *Sunday*."

"Well, I'm plumb tuckered out," stated John, "and I don't aim to clean up *anythin' tonight!*"

"Just think," mused Eben, "Mother does all this *every day* and we never hear her complaining. Maybe it's a good thing she went away, so we could see how much she's always doing for us."

"I guess we never rightly understood it before," said John soberly.

Looking from table to dresser Peter remarked, "I didn't know we had so many dishes in the house. Do you s'pose we've got enough more to eat breakfast off of?"

"If we haven't, don't let's eat!' groaned John.

From force of habit the boys tended the fires carefully and put out the lamps before they stumbled wearily up to bed.

Monday afternoon the boys walked home from school with slow and dragging steps, thinking of the disorderly kitchen and sinkful of dishes that awaited them. When they went in the south door they stopped short, afraid to believe their eyes, for Grandmother had sent Deborah over and she was very briskly making everything tidy once more. She grinned and shook her dishcloth at them as they dashed through the kitchen and out in the back yard, yelling with joy. Before many minutes had passed they were out in the *Rambler,* headed for the flat-fishing grounds.

On Wednesday they had a letter saying that, if they had fair winds, the *Good Fortune* ought to reach Boston by the first of the following week. That suddenly made the home-coming seem very real and near and the boys realized how much they had to do to get ready for Mother's and Father's return. The days flew by and the good weather continued so the boys were confident that the *Good Fortune* was having fair winds. But Saturday afternoon the wind shifted to the south-east and toward night the fog began to pour in. When the boys were out doing evening chores they saw the white mist creeping up the river and before they went in to get supper they sniffed the cool, moist saltiness of the air and noticed that the lamp-lit windows in neighboring houses were only blurred yellow patches in the greyness. While they studied their Sunday School lessons that evening they could hear the distant moan of the foghorn on the Pollock Rip Lightship answered by the blast of the one on Shovelful.

After fidgeting in his chair John finally burst out, "Golly, I hope this ol' fog won't bother the *Good Fortune* any!"

"Of course there isn't anything *dangerous* about it,"

asserted Peter, "'cause Father's always cautious in thick weather—"

"Yes," interrupted Eben, "and he'd be extra careful with Mother aboard, but—"

"But I don't want them to be *delayed* any," exclaimed John. "Seems like I'll *bust* if I hafta wait *much* longer for 'em to get home!"

"Maybe it's just a Cape fog and they aren't even getting it," suggested Eben hopefully.

"Well, I wish those ol' foghorns would hush up! They're dreadful mournful-soundin'," complained John.

"Huh, you'd better be thankful they're there, hollerin' out their warning of the shoals," Peter retorted. "The *Good Fortune*'s a considerable sight safer just because of their doleful old moaning."

The next day was still foggy. The boys went to Sunday School and church and then to Grandmother's for dinner. In the afternoon Grandfather and Grandmother had to drive over to Harwichport to take supper with some friends, and for the boys, left alone, the grey afternoon seemed to drag endlessly. They could not settle to reading and, after they had all wandered restlessly around the house and garden for an hour, Eben proposed that they take a walk. Peter and John agreed without much enthusiasm and they set out down the lane to the fish wharf where they could spend some time looking over the fleet. The little vessels were beginning to look very brave, with fresh paint, scoured decks and new rigging.

Leaving the fish wharf the boys climbed the hill and sauntered along the river bank to the salt works which would soon be opening for the season. From there the path led into the pine woods. "Let's follow the path all the way to Sears' point and then go home by the road past the cranberry bog," suggested Peter.

"I haven't been this way for a long spell," commented Eben; "we usually go just to the fish wharf or the salt works and right back again."

Suddenly they came out into a clearing and saw before them an old house. "Why, this must be the old Eldridge place that Aunt Betsy Ann was talking about living in," exclaimed Eben.

"I don't think I've ever been here before," said John, slightly mystified.

"You'd recognize it from the other side, the path that leads up from the bog road," reasoned Peter.

John's curiosity was stirred and when he said, "Let's go up close and peek in!" the other boys joined him readily. The poor old house looked awfully forlorn and neglected, as Aunt Betsy Ann had said.

"It's falling to pieces and no mistake!" remarked Peter as he poked around the sagging blinds.

John had disappeared around the corner toward the rear of the house and now shouted back excitedly, "Hey, come on! The back entry door is all stove in!"

Peter and Eben pounded around the house and found John examining the door that was split and hanging crazily by one hinge. They decided that it must have come unlatched and been banged back and forth by the wind until it was smashed.

They tried the inner door to the kitchen and found it unlocked. Since it opened so readily it did not seem wrong to satisfy their curiosity and look around inside. Some old furniture had been left standing about and, in spite of the dirt and disorder, it was easy to see that the rooms had once been homey and comfortable.

Eben, going ahead into the sitting room, called out, "Gee, what a dandy fireplace!"

Hurrying after him, Peter and John whistled in amazement. It was a huge, wide fireplace with an iron crane from which still hung an iron kettle, and at one side was an old brick oven with an iron door. By crouching down the boys could get inside the fireplace and look up at the sky through the wide chimney.

After examining the oven Peter and Eben went on into the other rooms but John lingered, fascinated by the cupboards that filled the wall space above and beside the fireplace. One was the "candle cupboard," John knew from the one like it at Grandmother's, and the boys always called the one at the opposite end of the mantel, the "maple-sugar cupboard" because in it Grandmother kept the store of sugar sent to her each spring by a Vermont cousin. John laughed at himself for wondering if it had been the "maple-sugar cupboard" in this house, too, and if perhaps they had left some behind when they went away.

Just for fun and curiosity John pulled up a chair and standing on it opened the cupboard door. There were several cardboard boxes on the lower shelf. He seized

them eagerly and opened them one after another but not a crumb of maple-sugar could he find! He thrust the boxes back in disappointment. As he jammed the biggest one in hard he stopped in surprise at the hollow sound it made when it struck the back of the cupboard. He pushed it again to make sure and thought he felt the board behind it give and shake a little. At that, he tossed the boxes out, helter-skelter, on the floor and reached in to investigate the back wall. One board was certainly loose and seemed to give along one edge. Pushing hard against it he managed to get the tips of his fingers in behind the edge. Gradually he worked them farther and farther in until it was plain that the loose board was really the door of a little secret closet set in the back wall of the cupboard.

At first it refused to open but John tugged and tugged with all his strength. All at once it flew open so suddenly that John almost lost his balance and fell back-

wards off the chair. When he recovered himself he peered breathlessly into the shallow, secret closet and found that it contained a shabby, black leather book, a packet of letters tied with red string, and a small, faded picture. John was on the point of tossing them back in disgust when his eye was caught by the picture and he paused a moment to examine it. It proved to be a picture of a three-masted schooner and on the back of it was some writing, a date, and the name—Elnathan Eldridge.

Suddenly he realized whose house this had been and to whom these papers belonged! Trembling with excitement he jumped down from the chair and shouted, "Peter! Eben! Come here, *quick!*"

The other boys were poking around upstairs when they were startled by John's cry. They came plunging down the stairs, wondering *what* could have happened to him. He ran toward them, flourishing the packet in his hand and shouting, "Look! Look! I've found Aunt Betsy Ann's lost papers!"

Peter grabbed them from him and stared at them incredulously. Then, wide-eyed with excitement, he exclaimed, "By golly, John, I believe you *have! Where'*d you find 'em?"

John showed Peter and Eben the cupboard and explained how he had discovered the secret closet. The three boys stood staring at each other, too amazed and excited to speak. Then it occurred to Peter that someone might come upon them there and ask a lot of troublesome questions, so he carefully put the packet into his inside pocket and suggested that they hurry home as fast as possible.

Once safely home the boys lighted the sitting-room lamp and, heads together, examined the papers more carefully. Several of the letters were from Captain Eldridge to Aunt Betsy Ann, and several were from his agents in Boston. The black book was a diary. The boys did not feel that they had any right to read the papers through, but they were convinced that they contained word of the purchase of the vessel in San Francisco and were all Aunt Betsy Ann needed to prove her claim.

"The letters were written from San Francisco, right enough, and the way they're all put together is sort of special and important-looking. Captain Elnathan probably put the bundle in that little closet thinking it was the best place to keep 'em safe for Aunt Betsy Ann," said Eben.

"Yes, and either he forgot to tell her where he'd put 'em or he *did* tell her and she just plumb forgot about it after all those years," added Peter.

"What'll we do with them now?" asked John.

After deep thought Peter said, "I think we'd better put them away, safe, till Father gets home and let him 'tend to 'em. If we give them to Aunt Betsy Ann right off, like as not she'll get all worked up and lose them again or do something foolish."

"Just a few days more can't make any difference," commented Eben.

"Anyway, Father was going to see those lawyers and he might have somethin' partic'lar he'd want to do with 'em," offered John, "but first off we've got to find a good safe place for 'em!"

They considered a number of different places and finally decided on the secret cubbyhole in Father's big mahogany desk. Very solemnly they stowed away the precious packet and closed the desk.

They hurried out to do their belated chores, their bobbing lanterns making glowing spots in the fog, and returned to the kitchen to speculate once more about the probable position of the *Good Fortune*. Now they were more impatient than ever for Mother and Father to get home!

A north-west wind blew away the fog and the boys awoke to a sparkling morning. Their spirits matched the day. With their wonderful secret and the prospects of the home-coming they were bubbling over with excitement and laughter. In the afternoon John went on watch in the scuttle so as not to miss the first gleam of the sails if by any chance Father should make the river. However, the boys felt pretty sure that Father would take the vessel directly to Boston, since the trip home in the train would be much easier for Mother than to have to go overside while the *Good Fortune* lay at anchor off the breakwater.

When it grew dusky John came down from the scuttle with nothing to report but they had not dared set their hearts on Mother and Father getting home today, so the disappointment was not so keen. Nevertheless, as they got supper they found themselves watching the road hopefully and listening for the sound of approaching wheels. But the evening stage brought no passengers for the Crosby house.

According to all their calculations Mother and Father must *surely* come the *next* day, so they set about making definite preparations. Peter decided to put beans to soak, although it was not Saturday, to have baked beans for the home-coming supper. He started them in the morning and they simmered in the oven while the boys were in school. When they hurried home at noon to go on scuttle watch Deborah came over with some raised rolls and a pie that Grandmother had made for them, to help out the festive meal. Once more the afternoon passed uneventfully for the scuttle guard. It was Eben's turn for that duty while Peter and John scurried around giving a last-minute check-up to the house and yard.

As twilight came on the boys were drawn irresistibly to the gate where they leaned and watched. When they saw the stagecoach swing into the lane from the main road they hardly dared believe their eyes, and they held their breath as the horses trotted toward them. It was not until they saw a head leaning out of the coach window and a handkerchief waving greeting that they let out all their pent-up excitement in a series of wild yells!

The coach stopped and Father jumped out and held up his hand to Mother who looked rested and pink-cheeked with the joy of coming home. In a bustle of joyful confusion Father, Mother and the luggage were gotten into the house and, somehow, they were all finally seated around the lamp-lit supper table. There was so much to tell and ask about they hardly knew where to begin. In a pause in the conversation Mother smiled at all of them as she said, "I declare, the very best part of going away is coming home again! You boys have got everything fixed just as nice as can be, but you don't mean to tell me you baked these beans yourselves!"

"Peter did the beans and John and I cooked and fixed the pickled beets," volunteered Eben.

"You'll have to look to your cooking now, Mother," laughed Father, " 'twon't do to be beaten by your own crew even if they did get their training at your hands."

Mother and Father were besieged by questions about every detail of the voyage, their luck in missing the storm, and the wonderful sights of Washington. Father undertook to give an account of all that had happened, helped out, here and there, by a word from Mother, and ended by saying, "Cousin Samuel and Cousin Dorcas want me to bring you boys down for a visit next spring. They've got a kind of notion that every boy ought to see the nation's capital. It's real funny—but—seems like I—*agree* with them!" and supper ended with a chorus of delighted whoops.

When they had left the table Father opened the portmanteau and Mother got out the gifts they had brought the boys. Holding in her hands three identical square boxes she said, "Father and I were so pleased with the way you boys took hold and fixed it so that I could go off, that we wanted you to have something that would always call to mind your 'special present' to me!" and she handed each boy a box. With fingers clumsy with eagerness they undid their packages and found a silver watch for each of them with his initials and the date engraved on the case! On all Cape Cod there were not three prouder or happier boys!

When they could get down to ordinary conversation once more Mother's face sobered as she said, "There's just one real *unhappy* thing about the trip—Father had a talk with those lawyer folks and they say that without the proofs they can't help Aunt Betsy Ann a mite! Seems real mean to me! Father's going over to ask Squire Nickerson if the neighbors can't take up that mortgage *without* letting her know about it. She'd never let us if she was to know! Deary me, I *did* have my heart set on bringing home good news for her."

All the while Mother was talking the boys were exchanging meaning glances, and when she finished Peter spoke up, trying to keep his voice calm and hide his mounting excitement, "While you were gone we boys had a kind of adventure. It's mostly John's story so he can tell it."

While John was telling about their going into the old house and his finding the cupboard and the secret closet, Eben slipped over and got the packet out of the cubbyhole in the desk. When John reached the climax of the story he handed the letters, diary and picture to Father. Then they waited with bated breath while Mother and Father examined the papers. Father's exclamations gave a clew to his astonishment and delight as he said from time to time, "I swan to man! . . . I want to know!"

Finally he looked up with a beaming face and said to John, "Son, you've done it! You've found Elnathan's missing papers. They prove right enough that he owned the schooner in 'Frisco and with that money Aunt Betsy Ann'll be safe and well-fixed as long as she lives!" Then, as he saw how filled up they all were with relief and happiness, he added, "Thanks to a big bump of curiosity and a taste for maple sugar!"

☼ 13 ☼

Sailors All

THE FIRST THING next morning Father hired Captain
Ed's horse and buggy and drove over to Yarmouth to
take Aunt Betsy Ann's papers to Squire Nickerson. He
had decided that it would be best to go over the letters
and diary carefully with the Squire before telling Aunt
Betsy Ann of the discovery.

Mother was so happy to be home again that she sang
to herself as she went about setting the house to rights,
pausing now and then to laugh over cluttered cupboards and other evidences of the boys' housekeeping.
Through the south window of the kitchen she saw
Father drive up the lane with Squire Nickerson beside
him in the buggy. They drove right on by and down
the hill to Aunt Betsy Ann's and Mother felt a great
weight lift from her mind at the thought of the good

[265]

news they were taking her. She marveled again that the boys should have gone to such an out-of-the-way place and stumbled on the missing documents. She laughed when she recalled Eben's and John's interest in secret cupboards and her own assurance that they would play no part in solving Aunt Betsy Ann's problem.

After their call Father had to take Squire Nickerson back to Yarmouth, so Mother and the boys were sitting down to dinner by the time he reached home. They all besieged him with questions, clamoring to know how Aunt Betsy Ann took the amazing surprise and how things promised to work out for her. Father told them, first of all, that the Squire had found the papers complete and in good order, definitely proving Aunt Betsy Ann's claim. It only remained for the lawyers to notify the firm in San Francisco and get the money for her. She would probably have enough to last her as long as she lived.

When it came to Aunt Betsy Ann's reception of the news Father laughed and said he didn't know that he could do justice to the scene! "She sure enough fetched up with all sails aback!" he told them. "She didn't know which part of it to be most dumbfounded about—to think of the letters being hid away in the old house, or to think of the boys going there of all places and finding them! Her thoughts were all a-skitter-scatter for a spell and then two things commenced to come clear in her mind. Her eyes flashed and she stamped her foot as she said, 'Now, those lawyer folks will see that I told the truth and remembered it all straight enough. I hope they'll be good and ashamed of themselves!' "

They interrupted the story with hearty laughter at this point, for they had all experienced Aunt Betsy Ann's indignation over the seeming slight to her honesty. But in an instant they were hushing each other up so that Father could go on and finish the account.

"The next idea that she made fast to," he went on, "was that it was *John* who really found the papers and she wanted me to tell her just how it come about. When I explained how he was kinda hoping to come across some abandoned maple sugar in the cupboard she seemed real put out to think he didn't find any."

Father paused to chuckle over John's expectant expression and continued, slowly and teasingly, "She set her mind to puzzling over it and she figured that a letter sent to Cousin Temperance in Vermont about this time of year might fix that difficulty."

Peter and Eben joined in John's joy over this announcement and began speculating about the length of time necessary for the letter to reach Cousin Temperance and the maple sugar to get back to them.

After the boys had clattered off to school Father sat in the rocker talking with Mother as she moved about clearing away the dinner. At length he rose saying, "Well, I reckon I'll look in the store a spell and go over the list of supplies for the fleet with Father. He wants me to help him chart a course among some of these newfangled things put up in tins that they're making such a talk about. We had some aboard the *Good For-*

tune last voyage and they're real tasty for a change. Perhaps I'll go down the road before I come home, anything you need down at Ezra Kelly's?"

Mother gave him a list of supplies she wanted to stock up her shelves again, and then sat down before a basket heaped high with accumulated mending, planning to keep her hands busy while she chatted with Grandmother and Aunt Ruth who were coming to spend the afternoon and hear all about her visit in Alexandria.

When they all gathered around the supper table that evening the boys noticed that Father seemed in especially good spirits. His eyes twinkled constantly as he joked and teased the boys, and they laid it to his satisfaction at having straightened things out for Aunt Betsy Ann. But, finally, pushing back his plate, he said, "As this day started off with a pleasant surprise for Aunt Betsy Ann, I figured it was a first-rate notion to keep up the good work."

With expressions of mingled bewilderment and expectancy the boys hung on his words as he continued, "First off I had a talk with Mr. Parker, after school, to see if his observations tallied with mine—"

At these words Peter went positively white, so Father hastened on, "—and sure enough they did! He said that the study of arithmetic had picked up considerable this term, and the other lessons are all shipshape. So, thinks I, it has come time for me to keep my promise. Peter, I'm ready to sign you on before the mast aboard the *Good Fortune*."

At this sudden realization of his long dream Peter was speechless and could only gulp and stare at his empty plate. But Eben and John more than made up for his silence by their excited exclamations over the news. Under cover of the commotion Peter somewhat recovered himself and finally was able to ask, "Wh— when do we sail, Father?"

"Well, as to that," said Father, "I reckon you've got a couple of weeks more at home. I'm joining the vessel day after tomorrow for a run to Philadelphia and then we're due to sail from Boston for a voyage to London. That's the voyage I'll be needing a first-class new hand aboard ship!"

Two weeks—it seemed an age to wait, and in the next instant it seemed far too short for all the things Peter wanted to do to get ready for his new life.

Eben's and John's tongues seemed to hang in the middle and wag four ways with all their questions and speculations, until Father interrupted their chatter to say, "Anybody'd think I was shipping the whole Crosby crew, judging by the lively goings-on. Come to think of it, Eben, you'll be promoted to first mate's birth here at home and John'll be quartermaster from now on."

Eben looked worried as he suddenly realized that the responsibility of the work would now be his and he said anxiously, "I dunno as I can plan things and fix to do 'em the way Peter has."

"Golly!" burst out John, "there'll be a dreadful lot of work for just two of us. Even if we was to take *all* our time, I don't see that we could do it."

"That's just about the way I sized it up, son," agreed Father, "and I stopped around to 'Lonzo Small's on my way home and dickered with him to come up and work around here two days a week."

At the look of intense relief on the two faces Father chuckled and asked, "What are you planning to do with all your spare time?"

"Fishing!" said Eben and John in one breath and were astonished at the shout of laughter with which Father greeted their statement.

"Well, I snum!" said he. "If that don't beat all! Here Grandfather and I were talking about that very thing just today. It seems that Silas Berry's retiring from the fleet this season and will stay at home while his son'll go as crew captain in his place. Silas is calc'lating to go deep-sea fishing off the Bishops, just to keep his hand in, and he's been puzzling over who he can get to go along with him. You don't suppose you two could see your way clear to sign on for a voyage to the ledge about once a week this summer, do you?"

Without a word John left his place, marched around the table and, planting himself firmly beside Father, demanded in a tone that he tried hard to keep from quivering with suppressed excitement, "Do you *mean* that, Father, honest to goodness?"

Meeting his eyes squarely Father answered, "I mean it certain sure, John."

With a whoop of suddenly released joy John executed a war dance around the kitchen. Then, pausing in the midst of his capers, he made a dive for the back stairs, pounded up to his room and was back in a moment, carrying his bank and his account book. Unmindful of waiting chores John sat down with Father to count over his share of the earnings of the Bass River Fishing Company and estimate the cost of a suit of real oilskins and some new cod line. When they had decided that there was money enough to buy the outfit that John felt was essential for a deep-sea fisherman, he heaved a sigh of entire contentment. He started out to do his belated chores with his mind so engrossed in thoughts of the hours that must elapse before he could get into Grandfather's store and commence his shopping, that only long habit enabled him to stumble through his work somehow.

Coming back into the house John found Grandfather there, talking over the Alexandria visit, the good news for Aunt Betsy Ann, and, last but not least, the adventures ahead for the boys. When he could get a word in edgewise John told Grandfather of his own particular plans and arranged to be in the store the first thing in the morning to try on oilskins before school. Even after that point was settled John lingered beside Grandfather's chair, fidgeting so uneasily that, at length, Grandfather looked up to say, "What's troubling you, John, can't you chart your course to suit you?"

With a gulp and a sigh John managed to reply, "I—I was just a-wondering if maybe this summer you could begin to show me how to keep the books in the store. The fishing part is just fun but I s'pose I've *got* to know the other part, too. I'm not awful good at arithmetic but *p'rhaps* I could learn."

"I presume likely you could, and this summer while business is slack will be a real handy time to get a start on it," answered Grandfather kindly, realizing something of what it had cost John to commit himself to regular vacation tasks in a subject as distasteful as arithmetic.

John was thinking rather dolefully that now he was in for it, when he caught an understanding look from Mother and suddenly felt unaccountably cheerful and satisfied again.

Peter had been impatiently waiting a chance to ask about the purchases he would need to make for his outfit and when his questions were answered Grandfather turned to Father and said, "I been aiming to ask you, Ben, about that change in the rigging of the fore and main tops—did you find it furthered her any?"

Grandfather's tone was skeptical and Father smiled as he replied, "Well, she handles just as pretty as ever, and I couldn't ask for her to answer any smarter than she did in the storm down among the islands, but I didn't figure I could tell much about her speed till I'd taken her on a long haul—like this run to London will be. What with Peter and the new rigging we ought to give a good account of ourselves that voyage and no mistake!"

Almost before the boys realized it Father had left for the short trip to Philadelphia, and Peter's days at home were slipping swiftly by. Mother was busy mending and marking his underclothes, shirts and socks, while Grandmother's fingers flew as she made him a little case containing needles, thread, thimble, scissors and a string of buttons for his necessary mending at sea.

Peter spent every spare moment in the workshop making himself a ditty-box to hold his small personal belongings. He took pains to make it carefully and was content to leave it plain and smooth, trusting to idle moments at sea for its decoration. In it would go his leather-covered diary, a pad and pencils for letters home, his best knife for carving and whittling, his silver watch and his sewing case. His clothing would be tightly rolled and stowed in the heavy canvas sea bag that he had selected from Grandfather's stock. Eben had made a stencil of Peter's name and was industriously painting it on every possible article of Peter's outfit.

The first thing they knew Father was home again and, for once, the excitement of the preparations for the double departure in a few days overshadowed the pleasure of his return. There was a hurry of finishing up last jobs and the hours alternately dragged and flew according to the occupations and thoughts of the various members of the family. And then it was the day of departure!

Father and Peter were to go to Boston by train, as John had done, and sail from there for London. Vividly reliving his adventure of a year ago John was seized

with a strong desire to be going too, and he watched
the final preparations enviously. Temporarily the fishing trips did not seem such a glowing prospect! He
loaded Peter up with innumerable messages to be delivered to Alec, all of which, under the stress of excitement, were promptly forgotten by Peter.

The stagecoach drove up and in a flurry of good-byes
and last-moment instructions they were off—leaving
Mother, Eben and John to face the tremendous change
and the sudden desolation of the homestead. Everything seemed dull and pointless for the first slowly-
passing, quiet days. Eben and John alternated between
wishing that they had been left with *all* the work to do
to fill up their time and thoughts, and feeling that even
the easiest chores were too much of a task for their list-
less indifference.

The second morning after Father and Peter had left
the boys woke up to the fact that things were at sixes
and sevens and that Mother was depending on them
to brace up and shoulder their new responsibilities.
They put their heads together and planned a new divi-
sion of work and chores. Eben was to have charge of
the work in the garden and around the house, laying
out the heavy work for 'Lonzo and apportioning the
lighter tasks between the two of them, while John
would be in command of the Bass River Fishing Company and direct all their fishing, eeling and clamming
expeditions.

Once they had faced their problem squarely their
spirits revived rapidly. They each found great satis-

faction in being boss of his particular job, and they were constantly discovering new bright spots in the changed situation. Now that there were only two masters of the *Rambler,* there were only two, instead of three, conflicting destinations to be considered each time they set out for a sail in her. Also, they could now include David and Joe in their pleasure trips as they had rarely been able to do before when there were three in the Crosby crew itself.

Joe was clamoring for Peter's place in the Fishing Company and John, hugely enjoying his new authority, gave the matter grave consideration before he decided to admit him and turn over to him Peter's list of customers. Joe's next request was that he be included in the much-anticipated deep-sea fishing trips that would start as soon as vacation time came. John consulted Grandfather about that and he seemed to feel that Silas Berry would have no objection to a third member of the crew.

Some three weeks after Father and Peter had sailed school was over and the longed-for summer stretched ahead of the boys. Coming into the store, the first day of vacation, after an afternoon of clamming on the flats, John found Grandfather talking to Silas Berry. John eyed the jovial crew captain expectantly and his heart gave a little whir of excitement at the captain's prompt inquiry, "How'd you boys like to go off fishin' next Tuesday if the weather holds good?"

"Oh *bully!*" exclaimed John, his eyes shining. "What time'll we start?"

"I haven't figured out the tide percisely but I calc'-late it'll be low water on the bar close onto seven o'clock," replied Captain Berry. "You boys better be over to the *Sarah B.* nigh about six-thirty so that we can get a timely start. You fixin' to bring your own bait?"

"Yes, sir," proudly stated John, "we'll have plenty of clams and fiddler crabs." With that he made for the door, turned to call back, "We'll be on hand Tuesday morning, right enough, Captain Berry!" and ran out to hunt up Eben and Joe and share with them the definite plans that for the first time made the trip a reality.

That evening John took down the *Old Farmers' Almanac* from its hook beneath the kitchen shelf and studied the weather forecast and the run of the tides. "Captain Berry was right," he called out to Eben, "it's low water on the bar at seven o'clock. If we get under way at half past six we'll get out of the river fine and dandy and then the tide'll run to the west'ard till after noontime. We ought to make the south-east buoy along about nine o'clock and have good fishing till 'most two."

Coming into the kitchen to verify John's reckonings Eben suggested, "Let's go over and ask Uncle Abner if he'll take us over the bridge to the *Sarah B.*'s dock in his lug-wagon? We'll have all the bait and our gear to take—"

"Yes, and he'll have to meet us again to bring home all the fish!" interrupted John eagerly.

As they went out of the kitchen door to carry out Eben's suggestions the boys called back to Mother, "We'll get the evening mail and be back directly."

When they came in again, later, empty handed Mother read their disappointment aright and said, "We can't begin looking for letters from Father and Peter yet awhile. Maybe in another ten days one'll be showing up but 'twon't do a mite of good to be impatient."

"I know," said John with a sigh, "but it seems like they've been gone for *ages!*"

"It's just twenty-nine days since they sailed," said Eben, who had been marking the days on the kitchen calendar. "I guess we were a mite hasty for they've hardly gotten there, let alone getting a letter back to us. It's bound to be a while yet before we hear!"

While he was talking John had reached down his new suit of oilskins from the hook in the entry and was trying it on for the dozenth time. Mother suppressed her dislike of the pungent, oily smell long enough to admire the stiff, clumsy coat and trousers to John's satisfaction, and secretly rejoice that they were not designed for wear in the house.

Eben had been unwilling to break into his "Boston" fund for a similar purchase, so he decided he would have to get along the best way he could with his oldest clothes and discarded boots and a jacket of Father's. John found it hard to understand this attitude for he took the prospective trips very seriously and to have just the right outfit and fishing tackle made them seem more important and business-like in his eyes.

Monday morning Eben, John and Joe overhauled their hooks, lines and sinkers and when their kits were in apple-pie order they trooped down to the Cove to get the bait. In all too short a time they were back with nearly enough clams and fiddler crabs to supply the fishing fleet, and then they were put to it to know what to do with themselves to make the lagging hours pass. They finally got through the day somehow and, satisfied that the weather promised to be fair, they went to bed extra early to make the morning come the sooner.

Mother was up at five o'clock, too, to get breakfast for the fishermen and to put up their lunch. The day before, Eben had brought down from the attic the wooden starch box, veteran of many of Father's boyhood trips, to be filled with a generous supply of sandwiches, pie and doughnuts, and the stone jug for hot, sweetened coffee, another long-anticipated symbol of their growing up.

Just as they had everything collected and ready Uncle Abner drove the rattling lug-wagon to the gate. He was wreathed in smiles not all due to the fine weather, as he promptly explained, but rather to his decision to go fishing with them!

"I haven't had a day's fishing these ten years," he said, "and, thinks I, here's my chance to see if I can still pull in the big fellers."

Uncle Abner laughed and slapped his knee in delight and Eben and John laughed with him for sheer high spirits as they loaded the back of the wagon with the buckets of bait and tubs of gear and then clambered to the seat beside Uncle Abner. After picking up Joe at the foot of his path they made the best speed they could along the main road, feeling certain that their rattling progress must be telling everyone that the Crosbys were off to the Bishops. As they jounced and clattered over the bridge the boys spied Captain Berry's catboat, the *Sarah B.*, at her dock below the bridge, and hailed the Captain who was already aboard, hoisting her sail.

They unloaded at the dock and while the boys stowed things aboard Uncle Abner put the horse and wagon in Captain Berry's barn for the day. The Captain chuckled with pleasure when he found that Uncle Abner was going along and the two old fishermen slyly poked fun at the boys for the amount of bait they had provided and their exaggerated expectations of the day's catch. But no amount of teasing could disturb the boys' good nature and confidence as they piled aboard the *Sarah B.* and cast off her moorings.

The strong southwest wind took them down river in long reaches and, once outside the mouth of the river and over the bar, Captain Berry let the boys take turns sailing her while he and Uncle Abner smoked their pipes and exchanged fish stories. The breeze was freshening and the *Sarah B.* dipped and swooped along throwing occasional sheets of spray to the delight of John who wanted his oilskins to be put to the proper test.

When they drew near the ledge of rocks, marked on one end by the tower of Bishops Light and on the outer end by the bell buoy known as the south-east buoy, Captain Berry took the tiller and headed her for the fishing grounds. As they rolled and slid toward their anchorage he asked the boys if they knew why their

forefathers had settled on the Cape. Knowing that some
tale or joke was in store for them they promptly said
"No," and Captain Berry sang in a roaring, lusty voice:

> *When our forefathers they came over*
> *They had no fish worth a-dishing*
> *So they took their sinkers, hooks and lines*
> *And went right out a-fishing,*
> *And as they had amazing luck*
> *And found the fish quite handy*
> *They thought they'd settle on Cape Cod,*
> *Although 'twas rather sandy.*

All laughing together they let the sheet down on the
run, heaved over the anchor and made a dive for bait
buckets and tubs of lines. In a brief time each one had
found a position, placed his gear handy, and, with legs
braced wide apart to meet the boat's roll, had his line
overside. Almost at once the fun began. Uncle Abner,
with a whoop of delight, caught the first fish and a moment later Joe got one. They began coming in so fast
no one could keep track of anything but his own bait-
ing and hauling and unhooking.

They fished steadily for nearly an hour and then suddenly John gave a shout as he was yanked nearly over
the side by an extra strong jerk on his line. Recovering
his balance and bracing himself he hauled in hand over
hand, gasping, "Golly, I got a buster this time!"

They all paused a moment to watch expectantly. All
at once John's line flew out of the water and at the
sudden release of the strain John lurched backward

and sat down with a crash and a splash in the midst of the fish flopping and slithering about on the floor boards.

They shouted with laughter at the comical picture he made and then their eyes followed his staring gaze and they found themselves looking in astonishment at the bodyless head of a huge tautog, fast to John's hook! The fish had been bitten off clean, just back of the gills.

Captain Berry was the first to hit upon the explanation, "That was a dog-fish shark done that, I'll warrant!"

"Yes, by cracky, and I've got him!" yelled Uncle Abner as he was dragged half overboard.

Eben and Joe jumped and grabbed him by the legs and, thus anchored, he managed to haul in his line. There, sure enough, thrashed a thin, grey-white, ugly-looking shark about five feet long. They dealt him a blow on the head and, hauling him aboard, made him fast atop the cabin.

"Well, leastways that mean-looking critter won't eat any more of our fish," stated Uncle Abner, surveying his catch in triumph.

By this time John had picked himself up and resumed fishing but he kept glancing ruefully at the big fish head and saying, "Gee, but that'ud been a monster one. I *caught* it right enough even if it did get et afore I could land it."

The fishing held good through the morning hours and the tub behind each fisherman filled steadily. From first one and then another would come a grunt of disgust at a lost bite or a whistle of pleasure over a whopper landed. After a while John tried a new ganging that Grandfather had showed him only yesterday. Captain Berry chuckled when he saw what he was doing and said, "You've got the hang of it, boy. It 'pears to me you've got the makings of a real fisherman."

That was the highest praise that John could have asked for just then and, to his own satisfaction, he justified it within the next half-hour by catching a fish very nearly as large as the bitten-off one. He was pretty certain in his own mind that it would prove to be the biggest one of the day's catch.

By noontime it was slack water and the fish ceased biting. Though it had been thrilling while it lasted the boys really welcomed the turn of the tide and the end of the day's fishing for legs and arms ached with the prolonged strain of bracing and hauling, yet they couldn't have been persuaded to stop as long as the fishing was good. Dropping their lines and ducking into the little cabin for their lunches, they flung themselves on the seats and realized suddenly that they were tired and ravenously hungry.

When nothing was left of their ample provisions but crumbs and empty jugs and boxes, they hauled up the anchor, hoisted the sail and headed for the mouth of the river, running easily before the wind. They took turns at the tiller while the rest of the crew cleaned ship. They reeled up the tangled lines, stowed away hooks and sinkers, and then set to work to apportion the extra fish that flopped around on the floor boards, having slithered off the piled-up tubs. When each fisherman had sorted over his own catch it was found that Joe had caught the most scup, Captain Berry had the most sea bass, and John's tautog was the biggest fish of all. Studying the whole gleaming, silvery "take" with a trained eye Captain Berry estimated that they had a liberal half barrel of fish, an excellent morning's catch.

When they had reached the dock in the river and made the *Sarah B.* fast Uncle Abner rose with a groan, admitting reluctantly that he *did* feel kind of tuckered out, but adding hastily that he hadn't had so much fun in years and meant to go again the following week if they'd have him.

Eben offered to go up to the barn and harness up and drive back to the dock while John and Joe fetched ashore the fish and all their gear. Uncle Abner accepted the offer gratefully and used the interval to limber up his stiffened joints by cautious and gradual exercise. By the time they were all loaded up and ready to start home he climbed to the wagon seat with almost his usual spryness.

The noise of their approach as they rattled up the lane drew Grandfather to the doorway of the store, where John hailed him with a lusty shout, "I got the biggest tautog all on accounta that new ganging you showed me!"

Grandfather laughed and exclaimed over their fine catch as he helped them unload the tubs of fish by the back gate. Uncle Abner and Joe drove off with their share still in the wagon, leaving John and Eben to sort their combined catch and decide which they would clean for their own use and which they would sell.

It was a difficult task to make the selection, for each and every fish looked valuable in the eyes of its captor. Setting aside a few choice ones that they would take pride in presenting as gifts to Aunt Betsy Ann and Uncle Aberdeen and Aunt Ruth, they filled two baskets with their reluctant discards and John set out at once to sell them, leaving Eben and Grandfather dressing the ones they would have for their own supper.

Mother invited Grandmother and Grandfather over to eat fried scup with them, that night, and they all pronounced them the sweetest eating ever, when they were served up crisp, brown and piping hot from the big skillet on the stove. During the meal John expressed the thought that was in all their minds when he said, regretfully, "Gee, I wisht Father and Peter were here to taste these scup! Father'd like it fine to know what a bully day we had."

When, after supper, Grandfather suggested that he go down to the road and get the evening mail he received grateful looks from two weary boys who were dreading the necessity of getting up to do their chores. They rose from the table in close imitation of Uncle Abner aboard the *Sarah B.* and recognizing the similarity they laughed each other out of the worst of their stiffness. Once outside they gave their evening tasks a lick and a promise and were back in the sitting room, yawning and stretching, when Grandfather came in and handed Mother a letter. Their eyes were closing so drowsily that they hardly noticed what he had done until they were suddenly startled broad awake by an exclamation from Mother, "Why, it's from Father, sure's I live!"

"From *Ben*—that don't seem possible!" said Grandmother.

"I couldn't figure I was seeing right, coming up from the mail," remarked Grandfather with a puzzled frown as he tried to count back to the sailing date.

Meanwhile Mother was tearing at the sealing wafer with trembling fingers. The paper rattled and then, in a voice quivering with excitement she read: "We have made a tip-top passage! a record breaker—Boston to London in seventeen days! We made the run from soundings on the Grand Banks to the Lizard in just nine days. It was the best passage I've ever sailed. Peter is well and he's some set up to think that between him and the new topmast rig they fetched us a record voyage!"

The Crosbys looked at each other, incredulous delight on all their faces, and then a chorus of exclamations broke out—"Peter's first voyage before the mast!" . . . "Boston to London in seventeen days!"

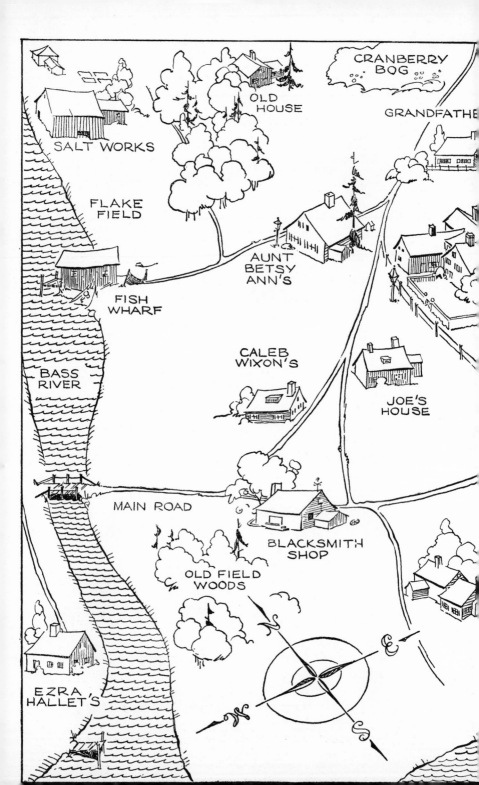

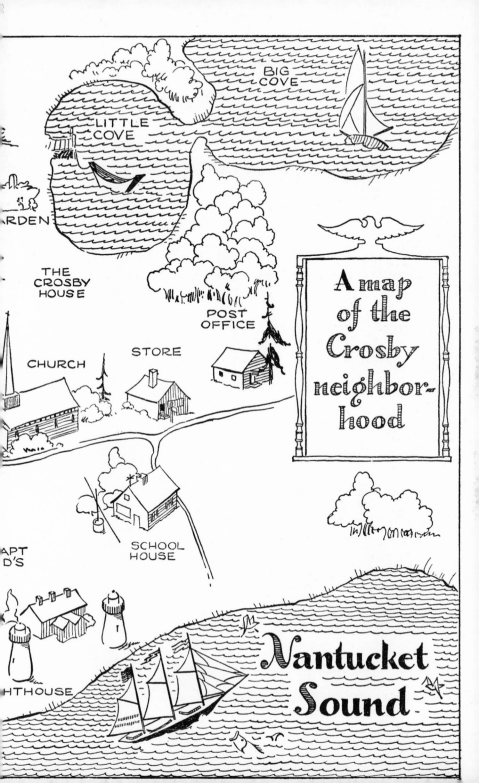